SHERLOCK HOLMES

Masters of Lies

ALSO AVAILABLE FROM TITAN BOOKS

Sherlock Holmes:
Gods of War
James Lovegrove

Sherlock Holmes:
The Patchwork Devil
Cavan Scott

Sherlock Holmes:
A Betrayal in Blood
Mark A. Latham

Sherlock Holmes:
Cry of the Innocents
Cavan Scott

Sherlock Holmes:
The Red Tower
Mark A. Latham

Sherlock Holmes:
The Vanishing Man
Philip Purser-Hallard

Sherlock Holmes:
The Manifestations of
Sherlock Holmes
James Lovegrove

Sherlock Holmes:
The Spirit Box
George Mann

Sherlock Holmes:
The Thinking Engine
James Lovegrove

Sherlock Holmes:
The Labyrinth of Death
James Lovegrove

Sherlock Holmes:
The Legacy of Deeds
Nick Kyme

Sherlock Holmes:
The Devil's Dust
James Lovegrove

Sherlock Holmes:
The Back to Front Murder
Tim Major

Sherlock Holmes:
The Spider's Web
Philip Purser-Hallard

SHERLOCK HOLMES

Masters of Lies

PHILIP PURSER-HALLARD

TITAN BOOKS

Masters of Lies
Print edition ISBN: 9781789099249
E-book edition ISBN: 9781789099256

Published by Titan Books
A division of Titan Publishing Group Ltd
144 Southwark Street, London SE1 0UP
www.titanbooks.com

First edition: May 2022
10 9 8 7 6 5 4 3 2 1

A CIP catalogue record for this title is available from the British Library.

Printed and bound by CPI Group Ltd in Great Britain.

PRELUDE

Dear sir –

The enclosed documents were left by our late client, John H. Watson M.D. Though my colleague Mr Swynge has arranged them to allow for greater readability, each is presented verbatim.

We would appreciate your urgent advice regarding their veracity and import. It is our professional duty to advise Dr Watson's literary executors on how far these, along with the other unpublished manuscripts in his possession at the time of his death, may legally be publishable, but in this instance we are unable to judge between us how best to fulfil this obligation. Any opinion you are able to give us on this matter will be most welcome.

The sensitivity of the overall account, relating as it does to scandal and culpability at high levels of the British government, will be apparent from the first, but it is not from this alone that our reservations arise. The manner in which this narrative differs from Dr Watson's other memoirs of his time in Baker Street became clear to us only gradually in reading, but caused us considerable disquiet, for reasons that will become apparent to you also.

We leave the material to speak for itself, and are confident that you will draw your own conclusions. Meanwhile, we shall await your advice.

J.M. Bodley, Esq.,
Swynge, Bodley & Sons, Solicitors

NOTE TO SHERLOCK HOLMES

Holmes—
Please be so good as to attend me at the Diogenes
Club at once. Loomborough.

NOTE TO JOHN H. WATSON, M.D.

Gone to the Diogenes. Do not follow. When I return I will tell you what to do. S.H.

NOTE TO INSPECTOR STANLEY HOPKINS

Hopkins, please come at once. I must discuss with you a matter of unparalleled urgency. Watson.

"I must agree with you, Watson," said my friend Sherlock Holmes, breaking a half-hour's silence. "General Gordon would not have shared such reservations. He would have been glad of anything that promoted present peace between the countries he loved, with the Future a secondary consideration."

I sighed, and set aside my newspaper. "Holmes," I replied, "I know perfectly well that I said nothing aloud, so how were you able to divine my inner thoughts and agree with them? No," I added, holding up a hand as he prepared to speak, "I know your methods by now. Let me see whether I can reconstruct your reasoning." Holmes smiled and gave a gracious wave of his pipe, granting permission.

We sat in our rooms at Baker Street on a warm Summer morning, the windows open to allow a breeze to pass. We had agreed between us to prefer the rich, if somewhat mixed, scent of the capital over the progressive closeness of a hot and stuffy room—in which, furthermore, Holmes had been trying out a new tobacco mixture of his own invention, that gave off a cloying rose-petal scent reminding me of Turkish Delight.

I had been reading *The Times* and had, I admit, fallen into something of a reverie, prompting Holmes into another display of the mind-reading trick he used as a form of entertainment, at times when he lacked any more consequential problem to stimulate his exceptional intellect.

"You read the paper earlier yourself, and so, I suppose, could see that I had reached the page with the piece about the expansion of our holdings in Hong Kong," I said. The story reported that our diplomats had lately signed an agreement to lease new territories on the Chinese mainland that, it was promised, would secure an enclave for the precarious but precious colony throughout the coming century. It was not the most prominent item in the paper, being upstaged by the charges against a pair of soldiers accused of perjuring themselves in a recent court-martial, and the announcement of the sale through Boothby's auction house of a supposed Shakespearean manuscript.

I continued, "I suppose, though I was not aware of it until you spoke, that I was gazing at the wall that holds the portrait of General Gordon, hanging opposite the one of Henry Ward Beecher which you so kindly had framed for my birthday."

"You have Mrs Hudson to thank for that," Holmes informed me, "for she was tactful enough to suggest the gift to me. The picture has been sitting unframed atop your bookcase for some years, and evidently dusting it has become a trial to her patience."

This explained Holmes' unusual consideration—he not being a man prone to the giving of thoughtful presents—but I was still attempting to follow his earlier insight. "Gordon's connexions with China are as well known to you as anyone," I continued, "so of course you would have realised that I was wondering what he would have made of this new arrangement. Such leases were unknown in his day, though I gather that they are now in favour with the Chinese government. What I cannot fathom is how you guessed that I was considering the question of reversion."

Though I am neither a diplomat nor a student of China, I have travelled in Asia and am familiar with the dangers facing the brave men and their wives, military and civilian both, who maintain our presence there. I assumed that to the negotiators a ninety-nine-year lease seemed as good as a perpetual one, but who knew what view the Chinese Emperor of the year 1997 would take when it expired? If he insisted on bringing the territories back under Chinese control, our grasp on Hong Kong would be as slippery as before.

Holmes smiled lazily. "Merely by following the movement

of your eyes, Watson, and your own movements this morning. A little after breakfast you opened the letter from your cousin in Melbourne, Mrs Deaver, and informed me that she was celebrating the birth of a male child, on which I dutifully congratulated you. The letters you wrote afterwards included a reply. As you and your relatives rarely correspond, it was natural to suppose that you took the opportunity to express hopes for good fortune in the infant's life to come."

"I see," I said. "And I suppose I looked again at the letter, after I read the newspaper article?"

"Not at once," he said. "After setting the newspaper down on your knees, you glanced first at the calendar, and then to the writing-desk where you composed the letter. Then you looked over to the table by the door, where it sits now with the others, addressed but awaiting its stamp. You glanced down at the paper again, and your eyes then wandered to Gordon's portrait, and remained there in contemplation before eventually returning to *The Times*.

"It was simple to deduce your train of thought. First you considered the passage of time: you and I shall not live to see the year 1997, and we have no descendants, though you and some future Mrs Watson may yet be blessed. Your new young relative's children or grandchildren, however, may very well see changes in their part of the world, arising from this short-sighted decision on the part of Her Majesty's colonial agents. You recollected your letter, and assured yourself that it would soon be on its way, but then your misgivings renewed themselves. You looked for reassurance to 'Chinese' Gordon—the saviour of Nanking and one of your own heroes—and after a little thought you realised that such concerns would not have troubled his spirit. Whereupon, I expressed my agreement with you."

"I see," I replied again. "Well, I am dismayed afresh to find myself so transparent."

"Ah, don't be downcast, Watson. The clearest waters are not always the shallowest, as any sailor could tell you who has had the opportunity to compare the South China Sea with the murk of the Thames. Besides, I admit that the ability to predict you arises in part from the closeness with which we are acquainted. Were you a stranger, the technique would be somewhat less reliable."

"I suppose that's something," I conceded. Though, in truth, the idea that Holmes knew me well enough to reconstruct my mental processes continued to unnerve me. I imagined him engineering a clockwork Watson in his mind, and setting the homunculus on its mechanical way, to think and act and speak as I would. The image of Holmes as a toymaker, moving me and Mrs Hudson around a doll's-house Number 221B, made me shudder slightly.

"But, Watson," said Holmes superciliously, again in response to no words of mine, "do not we all do the same in some degree? Is that not what you were doing when you imagined the responses of the late General Gordon to the developments of the present day?"

Coming on the heels of his previous ostentatious display, this irked me, and I was on the verge of an angry retort which might have spoiled the morning. I kept my temper and my silence, however, and held my tongue along with the newspaper, which I commenced reading once more.

A moment later I was reprieved by a knock at the door. Mrs Hudson hurried in, bringing an urgent missive that had arrived with a messenger.

"Brother Mycroft's writing, I declare!" exclaimed Holmes, tearing it open as our redoubtable landlady bustled away, taking the letters I had written earlier. "I have been expecting something of the kind. I have heard this morning of a death that is likely to interest him."

He perused the message swiftly, then handed it to me. As

he had predicted, it was from his brother. Mycroft Holmes requested—"demanded" would not be an unduly strong word— our presence at his club, with all dispatch. As he was a senior, though unacknowledged, official in the workings of Government, Mycroft's summonses generally portended some crisis of state significance, and were not to be ignored even had we been so inclined. As it was, Holmes seized upon the distraction with relish, and we hailed a cab.

It was a journey of only a few minutes, down past Baker Street's coffee-shops and newsagents, then through Mayfair and its grand garden squares, passing by the new Connaught Hotel, Pugin's grandiose Gothic Church of the Immaculate Conception, and a particular house in Berkeley Square in whose supposedly haunted attic Holmes and I had once spent a trying night. From there our cab continued past Walsingham House and the Bath Hotel and into St James', where the capital's most prestigious gentlemen's clubs are located.

A moment later we had alighted, and were passing into the hallway of one such, which Holmes had once described as the queerest in London. Glass panelling gave us a view of the reading room, in which the unsociable members of the Diogenes Club sat in their separate bays of books, newspapers and magazines, each with its single leather armchair, in absolute isolation from one another. With the glass between us, I was irresistibly reminded of fish skulking in their little caves in an aquarium.

Then Holmes knocked cheerfully on the window, eliciting a flurry of glares and shaken heads and the immediate attention of a plump attendant. Like all those at the Diogenes Club, he wore soft carpet slippers to muffle the sound of his footfalls. He ushered us with silent disapproval into the Stranger's Room overlooking Pall Mall, the only room in the building where conversation was permitted. A moment later we were joined by the considerable presence of Mycroft Holmes, who gestured at the man to bring us tea.

"An ambitious fellow," Sherlock Holmes observed as the servant hastened away. "His parents may have been in service, but I'll wager his child will not be."

"Ah, so you noticed that," Mycroft replied. He settled his enormous body into a freshly polished leather armchair, looking rather like a hot-air balloon that I had once seen descending to the Earth, and gestured to us to sit as well. "The skin above the ears, of course, and the squint."

"Together with the left middle finger," Sherlock agreed lazily.

"Naturally. Well," said Mycroft, "thank you both for coming here so promptly. You are both well, I trust?"

As I understood it, Mycroft Holmes was the linchpin around which the British establishment revolved, the weighty and immobile foundation upon which everything else was built. Like everyone but himself, I could comprehend only a small portion of his function, but I knew his mind to be an entrepot of reports and memos, records and instructions that drove the flow of information across our global Empire. If there was a correspondence to be discovered between the declining output of a sawmill in Manchester and the failure of a military sortie in Bengal, or between the price of cattle in Adelaide and the fall of a sparrow in Putney, Mycroft was the man to spot it, to tell you what its consequences might be and how they might be avoided. He was as indispensable to Great Britain's interests across the face of the globe as his brother was to the thwarting of her criminals.

"Quite well, brother, thank you," Sherlock Holmes replied. "I have been occupied with a number of pretty problems recently, but as it happens you find me free this morning. May I assume that Her Majesty's Government is in need of my services once again?" Though I knew the brothers respected one another, neither was a man to waste his time in idle chit-chat.

"That is putting it rather more grandly than I should myself," Mycroft told him, "but your surmise is correct. Thank you, Jennings, that will be all." He waved away the allegedly ambitious attendant, who had returned with a tea-tray. "You have heard, perhaps, of the death of the Honourable Christopher Bastion?"

"I believe I have encountered some intelligence to that effect," his brother admitted. "Perhaps, though, for Watson's benefit, you could summarise the salient details?"

Mycroft nodded cordially. "Very well. Bastion was found by his manservant in his study at home this morning. He had taken prussic acid, and had been dead for some hours. He was the middle son of the late Viscount Agincourt, and his older brother is the current holder of the title. The family is ancient and distinguished, and notable for its long history of service to the nation. Christopher Bastion was until last week a senior civil servant at the Foreign Office, and had been one of its chief assets for many years, thanks to his political incisiveness and expert knowledge of affairs in many parts of the world. He was trusted with the most sensitive matters of policy, in both the diplomatic and the military spheres. He had, however, a long and unfortunate susceptibility to the company and charms of women, and this had recently led him sadly astray.

"A few weeks ago, Scotland Yard arrested a foreign spy, known by the alias 'Zimmerman', on whom they had had their eye. Thanks to the speed and efficiency of the operation, the man had scant warning of his arrest, and was hurriedly burning papers when he was caught. Among those he had not yet destroyed, the police found a recent letter from none other than Christopher Bastion, implying in no uncertain terms that he would be willing to sell government secrets to Zimmerman's masters for a high enough price. Hitherto Bastion's probity had never been questioned, so I am sure you can imagine the shock and upset with which this news was received in Whitehall."

"Had he a reason to want for money?" Holmes asked sharply. "Has the family fallen upon hard times?"

"Not the family," said Mycroft, "but Bastion drew no allowance from the Agincourt estate, preferring to earn his own keep. His salary was not extravagant, and he was fond of the expensive things in life, including a young woman with whom he had recently formed a most unsuitable attachment. She had become a significant drain on his finances, as unsuitable young women are wont to be."

"He admitted this?" asked Sherlock.

"Openly and without reservation, on being questioned. He was most insistent, however, that he had not written the letter to Zimmerman. In deference to his unblemished record, two experts in handwriting were consulted, independently of one another. Both confirmed the hand as his. Bastion was quite indignant when he learned that he was not believed, although he must have seen that we could not possibly take the risk of retaining his services. He was discreetly dismissed, and it seems the young lady, recognising that the wind had changed, left shortly thereafter. His valet attests that he has been in low spirits since then. It would seem that in view of his disgrace, his financial ruin and his romantic disappointment, Bastion had no interest in continuing his life."

"It sounds an open-and-shut case," I agreed, bracing myself for the pair of scathing contradictions that I invited in making such a statement in the presence of both Holmes brothers.

Mildly, Sherlock said, "Hardly, Watson. While prussic acid is best known as a method of suicide, its use as a weapon of assassination is not unknown. Furthermore, I count at least six possible motives for murder, the likeliest being romantic jealousy of Bastion, retribution for an unpaid debt and a wish to silence him for something he knew. Was he alone in the house?"

"Other than the servants, quite alone," Mycroft confirmed. "As you will have gathered, he was unmarried, and he maintained a bachelor establishment near Piccadilly. His lady friend is no longer in the picture. His suicide is not in doubt, however," he declared, to my surprise and his brother's evident annoyance. "Bastion left a note. His death concerns me and Her Majesty's Government only insofar as it is lamentable to see a trusted ally so fallen. Our interest is in how far he was compromised beforehand. Specifically, in what secrets he might already have divulged to Zimmerman, or to others with whom Zimmerman placed him in contact."

"One assumes that, had he done so, his monetary difficulties at least would have been alleviated," Sherlock pointed out sharply. "And with them his romantic ones, if your description of his young friend's character is accurate. Are you certain that she is not herself a spy, incidentally?"

"It seems peculiarly unlikely," said Mycroft. "She is a dancer with pretensions to becoming an actress. She was christened Gillian McGuire, but Bastion knew her by the ridiculous name of 'Adorée Felice'. We have spoken to her, naturally, and are keeping her under observation, but we are satisfied that she had no knowledge of Zimmerman or his schemes. She appears to be a vulgar little creature from a humble Irish family, and in our estimation that is exactly what she is."

"I see," my friend said. "Zimmerman himself has been uncooperative, I suppose."

"As the grave," agreed Mycroft sombrely. "He essayed an escape from the police-wagon on the way to the station, and was trampled by a coach-and-four following close behind. He did not long survive the experience, and we got nothing from him before he died."

Sherlock frowned. "How inconvenient. And Bastion's finances?"

"We have spoken to his bank manager, and he was certainly in dire straits. There have been no unusual sums of money paid in recently, though Miss Felice had caused unprecedented outgoings. However, that in itself does not mean that Bastion took his secrets to the grave. If he handed them to a foreign power for promise of payment, there is no reason to assume that promise would have been honoured. Zimmerman's possession of his letter would have been enough to secure his cooperation, if he wished to retain his reputation and position."

"Indeed it would, before he lost them. But if he had already betrayed that trust, why did he not confess as much to his superiors when he admitted his unwise entanglement? If he was as astute as you say, he must have known that they could never keep him on, so he had nothing to lose. Yet why would such a man be so rash as to write such a letter in the first place? The criminal underworld has many channels of communication, and most do not involve signing a letter in one's own hand."

Mycroft sighed heavily. "This is where our approaches differ, Sherlock. Your interest in the workings of the criminal mind is admirable in its way, but sometimes excessively analytical. In my position, I am forced to be practical. It is clear that Bastion did write the letter, and that he did not confess the fact. Since his reasons for these decisions can form the basis of no future actions on his part, they have become immaterial. What we need to know presently is to whom Bastion has spoken recently, what he might have told them, and what their affiliations may be. If it appears that he may have divulged privileged information, I must act to limit the damage done. The success of many a diplomatic endeavour, not to mention the lives of certain of Her Majesty's agents, may depend upon it."

Sherlock Holmes inclined his head. "Very well. However …"

His brother raised a pudgy hand. "Oh, I know that you have your own methods, Sherlock. Your sources of information among the criminal classes of London are equal to my own among persons of influence, wealth and power across the globe. I would not dream of telling you how to conduct your investigation, provided only that it produces results. I shall require frequent reports to that effect."

"Then we are in accord," said my friend. "Has Zimmerman's headquarters been preserved?"

"If you can call it a headquarters. It's a rather dismal room in Hackney. But yes, it has been kept under police guard. His effects are now at Scotland Yard, where they have been inventoried and examined thoroughly."

"And the scene of Bastion's suicide?"

"The police are in attendance still. I expect you will find a friend of yours there. I have given instructions that the body must not be moved until you have examined it. I knew that the lure of a recent corpse would exert more power over you than any less sensational avenue you might pursue."

"Since the evidence there will be fresher," Sherlock said, "I would be remiss not to attend directly. Indifferent to Bastion's death Her Majesty's Government may be, but you must see that his state of mind in his last hours could have a crucial bearing on his relations with these foreign operatives."

Mycroft inclined his massive head, his chins rippling in waves. "Very well, Sherlock, you must tackle the case in your own *métier*. I have let the police know that you have absolute authority to investigate the matter."

Given the confidential position Mycroft held, I could not help wondering how the constabulary could be assured of this, but doubtless there were channels through which the elder Holmes made his wishes known.

Certainly Sherlock seemed in no doubt. "Come then, Watson," he said. "We are to view the aftermath of a most tragic suicide—unless it proves yet to be a most clandestine murder. We shall apprise you of our progress," he assured his brother.

"You always know where to find me," Mycroft acknowledged as we left.

Holmes led me out of the Stranger's Room, past a still disapproving Jennings, and away from the Diogenes Club. I paid off the cabman, who had been waiting for us, while Holmes lit a cigarette.

"Holmes, that attendant," I asked, reminded of his earlier conversation with Mycroft. "Jennings. However did you—"

My friend sighed as he shook out his match. "Dear Watson," he said, "your inability to perceive what is perfectly apparent never ceases to confound me. Jennings has shallow grooves above his ears, symmetrical on each side. What does that tell you?"

I frowned. "Has he been keeping pencils there?"

Holmes laughed. "Oh, my dear fellow, no. Marks such as those are seen when a plump man wears ill-fitting spectacles. He does not need them for his work, so we may assume that they are reading-glasses. The shallowness of the marks shows that he has not been wearing them for very long, yet he has the squint of one who has been short-sighted for many years. I have not seen him at the Diogenes Club before, and while I would not expect to recognise all their employees on sight, I could not fail to observe that his livery and especially his slippers showed little sign of wear. He has the bearing of a lifelong servant, yet he has evidently been well fed for some time, suggesting employment in a well-off household. Given his age and current duties, he was most likely a footman.

"The Diogenes pays its staff unusually well for their discretion and tolerance, but spectacles and books do not come cheaply, and are not bought on a whim. Nor is a myopic footman likely to have acquired the habit of reading for pleasure. His family has recently expanded, so his household expenses have not become any lesser of late. The obvious conclusion is that Jennings, having recently secured a position with an increased income, is taking advantage of it to better himself and his young family through education."

"I see." I cast my mind back to the brothers' observations. The squint and the skin above the ears were explained, at least. "And his middle finger?"

"Small bite-marks," Holmes replied, "undoubtedly left there by a teething infant. Really, Watson, this is trivial stuff."

We had set off by now, walking the short distance to the Piccadilly address that Mycroft had given us. Holmes was ever a brisk pedestrian, and I had to hurry to keep up with him. He fell silent, seeming distracted, but soon I heard him mutter, "But—a case. A case from brother Mycroft!"

He had an exultant gleam in his eye which seemed to me out of proportion to the sad and sordid circumstances of Bastion's death, whatever had occasioned it. "Oh," he added aloud, "he loves to have me dance to his tune, Watson, but how invigorating the measure is!"

THE DAILY GAZETTE
16th May 1898
WOUNDED ZULU WAR HERO WALKS FREE

Robert Foxon, the self-made ivory magnate and former sergeant in the Second Warwickshire Regiment, who still bears the wounds from his distinguished service in the Zulu War of 1879, has been exonerated by a court-martial of all charges relating to the unfortunate deaths of native women and children.

Mr Foxon had been accused of ordering the shooting of some forty inhabitants of a Zulu village near the Buffalo River. Two men who served in his company made statements to the effect that they had taken part in the shootings at Sergeant Foxon's orders, but an affidavit sent by an officer, a Major Macpherson, now resident in Lahore, India, absolved him of any involvement in the regrettable incident.

Major Macpherson, who in 1879 was a lieutenant with the Warwickshires, attested that Foxon had become separated from his company in the disorder following a temporary setback at the hands of the savage forces, and had been many miles away at the time of the occurrence. His deposition spoke movingly of how Sergeant Foxon had, "abandoned his position along with his hopes of Victory, though never his Duty."

The Major's conclusion was that Sergeant Foxon's men, leaderless and lost, had acted under their own initiative and that no blame could attach to their absent sergeant. The two who went on to testify against him were, he could only conclude, motivated by malice. The court-martial's verdict agreed with this assessment, and exonerated Mr Foxon, who walks away today a free man, without a stain on his character.

While simple decency demands that the full force of the

law should be brought to bear against those who bear false witness, it is to be hoped that this unfortunate affair will further serve as an instructive moral lesson against those who would see men persecuted for decisions taken on the spur of the moment and under great strain at time of war.

In such cases, a vindictive zeal for vengeance in the guise of justice must be sternly rebuked, and understanding extended to the heroic men of the British Army, whose occasional lapses from the most rigorous application of the moral principles that would apply during peace-time are a small price to pay for their staunch and tireless defence of our great nation against her enemies.

The Honourable Christopher Bastion's townhouse was a compact but desirable residence from the early part of the century, perfect for a well-heeled bachelor. We found it set back in a side-street, a moment's walk from both the bustle of Piccadilly proper and the soothing calm of Green Park.

The police constable on the door was at first inclined to be obstructive, the word from Mycroft having not apparently penetrated to his rank. But he was soon overruled. "Mr Holmes and Dr Watson!" cried an energetic young man, bounding from the house and shaking our hands, and I was pleased to recognise Inspector Stanley Hopkins. In deference to the heat of the day, he had exchanged his habitual tweed suit for a lighter one in grey. "I am surprised to see you here, though I know you would not have come without good cause. I suppose it is about the late Mr Bastion?" He sounded doubtful, and understandably so if the suicide was as far beyond question as Mycroft had led us to believe.

Stanley Hopkins was one of the most promising of the younger generation of Scotland Yard inspectors, an ambitious detective who embraced the modern developments in policing methods, such as fingerprint identification and crime-scene photography, that baffled and vexed old-timers like Bradstreet and Athelney Jones. He was also a keen student of Sherlock Holmes' techniques and methods, and had called on our help on many occasions. Holmes had taken a lively interest in Hopkins' career, as had I. Though pleased to see him here, I was equally surprised that the Yard had tasked one of its most able officers with investigating Bastion's suicide.

"Please come in, both of you," said Hopkins, ushering us through the front door. "The body hasn't yet been moved, as I called in a photographer to record the scene. It might seem excessive, but I thought it best to be meticulous given the importance of the deceased."

"I'm sure you're always meticulous, Inspector," I told him.

Hopkins grimaced. "I wish we'd all been more so when we were transporting Zimmerman. You know about Zimmerman the spy? I see you do. His death was a real loss to our investigation, though I'm not so keen to mourn him as I am this poor fellow. Although, of course, Mr Bastion had succeeded in quite destroying his life already."

A pair of uniformed police stood in the hall, and Hopkins introduced them. "These are Sergeant Douglass and Constable Fratelli, who have been helping me in this matter. We've been assigned to Bastion's case since the beginning, you know, since it arose from our arrest of Zimmerman. It was the letter we found in his possession that put us on to Bastion in the first place."

"I should have surmised as much," Holmes murmured to me, "when Mycroft told us that the police had been speedy and efficient. Hopkins is one of the few capable of such."

The young Inspector led us through into the cosy, book-lined study where the Honourable Christopher Bastion had met his end. That distinguished civil servant lay slumped across his desk, a fountain-pen in his right hand. His head was turned to face the door, and I could see that he had been a handsome man, in his middle fifties with a fine beard, once fair and now mostly a distinguished grey. He wore a shirt and tie; his jacket hung on a peg by the door. As we drew closer I saw that to his left lay a small bottle, now empty, whose contents had stained the dark cherrywood of the desk top. I smelled the distinctive odour of almonds which always accompanies prussic acid, and shuddered.

A man I recognised as the photographer regularly employed by Hopkins for his crime-scene work was packing his equipment into a sturdy wooden case, helped by a tall, thin servant who I guessed to be Bastion's valet. The latter's face was downcast and tear-stained.

"This is Probert," Hopkins told us, calling the valet over. "I wouldn't have asked him to stay in the room with the body, but he's insistent on helping us in any way he can. Probert, these are Mr Holmes and Dr Watson. They'll be working with us on this case."

"Good morning, Probert," said Holmes, shaking the servant's hand energetically. "Can you bear to tell us once more how you came to find Mr Bastion like this?"

Probert blinked rapidly as the tears threatened to come again. "I left him last night, sirs, reading late." His voice was deep and Welsh, and husky with emotion. "He often liked to, and lately he'd been quiet and melancholy, like. You know something of his troubles, sirs, I dare say. I made bold enough to warn him about that young hussy, Miss Felice, but he wouldn't have none of it, and look at him now ..." His voice began to crack.

"What was he reading?" Holmes asked sharply, stemming the threatened flow of emotion.

Probert collected himself. "Why, a book of poems in Latin, sir. Very fond of them he was, Ovid and Virgil and them. He read some out loud to me. He had a lovely reading voice, although I couldn't understand a word, of course." Probert looked around the room. "See, there's the book, on the floor by the desk. Normally very tidy he was, but ..." Words seemed to fail him.

"Quite so," said Holmes, bending to inspect the book. It was, I saw, a volume of Catullus. "So you left him in the study last night. Was he dressed as he is now?"

Probert seemed to falter again, and swallowed. "Just the same, sir. His bed hasn't been slept in either. I went in to wake him this morning and he wasn't there. Well, that alarmed me, knowing he was in the house, like. I keep the keys, you see, the household not being big enough to need the services of a butler, so I knew he hadn't gone out. Not that he would have anyway, so late at night. So I came down to see whether he'd fallen asleep here, not that that was a habit of his, sirs, I promise you. And when I opened the door—"

His face began to crumple again, but once again Holmes stepped in with a question. "The door was closed?" he asked. "Is that how you left it? And the windows, as they are now?"

"Yes, sir. All as I left them. It was a close night, but I'd shut the windows. Mr Bastion complained of the heat, but he relented, like, when I reminded him how much he detested the smell from outside. And then I'd shut the door on him when I went to bed."

"Were the doors of the house locked?"

Probert looked most affronted. "Of course, sir. I lock them every night, and last night was no exception. Why would it be?"

"And this morning you found him exactly thus? You moved nothing?"

"No, sir. I mean, I could see straight away he was dead, and like I say he's been so ... out of spirits ... it wasn't hard to guess why. I was so upset I had to sit down for a moment, right there in the doorway. But then I thought of how it would look if the maid found me like that, so I stood up and went over to him. I took his wrist just in case there was a pulse, but he was cold. And then I saw the note ..."

A handwritten rectangle of notepaper lay, I now saw, close to Bastion's outstretched right hand.

"You picked it up to read it?" Holmes asked the manservant.

"Well, yes, sir, I did do that. But then I put it back just where I found it. I realised right away I'd have to call the police, and they always say to keep things like they are, don't they, sir? I did right there, sir, didn't I?"

"You did very well, Probert," said Hopkins. "Nobody could reproach you for having left him alone. You weren't to know he'd do something like this."

"No, sir." Probert was crying again now, the tears running down his cheeks. "I didn't think he'd be so stupid, begging your pardons, sirs. Excuse me, I—" And he left the room, quite suddenly.

"He must have been touchingly fond of his master," I observed, "to be so affected by his passing."

Holmes' mouth quirked in amused irritation. "Try not to be quite so sentimental, Watson. Such a scene as this would unnerve anybody."

Not in the least unnerved, he afforded the body a casual glance before checking the study windows, which gave onto a small but well-kept rear garden and mews. Holmes' interest was in the catches, however. "Firmly fastened," he pronounced after a moment's inspection. "These locks are of a modern brand, and normally reliable. Mr Bastion was careful of his security."

"It's the same throughout the house," said Hopkins. Used to Holmes' ways, he added mildly, "We have checked all the windows, you know. Will you tell Mr Holmes what you found, Fratelli?"

"All secured just the same, sir," said Constable Fratelli. "No sign of forced entry anywhere. And Mr Probert has the keys, like he said."

"He has them now," Holmes pointed out. "That does not prove that he had them for the whole of last night. Where does he keep them when asleep?"

"On a hook beside his bed, sir," said Fratelli. "I suppose one of the other servants could have crept in and took them, but I don't see why they should." His scepticism was polite, but clear. Thus far we had seen no reason to imagine that anyone had been in the house that night other than the staff and Bastion himself.

The photographer finished his packing and was shown out by Fratelli. Sergeant Douglass remained with his superior as Holmes finally turned his attention to the deceased. "Some pinkish discolouration and a characteristic odour of bitter almonds," he announced, peering at Bastion's face. "The fingers of the left hand slightly blistered where he held the bottle. A chemical analysis will confirm it, of course, but I have little doubt that this is indeed a case of cyanide poisoning. Watson, do you concur?"

I agreed that all the visible indications were consistent with that diagnosis.

Holmes turned to the note, first examining it where it lay on the polished surface of the desk. "I suppose Probert has confirmed that this is his employer's writing?" he asked Hopkins, who nodded. "A sad apologia for a life," Holmes added, a little dismissively, after reading it through. "I should like to see the letter that was found with Zimmerman also. Inspector, do you know where it has ended up?"

"I believe it's still with the Foreign Office," said Hopkins. "Bastion's minister was Sir Hector Askew. I could contact his office and ask for an appointment for you."

"I dare say my brother can arrange that," my friend replied.

He passed me the dead man's final communication, and I read it, shaking my head sorrowfully. I found it poignant that a life could end on—and in—so impersonal a note, as if the public service to which the better part of it had been dedicated had left Bastion no pride at the end but in his neglected decorum.

Holmes had not stood idle, and was rooting through the drawers of the desk. He withdrew an appointment-book, which he flipped through swiftly. "No meetings noted for last night," he observed, "and nothing mentioning Zimmerman by name or initial, though that is only to be expected. A good many appointments with 'A', though—presumably the *soi-disant* Miss Adorée Felice—mostly in night clubs or restaurants, few of them reputable."

A thought seemed to strike him and he set the appointment-book alongside the letter, leaning in closely to scrutinise the handwriting. Then he dropped abruptly to his hands and knees and began to examine the floor between the door and the desk. However, he soon desisted with a sigh. "Hopeless," he said. "A carpet retains marks imperfectly at the best of times, and there are far too many tracks of servants and policemen and photographers to detect anything else."

"What are you expecting to find, Mr Holmes?" Hopkins asked curiously. "Have you some reason to suppose there's been foul play? I'd say it was certain that Bastion killed himself, or as close to certainty as anything comes in police-work. What makes you suspect otherwise?"

"I suspect the fountain-pen," declared Holmes. "Bastion clutches it still, yet he must have written the letter before taking the prussic acid. It is a fast-acting poison and he would not have had the leisure afterwards. But in that case, why did he continue to hold the pen while unstoppering the bottle and drinking? It would have been quite inconvenient, and he had no further use for it."

"Perhaps," I speculated, "he thought of some amendment to the letter after taking the poison, but didn't have time to make it before he lost consciousness."

"Or he simply clutched at the nearest object during his final moments," suggested Hopkins sensibly. "Who knows what impulses drive a dying man?"

"Indeed," said Holmes. "One so rarely gets the opportunity to consult them on the matter," he added macabrely.

"If there are to be any surprises, Mr Holmes, I'd be rather grateful if you were to give me some warning," said Hopkins. "Our Commissioner is taking quite a close interest in this case. Between ourselves, he seems a little agitated about it."

"It seems to me that Bastion took the only option," I said. "The honourable way, as far as such a thing was still available to him. That can't reflect badly on the force, surely? As you say, he was the architect of his own downfall."

"That's certainly my hope. The Commissioner has reasons to be sensitive about this whole business, though. Bastion is—that is, he was—an old schoolfriend of Lord Loomborough, the minister in charge of the police."

"Lord Loomborough," noted Holmes. "Well, there's a coincidence. We saw him this morning at the Diogenes Club, Watson—do you remember? He was sitting in the next bay along from his colleague Lord Caversham, ignoring him entirely of course, with the eminent biologist Scaverson dozing away in the next." Of the three gentlemen Holmes mentioned, I had recognised only the Earl of Caversham, whose son Lord Goring we had assisted in the matter of a murder the previous year.

"Yes, I understand he's a member," Hopkins said. "The late Mr Bastion was not, though they had other clubs in common. I don't know whether they were close friends, but they were at Eton together also. The Commissioner's concerned that their relationship might lead the Minister to become personally involved. His Lordship's shown a sight more interest in the details of our operations than his predecessors, I have to say." He sighed. "You're fortunate that the politics of policing aren't something that much troubles you, Mr Holmes."

But Holmes was abstracted, tapping his fingers in a rapid rhythm against the wood of the desk. "What troubles me, Hopkins, is this tableau. The pen seems altogether too perfect a touch. Does it not strike you so?"

Hopkins' honest face frowned. "To be frank, no. You know how I respect your methods, Mr Holmes, and you know I won't rest if a shadow of a doubt remains, but if there's any shadow in this case I've yet to see it. We know nobody broke in. All the signs confirm that the deceased succumbed to poisoning from prussic acid, administered by his own hand. The note alone would more than satisfy a coroner. I see no reason not to accept that Bastion committed suicide, and continue our investigation into the late Zimmerman's other contacts."

"A sad comedown," I observed, "from his position beside the seat of power."

Holmes stared distractedly at Bastion's straight-backed desk chair, and then his brow wrinkled. Once again he fell to his knees, drawing his magnifying-glass like a pistol.

The chair was elderly rather than antique, worn well from being sat in often, and becoming a little loose at the joins. Perhaps Bastion shared Holmes' dangerous habit of leaning back on two of its legs to cogitate, which I have noticed causes similar loosening. Indeed, I worry that one day a distinguished client will seat himself on an item of furniture that Holmes has thus abused once too often, and that it will collapse beneath him into its constituent timbers.

In this instance, where one side of the slatted seat-back met the seat, a few strands of thread had become caught in the loose joining. Holmes removed them carefully with a pair of tweezers, then set them down on the blotting-pad on the desk. He passed his magnifying-glass to me—Hopkins had his own. We saw that the strands were coarse wool, of a greenish-brown colour.

"Tweed," said Hopkins, who habitually wore the stuff himself. "I suppose he had a tweed jacket."

We all looked at the jacket that hung by the door. It was of a black cotton cloth, distinctly better suited for Summer wear than was the warmth of wool.

"I imagine he did," said Holmes, "though it would be unusual for a gentleman to wear it in town. One might as well wear a deerstalker hat," he added with a faint smile. "Still more so to wear it in his study, I think. This chair was repaired and revarnished a month or so ago, from which I conclude that Bastion used it often, and not gently. These threads have no varnish on them.

They were left there recently, but the weather has been excessively clement for some time now. There has been no occasion to force Bastion to wear an unseasonal tweed jacket indoors."

Hopkins exchanged a glance with me. Both of us, I could see, feared that Holmes was overreaching himself here. But, having been proven wrong so often in the past, we were each reluctant to say so.

Holmes crossed to the clean and empty grate, where clearly no fire had burned since the Spring. He gave it a swift perusal, then asked abruptly, "How is the hot water for the house supplied?"

Hopkins blinked in surprise, then responded in the time-honoured fashion of a senior policeman caught out by a difficult question. "Sergeant?"

Sergeant Douglass checked his notebook. "There's a boiler in the cellar, sir, coal-burning. Some of the lads looked at the coalhole earlier for any signs of ingress, but there's bolts on the inside there, too."

"Come, Hopkins!" exclaimed Holmes, and hurried from the room.

Hopkins frowned at me. "What's he …?" he began to ask, but Holmes barked, "You too, Watson!" and the pair of us hurried after him like the faithful hounds we were.

In the stifling cellar, Holmes hauled open the heavy iron hatch on the front of the boiler and seized a pair of coal-tongs. The fire inside was burning low, warmth radiating from the cylinder tank above it. Holmes knelt down yet again, heedless of the heat on his face or the coaldust on his trousers, and started poking about among the flames.

"Aha!" he cried triumphantly, and used the tongs to lift a blackened scrap of fabric from the fire. He rushed with it to the cellar steps and up into the kitchen, trailing smoke behind him. I shut the boiler hatch with a familiar sigh, and followed.

Holmes had spread out the material on the tiled floor of the kitchen. It had not stopped smoking, and smelled unpleasantly of singed wool. In the sunlight, it was evident that it was a few square inches of charred tweed.

"There are more scraps in there," Holmes assured us. "Not much remains, but enough that we may be confident that the jacket Bastion wore was burned there. Something else, too." He hefted the tongs and started back down the steps.

"But why would he have been wearing a tweed jacket?" Hopkins asked, bewildered. "Probert said he complained about the heat."

"Call Probert," Holmes instructed him shortly from below. "Have him await us in the drawing-room, with a constable on hand, and search his room. Bastion's wardrobe also. Watson, I need you to have a closer look at the body. Pay particular attention to the wrists, if you please."

Bewildered, I returned to the study, where Fratelli had arrived with a stretcher. He and another constable were beginning to lay out the body, but I asked them to desist for a moment while I did as Holmes had asked.

A few moments later, I was sure of what Holmes had had in mind. The clues were subtle, a slight reddening of the skin rather than any obvious weals, but Bastion's wrists were chafed. It was a sign that any but the most scrupulous medical examiner might have overlooked or dismissed, in the absence of any stronger reason for suspicion.

The chafing could well have come from a rough fabric like tweed, but only if it were forcibly rubbed against the skin. Simply wearing it would not have sufficed. It seemed that Bastion's arms had been constrained by something outside the tweed jacket, and that he had struggled against it.

"Good God," I breathed in realisation, and looked up to see Holmes and Hopkins standing at the door. Holmes' face was blackened from the soot as he bared his teeth in a terrifying grin of triumph.

In the tongs he held a short and singed, but clearly recognisable, length of rope.

NOTE FOUND WITH THE BODY OF THE HONOURABLE CHRISTOPHER BASTION

To those who survive me —

Over the past weeks, the reasons I have to prefer the continuance of Life to its alternative have by turns shown themselves false. Though the action I am about to take, along with my life and my leave of it, occasions me no greater unhappiness than I already suffer, I am aware that it will bring distress to my family and other connexions, and that I regret. I must particularly apologise to the servants who will doubtless discover my body, this not being an experience I should care for myself.

I ask my elder brother Julian and his children to preserve the Honour of the Family — as I have failed to do — and I hope that he, my younger brother Rupert and our dear Mother may yet forgive me the disappointment I now occasion them.

Pray for my soul, if you can find it in your own to do so.

In sorrow,
Christopher Bastion

Holmes' fingers were tapping at the desk again, a fast measure of the sort I associate with dances from the Southern Americas.

"So the murderer brought a jacket with him," Inspector Hopkins said, puzzling the matter through. "Or more likely he found it here among Bastion's things. The cotton one wouldn't do, though. It had to be a thicker cloth, like tweed, so that the rope-burns would be almost undetectable as such. Obvious marks would have shown that violence was done. He made Bastion wear it, somehow—at gunpoint, I suppose—and forced him to write the letter. Then he tied him up, and administered the poison while he struggled. He wouldn't swallow that stuff under duress, after all, even if the alternative was shooting. Why should he? He'd be dead either way."

"Unless his state of mind were genuinely suicidal," I ventured.

Unexpectedly, Holmes laughed. "A provoking waste of the murderer's effort if it was. But no, he could hardly have relied on that. Almost anyone would struggle against such a fate."

"Then," Hopkins went on eagerly, "once Bastion was dead, the killer removed the rope and jacket, burned them both to hide the evidence, then posed him as if he'd just written the letter."

I shook my head. "How diabolical." Then, considering the matter further, I added, "They took a chance, though, even so. What if Bastion had refused to write the note? The murderer could hardly do that for him. And I suppose he must have dictated it to him word by word, to make sure he didn't smuggle in some secret message to show he was being murdered. After all, Bastion was a resourceful man when not being led astray by his appetites, and he must have known some spy-craft."

"An intriguing thought, Watson," said Holmes. "At first sight I detect no sign of any code or cipher, but the question will bear further investigation. May I keep it, Inspector?"

Hopkins shrugged. "It's been photographed *in situ*. We'll need it for our records eventually, and of course if it becomes important as evidence, but you're welcome to it for now."

"But how did they get in, Hopkins?" I asked. "I thought your men eliminated all the doors and windows. Not to mention the coal-hatch."

"That problem, at least, is elementary," murmured Holmes.

"Oh, yes," Hopkins agreed at once. "It can only be Probert. He has access to Bastion's clothing, and he keeps the house-keys. Either he killed his employer himself, or he allowed someone else into the house who did."

I was shocked. "But he seemed so upset at his master's death."

Holmes tutted. "Come, Watson. We have both known murderers who were the most consummate actors, and others who felt actual grief for their victims. It is clear enough that Probert was involved, even if he was coerced by another. I suggest we put the question to him."

We found Probert waiting in the drawing-room as Holmes had instructed, with a solidly built policeman—introduced to us by Hopkins as Constable Vincent—standing meaningfully at hand. Where Bastion's study had been comfortably functional, with unshowy furniture and paper files on display alongside the books, the drawing-room was obviously intended to impress. Portraits hung on the flock-papered walls, and a bust of one of Bastion's ancestors sat in an alcove above the fireplace. Under its stern gaze, the manservant sat trembling on a velvet chaise-longue.

His face was as white as a snowcloud. Holmes—whom I had persuaded at least to wash his own face before the interview, so that he would appear somewhat less demonic—sternly tossed the charred remnants, the rag of tweed and the twist of rope, at Probert's feet.

He said, "I do not think I need to tell you the trouble you are in, my man. If you cannot give us a satisfactory account of what occurred last night, you will certainly hang. You may hang in any case, but if you tell us the truth it is at least possible that someone more culpable will swing alongside you. But you must begin now."

"Oh, sirs, forgive me," babbled Probert. "For lying, I mean— no man can forgive the rest, nor God either, I'm afraid—O God! I'm so afraid. It was my niece, you see, little Lucy, my sister Nancy's girl, God rest her—she's in service in Cardiff and they told me they'd taken her there, that she'd die if I didn't do what they said, and—"

"Probert!" snapped Holmes, and held up a hand. The valet subsided into tremulous silence. "We can learn nothing from this stream of blather. Pray tell us the facts, and in the correct order if you please. Start from the beginning. Who are 'they'?"

Probert gaped. "I never knew their names, sir. They called round yesterday while Mr Bastion was out at the Ministry. Two big, burly lads, dressed like salesmen. They said they were selling tea, with samples. Mr Bastion's always wanting to try new blends, so I let them in."

"What were their appearances?" Holmes asked crisply. "Their accents? Their ages?"

"Oh, both in their late twenties, they could have been," the valet said, screwing up his eyes to bring them to mind. "One fair, one dark with muttonchops—not black, but dark brown, like. Brown serge suits they were wearing, double-breasted with black buttons and lapels, and brown bowler hats. They talked like Londoners, as far as I could tell."

"So far, so anonymous," Holmes observed grimly. "Please proceed."

"Well, as soon as they were inside I could tell they were up to no good," said Probert. "They started moving ornaments around, making offensive comments about the servants' cleanliness and the master's taste. I could tell they were wrong ones then. But no-one else was in except the maid, and I wasn't going to call on her to help, was I?" He faltered, staring at us in appeal, but nobody reassured him on this point.

He continued, "Well, after a bit they got to the point, like. They knew who I was, and they knew about my family. They knew my only living relation—apart from her father, my brother-in-law, who I'd be glad to see the back of, to be honest with you, drunkard that he is—was young Lucy. She's my goddaughter as well as my niece, and she's meant the world to me since her Mam died. She's only seventeen, sirs, and housemaid to a very respectable family in Cardiff, like I said. They told me that some friends of theirs had her in their house, they showed me a lock of her hair—"

"How did you know that it was hers?" Holmes interjected.

Probert shook his head convulsively. "I asked myself that afterwards, Mr Holmes. It was brown and curly like hers, but of course you're right, it could have been anybody's. At the time, though, I believed them—and afterwards, well, would *you* have taken the chance?"

I said, "Did you not think to send a telegram to Cardiff, man, to ask after your niece and confirm their story?"

"It all happened so fast, sir. The idea didn't come to me till later, once all the Post Offices were closed."

"Find out at once," Hopkins ordered Constable Vincent, who left the room with alacrity once Probert had supplied the address. "Please go on, Probert."

"Well, the men looked round the house, sir, even going down into the cellar. Then they told me they'd be coming again that night, after Mr Bastion was asleep, to take away some share certificates they reckoned were in his study, and they said if I knew what was good for me and for little Lucy, I'd leave the servants' door unlocked for them. They told me to expect them at one in the morning, and to lay out a thick outdoor jacket in the kitchen. I said that Mr Bastion wouldn't have retired by then, night owl that he was, but they said that was all the better, as he could show them where the papers were. All I had to do was let them in and keep out of their way."

"And you complied, of course," Holmes scoffed.

"Like I said, sir, I didn't see that I had a choice, not if I wanted to keep Lucy safe. They said they only wanted the shares, you see—I knew Mr Bastion had money troubles, and I thought they were from his creditors. And if so, well, it was only what he owed, wasn't it?" A faint look of disapproval entered Probert's expression, and I wondered whether he harboured that Puritan streak that I have found common among his countrymen. A belief that Bastion had brought this trouble upon himself would have made it easier for him to betray his master in this way.

Holmes was asking, "Did Mr Bastion in fact keep share certificates in his study, to your knowledge?"

"Well no, sir, but he didn't confide in me about everything. I only know about his money difficulties because he sent me to the bank to collect some of his savings."

"So you left the servants' entrance unlocked, as instructed, and left the tweed jacket to hand. Why did you suppose it would be needed?"

Probert quailed. "I hadn't a clue, sir. I thought perhaps they planned to take him to see their employer, whoever he owed money to. But I didn't want to speculate, sir, nor argue either. I just did what I was asked."

"Thus making yourself, by your own admission, a willing accessory to kidnapping at the very least," Holmes sighed, with a glance at me. "And did the men arrive at one o'clock?"

Probert looked even more ashamed than before. "Sir, I

couldn't bear to listen. I left the door unlocked, took a sleeping-draught and went to bed. I wanted to sleep through it all, you see, and hope that all was well in the morning."

"And instead you awoke to find your master killed," Holmes concluded remorselessly. "Well, Probert, I am not surprised that you were upset. The realisation that the crime you were in fact an accessory to was murder cannot have been a pleasant one."

"I thought … I still hoped perhaps, that he'd killed himself," Probert admitted. "I thought perhaps losing the last of his money had been the final straw, like. I wasn't sure of it until you showed me the rope."

He broke off into sobs, and none of us felt especially inclined to comfort him.

After the manservant had been arrested and taken away, Hopkins confided to Holmes, Douglass and myself, "On the whole I believe him, even so. He's a craven specimen, not a malicious one, and I don't think he has the wit to invent such a convoluted story. My guess is it's true, as far as it goes."

"We cannot be certain until we find the men he described," Holmes observed.

"That's true, of course. I mustn't become complacent, especially after you've proved my first assumption wrong."

"Nonetheless," Holmes admitted, "I too believe that there is more to this crime than a simple matter of a servant killing his master. We have no indication of any grievance against Bastion on Probert's part, and your men's search found no gun or other weapon in his room."

"He could have disposed of it somehow," I said. "Thrown it into the Thames, perhaps."

"Then why not rid himself of the rope and jacket in the same way?" Holmes asked rhetorically. "Perhaps indeed a gun will appear yet—I recommend a thorough search of the house, Hopkins," he added, as if the Inspector would not have considered such a measure without his expert advice "—but in the meantime we should look out for two burly murderers in serge suits."

Holmes then asked to be taken to see the address in Hackney where Zimmerman, the spymaster who was believed to have recruited Bastion, had been based. Mycroft had assured us that no expense would be spared, so we sent Constable Fratelli to procure us a cab. "You won't see very much there, though," Hopkins warned us meanwhile. "We've cleaned out his effects. If you want material evidence you'll need to come to the Yard."

"I intend to do so," said Holmes, "but even so, I should first like to see the location of the arrest. Was anything of interest found on Zimmerman's body, after his ill-fated escape attempt?"

Hopkins shook his head. "Nothing but the clothes he stood up in, and those were ordinary enough—an inexpensive suit, bought off the peg at a local tailor's."

"And the body itself?"

"We looked for anything that might distinguish it, but there was nothing out of the ordinary. All we can say is that, before the horses trampled him, he was a healthy man in his thirties, with no signs of serious injury or illness in his past. I suppose if I were to die suddenly and anonymously they'd say the same," reflected Hopkins ruefully.

"'Zimmerman' was a code name, of course?"

"So we assume. He was reclusive and never left his room, and the German for room is Zimmer, you know. His agents, or their messengers, met him there, and all his food and other goods were delivered."

Holmes frowned. "That is most remarkable. I presume the body has been disposed of by now? Quite so. Well, it is a pity, but not to be helped."

Our cab had arrived, and Hopkins accompanied us to the house. As we travelled from the gentility of Mayfair through Holborn and into the altogether less salubrious surroundings of the East End, the Inspector apprised us of how he had come to be involved in the events surrounding Zimmerman's death.

If Hopkins' reputation as one of the brightest of Scotland Yard's rising stars was based partly on the murder investigations with which Holmes had assisted him early in his career, it was also well earned by his own merits. It seemed that his more recent work had involved a series of assignments to cases considered out of the ordinary by his superiors. In recent months he had investigated a particularly vicious blackmailer, an outbreak of counterfeiting, and more recently a series of arsons across the capital which had done great damage and claimed several lives.

It was this last case that had led Hopkins to Zimmerman, after one of the victims, Konrad Wendt, was identified as an agent in the service of a foreign government. The spymaster was now presumed to have organised the entire prolific arson spree merely to rid himself of this troublesome rival. Hopkins and his superiors had considered the idea of waiting and watching Zimmerman to identify the members of his spy ring, but felt that the risk of alerting him to their presence and causing him to abscond was too great, leading to the speedy apprehension Mycroft had told us about.

The cabman called to tell us that we had arrived, and we alighted to find ourselves outside a grimy terrace in one of the better parts of the East End. At one end stood a grocer's shop, at the other an unprepossessing public house.

Another policeman, introduced to us as Constable Kean, now stood guard at the door of the house where Zimmerman had rented his rooms—in case, Hopkins told us, any of the spy's colleagues might come looking for something that they thought the police search might have missed. Constable Kean accompanied us inside, together with the landlady, who stood with her arms folded as if we were imposing upon her time, though nobody had asked her to be present.

The rooms were sparse and meagre, with the only furniture remaining being a hard wooden bed, a table and chair. The fireplace where the frenzied Zimmerman had been found burning his papers had, to Holmes' disappointment, been swept thoroughly clean, though Hopkins assured him that the ashes had been sifted and all surviving fragments of paper recovered. Over the landlady's voluble protests, Holmes prised up a loose floorboard, but found the space beneath it empty. He replaced it with a dissatisfied sigh and began to knock listlessly at the walls.

For my part I was struck by how mean and miserable a life Zimmerman must have led, confined by necessity to the four walls of such a room, lit dimly through its coke-smeared windows even on so bright a day as this. This morning we had visited Mycroft Holmes, enthroned in luxury and comfort at the Diogenes Club, while here a man who was his professional counterpart had lived in squalid isolation.

The landlady, an unedifying specimen of cockney womanhood but garrulous enough in the presence of money, acknowledged that she, too, had known her tenant as Mr Zimmerman. Asked to describe him, she shrugged and said unhelpfully that "he looked like other folk, I suppose." In the months he had been lodging with her she had rarely or ever known him to leave his room, yet he was no hermit, receiving visitors at all hours of the day and night. "And queer enough some of them was," she noted derisively. "Covering round with scarves and such in the middle of Summer, like they didn't want no-one to recognise them. Who did they think they were, then, eh, the Duke of Wellington?" She admitted that her lodger had, however, paid his rent regularly and on time, "which is more than what I can say for some."

Hopkins reassured her patiently, and I sensed for the umpteenth time, that the police would continue to cover the rent for as long as the investigation continued. This seemed to mollify her, though Holmes' sudden move to dismantle the bed had the opposite effect. Again, though, he found nothing, and left Constable Kean to reassemble it. "I can only compliment your men on the thoroughness of their search, Hopkins," he told him peevishly. "If there are any clues remaining here after so long, they are beyond my ability to detect."

We returned with the Inspector to Scotland Yard, where we were told by Constable Vincent that a deputation from the Cardiff police force had found Lucy Evans, Probert's niece, going peaceably about her domestic duties at her employers' house, and that beyond her understandable distress at the news of her uncle's arrest she had experienced nothing untoward over the past few days. We could be thankful for that, at least.

While Hopkins set about instigating a search for the men whom Probert had described, Vincent led us into the room where the late Zimmerman's effects had been stored. Holmes nodded with approval, and pitched himself into searching through the neatly ordered piles and throwing them into utter disarray.

He quickly confirmed what Hopkins' men had already established, that there was little here to connect the spy with Bastion. Apart from the civil servant's letter to Zimmerman, now in the hands of Sir Hector Askew, none but the most routine correspondence had been found, and nothing else bearing Bastion's name. The only papers here were invoices for goods and services, playbills and advertisements and the like, old newspapers and some recent issues of *Punch* magazine. There were a few, very conventional, books—some novels of Dickens and Scott, the poems of Wordsworth and Tennyson, and a volume of Shakespeare. Holmes flipped through them in search of any indication that they might have been used to generate a book-code, but if they had then our spy was too wily to have left traces of the fact. The police had spoken to the tradesmen whose invoices were represented, cobblers and stationers and grocers and the like, who all told the same story of receiving orders via a messenger and delivering their goods to Zimmerman care of his landlady.

It did appear as if Zimmerman had gone through a great quantity of tobacco, and his liquor cabinet had also been better stocked than one might have expected for a man in his situation. The better, I assumed, for plying his informants and agents with. He had few clothes—as I supposed befitted a man who rarely went outside—some of which had been retrieved from his regular laundry by the police on the basis of the receipts they had found. Like the clothes he had died in, all were cheap, though not of especially poor quality, and none had been tailored for his wear.

Finally, Holmes turned his attention to the charred scraps carefully preserved from the ashes in the spy's hearth. There, too, he found precious little encouragement. The signs suggested that Zimmerman had destroyed the most sensitive materials first, reasonably enough, but a few fragments remained. The most intact appeared to be records of financial transactions, but even there, where one might optimistically have hoped for names, or at least for code names, Zimmerman had frustrated us once again by using an arbitrary system of non-alphabetical symbols that bore no relation to any scheme we could identify.

"A most anonymous man," Holmes observed. "Indeed, a very dull one in most respects, his only points of interest being the pains he took to remain anonymous. I assume that the body was photographed, Hopkins?"

"Oh yes," the Inspector said, "though it's no help as far as his face is concerned. Those horses gave his head quite a hammering."

THE DAILY GAZETTE

21st October 1897

DISCREDITED BARRACLAGH CLAIMANT GOES MISSING FROM HOME

Mr Leonard Griffon, whose supposed inheritance of the Barraclagh earldom and its associated Irish estate was discredited in court, has gone missing from his Finchley home and has not been seen for some days.

Mr Griffon is understood to have been financially embarrassed prior to his discovery of a marriage-certificate that might have placed him in line to inherit the title and its lavish holdings, had not an earlier certification been discovered that invalidated it. It is widely speculated that the document first discovered was a forgery, although one that convinced the legal experts who swore to its authenticity in court.

While his temporary notoriety as the so-called "Barraclagh Claimant" somewhat alleviated Mr Griffon's money troubles, his neighbours attest that his income had "dried up" of late, and that some crisis may have ensued. A police investigation is in progress. The officer in charge, Inspector Bradstreet, told our reporter that he is still learning about the ramifications of the previous case and how they may have affected the missing man's behaviour.

It is to be hoped that Mr Griffon is safe and well, and that there is a perfectly harmless explanation for his disappearance.

A messenger had appeared while Holmes was occupied with Zimmerman's possessions, and informed us that Mycroft had arranged our appointment with Sir Hector Askew, the Foreign Office Minister who had been Bastion's immediate superior. Together my friend and I proceeded by cab to Bloomsbury, where Sir Hector's townhouse was located. We drew up shortly between one of those small, leafy parks with which the wealthiest parts of London are dotted, and the large corner house of a Georgian terrace.

Inside the latter we were swiftly ushered into the presence of Sir Hector, a man of fretful appearance in his late middle years, whose luxuriant grey beard was poor compensation for a pate on which the hair grew sparsely. He greeted us with some reserve, adding even more diffidently, "You come to me highly recommended by your brother, Mr Holmes, and I trust that he has not been swayed by family partiality. I must particularly enjoin you not to inquire into the nature of the state secrets held by the late Mr Bastion unless it becomes necessary to do so, strictly necessary. Have I your assurance on that point?"

Holmes inclined his head gravely, and Sir Hector proceeded. "This is a terrible business, simply terrible, and I am quite exhausted by dealing with its ramifications. Both the Government and I personally shall be most grateful for anything you can do to help limit the damage. Bastion was my right-hand man, and had been to several ministers before me. The harm he may have done by intemperate disclosure of all he knew is incalculable, quite incalculable."

"So we gather," Holmes replied. "Some people might even suggest that allowing a man with his weaknesses to hold such a position of responsibility argues some negligence on the part of those predecessors of yours."

Askew looked shocked. "But there was never a hint, not even a breath of a doubt of Bastion's reliability. He was of one of the oldest families, the noblest, of a reputation quite above reproach. Why, his grandfather served with mine during Lord Palmerston's administration. He was considered by all my forerunners to be absolutely trustworthy."

"It must be some comfort to them that it was you he eventually betrayed," Holmes observed drily. "I understood, however, that Bastion's weakness for the fairer sex was well known?"

Askew coloured. "Well, to be sure he enjoyed the company of women, but such a predilection was considered … harmless, relatively harmless … quite acceptable, in fact, compared to the vices that some men harbour. I have inquired among my predecessors, and they were aware that he had had … mistresses … before. None of those had shown the slightest sign of compromising him as this one did. Throughout his prior affairs, his conduct in office was unimpeachable. As far as his professional life went, he was …"

"Trustworthy?" suggested Holmes puckishly. "Above reproach? Of undoubted reliability? I am hearing such opinions expressed a great deal about the late Mr Bastion, and yet the evidence of reality is lamentably lax in bearing them out. Errors of judgement were made, Minister, and they were surely not Christopher Bastion's alone."

Sir Hector subsided, tugging ruefully at his beard. "I cannot deny the justice of that, Mr Holmes. I fail to see, however, that it gets us very far with the practical problem at hand."

"I agree, unless it turns out that some of those who contributed to his installation—and continuation—in this position of trust are themselves compromised. That, I feel, is something that my brother, and Her Majesty's Government, should properly take an interest in."

Askew paled. "Mr Holmes, you are surely not suggesting …"

"I suggest nothing, Sir Hector. I merely note possibilities. Prior to the scandal, had Bastion seemed preoccupied to you?"

The Minister seemed disconcerted by the sudden turn in the line of questioning, as well as by uncertainty over whether he himself was under suspicion. I had already known that the mere mention of Mycroft Holmes' name could strike fear into the functionaries of the Civil Service, but I had not realised that it was sufficient to make government ministers themselves quail.

Sir Hector shook his head distractedly and replied, "On the contrary, he seemed in good spirits, excellent spirits. At the time I had no idea that there was any special reason for this. I assumed that it was because of the success we have had in certain of our recent endeavours abroad."

I wondered how far Bastion and Askew had been involved in agreeing the lease of our new territories in Hong Kong, but the Minister was still speaking. He said, "Knowing what I now do, I assume that his association with the young person was proceeding to his satisfaction. She must have been excessively beguiling, I suppose, to offset the pecuniary expense, but I understand that … well, let us be charitable and call it love … can have extreme effects upon a man."

"I have often observed it to be so," said Holmes drily, "though never at first hand, I am relieved to say. Are you yourself married, Sir Hector?"

Askew looked shocked at the idea that the question of love might be relevant to his marriage. "I am indeed," he said stiffly. "But I too am fortunate enough to keep my head in such matters. Bastion's failings are not my own, I am pleased to say. Still," he added hurriedly, "I cannot find it in myself to judge him too harshly. Too often the flesh is weak, Mr Holmes, sadly weak."

"Well, then," said Holmes, "let us trust that Mr Bastion's is the only flesh whose weakness proves relevant in this matter. So you saw no deterioration in his mood as the discovery that led to his dismissal approached? He said nothing that might have alluded to a crisis to come?"

"Nothing at all, as far as I was aware. To me he spoke of state matters with his usual gravity, and treated them with the seriousness they warranted, just as he always had."

"He made no attempt to find out any information to which he would not normally have been entitled?"

"Not that I knew. There was little to which he did not have access in any case, within our Ministry at least. Very little."

"I see." Holmes frowned. "It sounds to me as if Mr Bastion took a very blithe view of his financial troubles, and of his decision to betray his country. That, he seems not to have treated with the seriousness it warranted at all."

Sir Hector Askew could do little more than shrug his agreement.

Holmes continued, "I am told that you have the letter he wrote to this man Zimmerman."

"It was given to me for safekeeping," the Minister agreed, readily enough, "while my Office made its internal investigations. I have it in my safe here, which is why I suggested we meet here rather than at my office—even though, as I have mentioned, I am extremely busy at present, quite exceptionally busy in fact. I felt that its contents were altogether too incendiary to risk their presence there."

"I am sure you are correct. I must ask you, however, to deliver it into my keeping for the moment. I need to understand its contents thoroughly." Seeing Sir Hector's hesitation, he added, "I can hardly imagine that Bastion would have revealed anything of vast national sensitivity in an initial approach. As I am an uninvolved party, you can hardly object to such an arrangement, I trust."

Sir Hector huffed and tugged his beard again. "I fail to see the necessity—"

Holmes sighed. "That is because you are not a detective, Sir Hector. I am, and I tell you that it is necessary. Please hand it over, or I shall be obliged to tell my brother that you have been uncooperative."

Again, I saw alarm in Askew's eyes. He stood and crossed the room to a painting of a picturesque moorland scene, which hinged aside to reveal a wall-safe. With a practised hand he turned the knob to the correct combination, and withdrew an envelope which he handed to Holmes. My friend opened it to examine the folded paper within. He replaced it and pocketed it with thanks, but not before I recognised the handwriting we had seen in Bastion's suicide note.

Then he bade a curt goodbye to Sir Hector and strode out into the hallway, leaving me to attempt a more conciliatory farewell.

"Holmes' manner can be brusque," I observed meekly as we followed, "but it arises from his zeal to prosecute a case. You may be sure that he will show far less courtesy to the wrongdoers when we face them, and you may be just as confident that we will."

The older man gave me a weak nod. "I thank you for your reassurances, Dr Watson. From his attitude I might have assumed that he meant to prosecute me. Ah, Jerome!" he added as a young man emerged from a nearby doorway. "Dr Watson, I'd like you to meet Jerome Windward, who's some sort of cousin of mine. Second or third, is it, Jerome?"

"First, sir, I believe, but two or three times removed," said Windward, in a light but steady voice. He was a handsome young man, curly-haired, with a noble brow and something about his sensitive mouth that put me in mind of the poet Shelley. "I'm delighted to make your acquaintance, Dr Watson."

Sir Hector explained that his relative was staying with him in town for the Summer. "I believe he's something of an admirer of yours," he added.

I looked around for Holmes, assuming that Askew was addressing him, but he had already left.

The young man said, "Indeed, Dr Watson, I'm quite the devotee of your accounts of Mr Holmes' exploits. I'm a writer myself, you know. It's a bit of a family tradition." As the older man bade me farewell and vanished back into his study, I recalled that Sir Hector had, early in his political career, achieved some small notoriety as the author of a pair of novels, *Davina* and *The Vintner of Slough*, which had received uniformly negative reviews.

"Cousin Hector talks a lot about Palmerston," Windward added, "but the premier who he really admires is Disraeli. Old Dizzy actually had some literary talent, though."

"He certainly had," I said, having long admired *Coningsby* and *Sybil* in particular. "I'm afraid I haven't had the honour of reading Sir Hector's work, though. Or your own, Mr Windward," I added, meaningfully, thinking perhaps to take this charming young tyro down a peg or two.

"Oh, I'm unpublished as yet," he admitted carelessly, "though in time I hope to make my name and my fortune—not to mention a better fist of the writing business than poor Cousin Hector. I'm sure the publishers will leap at the chance once they see what I'm offering. I craft stories of crime and mystery, Dr Watson, like your own, but mine are fiction, unfettered by your need to remain faithful to the facts. Arthur Morrison and Max Pemberton are my models for plot—though yourself, naturally, for style."

"I see," I said, as Holmes' irritable cry of "Watson!" resounded from outside. "Well, it has been delightful to make your acquaintance, Mr Windward, but as you can hear I am needed."

"Here, Doctor," the young man said, suddenly depositing

in my hand a heavy envelope, "one of my recent efforts—*The Assassins' Dagger*. Perhaps you could glance through it, if it won't occasion you too much inconvenience, and give me your opinion? I should be most grateful. As I say, you are one of my literary masters."

Flustered yet flattered by his forwardness, I promised that I would do my best, and once again hurried after Holmes.

The rest of our afternoon was spent in calling at each of the venues mentioned in Bastion's appointment-book, asking about the civil servant's visits. As Holmes had noted previously, many of these establishments were insalubrious, and accordingly unwilling to divulge information about their patrons' habits and associations—even when presented with pecuniary incentives, and certainly not when imposed upon by threats of the police. From the partial information we could gather, it seemed that on the rare occasions when he had not been seen with Gillian McGuire, alias Adorée Felice, Bastion had been living his normal social life, associating mostly with friends of long standing, nearly all of whom were either equally trusted public servants or visitors from outside London. None of them seemed promising as conduits for privileged information between a spy and his handler. Hopkins' inquiries among Bastion's colleagues at his work, and his grieving relatives, were to prove equally fruitless.

After the long, hot day the evening was cool. Holmes spent most of it minutely perusing the civil servant's supposed suicide note. First, he copied the contents and laid out the words in various grids, in different combinations and permutations, doing the same with their first letters, their second and so forth, counting first from the beginning and then from the end of each word. This laborious procedure produced no indication that the letter had been written in any kind of code.

"We cannot exclude the possibility that the wording may

convey a private meaning to some friend or colleague," he noted, "but otherwise, I think we may dismiss the notion of a secret message here."

He then set up a bright lantern on his writing-desk, and examined the note closely with his magnifying-glass, lighting it from various angles and from behind. He did the same with Bastion's letter to Zimmerman, and with the appointment-book, which he had retained with Hopkins' permission. After examining them closely, together and separately, he snipped off tiny fragments of the paper, and scraped off samples of ink, and subjected them to chemical analysis. He attempted, with a variety of pens and on several paper types, to reproduce the exact shape of some of the letters. He consulted textbooks of graphology in various languages, and his own copious notes upon the subject. In increasing annoyance he flipped through the appointment-book, comparing individual pages with one another.

Finally he threw down his glass with an exclamation of frustration. I looked up from young Windward's manuscript, which I had been reading with, to my surprise, considerable enjoyment.

"I am confounded, Watson," he confessed with a growl. "I have reached the limits of my expertise. My knowledge of handwriting is both broad and deep, but in the end I am a generalist. My graphological knowledge rooms in my head with companion subjects as diverse as criminal history, toxicology and the physical properties of mud. I have reached the limits of its permitted space and must, to my frustration, consult some specialist who has seen fit to grant it sole occupancy."

This happened rarely, I knew, but it was not unprecedented: Holmes had in the past been forced to approach experts in, for instance, the fields of mycology and herpetology when his knowledge of fungal growth and reptile behaviour had, even with the assistance of his textbooks, proven inadequate to the task in hand. When he discovered such lacunae in his own compendious expertise, he responded with shame and dismay, as if they were a moral failing, or perhaps a personal affront.

I had been wondering about his activities for some time. "Do you suspect, then, that the letter to Zimmerman was forged?" I asked. "I understood that it matched the other samples of Bastion's writing."

"These three samples match one another perfectly, at any rate," Holmes admitted. "More perfectly than they should. A man's moods leave their traces in his script, Watson. A man in a state of cheerful excitement shapes his letters with an energy and vigour that are absent in his more depressed hours. A tired or drunken man writes more erratically than he would when alert and sober.

"If we are to believe what we are told, then the handwriting in this letter, in which Bastion betrayed his country, and this, which he wrote at the point of death, reproduce perfectly that seen in his appointment-book, in which he recorded perfectly mundane matters of daily routine. There is no sign of stress in any of them, no more deformed letters or slapdash shortcuts in one than another. Either Bastion had nerves of such firm steel that he wrote with perfect calm when anticipating his own death at gunpoint, or these materials were not written under the circumstances we have been led to believe. I was a fool to miss such an obvious point before."

"But the writing matches nevertheless?" I repeated, trying to grasp what my friend was implying.

"As I have been saying, it is identical," Holmes snapped. "As identical as one might expect from an accomplished—no, I would say a technically perfect—forger imitating Bastion's hand."

"Good heavens," I said. "But that might mean that Bastion was not a traitor at all."

Holmes nodded. "Perhaps. It means that the suicide note

need not be genuine either—that is, that Bastion may not even have written it to the murderer's specification. It would have saved him some little effort and unpleasantness at the scene. Who knows, perhaps even the appointment-book is falsified, to conceal some meeting of greater import. I will try to obtain more samples of Bastion's hand from his office, assuming that we can trust even those to be genuine."

"He had family," I reminded Holmes. "Perhaps Mycroft could ask his relatives whether they have kept any letters of his?"

"A good notion," Holmes agreed. "I should prefer not to involve them, but it may come to that."

It was late and I was prepared to retire, but Holmes had begun pacing about with a nervous energy that I found bordered upon the manic. "Graphology is a closed avenue for tonight," he said. "I must find another to explore."

He vanished into his room while I continued to read Windward's tale of crime, *The Assassins' Dagger*. As the young man had promised, it was a gripping yarn, mixing peril and tension with the intellectual fascination of a puzzle whose solution I glimpsed in part as I read, but remained unable to fully grasp. It reminded me of nothing so much as my own accounts of my cases with Holmes, but with the additional intrigue, for me, of not knowing in advance the answer to the conundrum or the climax of the plot. For a novice author, he showed astonishing talent and promise, and it seemed to me likely that he had Great Things in his future.

After a few minutes, a stranger emerged from Holmes' room, a ratty, whiskered fellow with a shabby coat, a stye in one eye and a complexion so poor it made my own skin itch in sympathy.

"I suppose you're going out, then?" I said, now well used to my friend's disguises—although if truth were known I would still have had trouble in picking him out in a crowd.

"That I am, sir, begging your pardon, sir," the man wheedled, rubbing his hands together nervously.

"Please, Holmes," I begged, "spare me the voice at least."

The man straightened and seemed to grow taller, more identifiably Holmes. "I find it helpful to associate a disguise with a specific character," he told me, a little disgruntled. "Breaking that association interferes with my method."

"I see," I said, though I did not. "Will you be back for breakfast?"

"Unless some unexpected crisis arises. We are due at Scotland Yard to meet Hopkins at nine," he reminded me.

With that he left and I settled down with Windward's masterpiece. So gripping was it that it was some hours later before I retired.

LETTER TO "ZIMMERMAN"

18th May 1898

Sir—

You may be surprised to hear from me. You have heard, no doubt, that I have of late been inquiring after you, or someone in your position, and have perhaps had misgivings that I was doing so on behalf of my employers.

But I can assure you that nothing could be further from the Truth. The time has come to show my true colours along with my hand—for however I might phrase the disgrace I now contemplate, it occasions me no greater sense of satisfaction—and you, if you are willing to review them, certain particulars of my work in connexion with the service of Government that I have been, and remain, under a solemn oath to keep concealed.

I admit my distaste at the expedient to which I am compelled—these circumstances, I confess, are ones I neither anticipated nor welcome—but I must be pragmatic. And I am forced to concede that your work is little different from that with which I have actively colluded. Only your loyalties differ, and what is loyalty? An admirable quality, no doubt, but soluble in the presence of money and of desperation.

The information I possess is of exceptional value, and I anticipate that the compensation I receive for it will be equally lavish. The details of this must be negotiated between us in person.

Yours

Christopher Bastion

When I awoke at eight I found Holmes already at breakfast, having returned at some point during the night, and seemingly not in the least tired. I knew that his indefatigable energy when engaged in a case that exercised his intellect was reflected in his lassitude at other times, and though I had found the former state exhausting on numerous occasions, I was glad for his sake to see it.

"Ah, Watson!" he cried. "You have some time for some of Mrs Hudson's excellent kedgeree before our appointment with Hopkins."

I mumbled an acknowledgement and poured myself a coffee. Unlike Holmes, I am not always at my brightest in the mornings.

After thus fortifying myself, I took some food and inquired after his nocturnal activities. He pursed his lips. "I have had but small success, Watson," he told me. "I have been haunting some of the lowest and most criminal public houses of our fine capital, in the hope of catching wind of the men who, if Probert is to be believed, menaced him and murdered Christopher Bastion. Unfortunately, all we know is that they are large and burly, one blond and clean-shaven, one brown-haired with muttonchop whiskers. Rather than work from such a vague description, I based my approach upon their known activities. Gambling that their grudge against Bastion is unlikely to have been a personal one, but was probably entered into on behalf of a third party, I offered myself discreetly as a thug for hire and asked where I might find those willing to pay me to commit violence.

"I then started trawling the establishments I was recommended in response to this, hoping that our pair might also be in attendance, seeking further work of the like kind.

"That gambit met with no success, which told me that either the men were paid well enough for Bastion's murder that they need no more work for the time being, or that they are long-term employees of whoever instigated it, rather than being freelance operators."

"Or that Probert is lying," I pointed out.

"Let us suppose for the moment that he is not. If such men exist, it is not unreasonable to suppose that they might be known to others who frequent such places, but asking violent men to identify other violent men is naturally a task requiring the utmost delicacy and caution. Accordingly, I pretended to be a pathetic specimen seeking help. I said that the men, who had not told me their names, had asked me to meet them for a job—I thought at the place in question—but that they had not appeared for our appointment and that perhaps I had been confused. I went so far as to hint that they had gained my cooperation as Probert told us they did his, with threats to my family members, in case that is a known *modus operandi* of theirs.

"After trying this approach in a number of exceptionally sordid hovels, I happened on a garrulous old fellow who seemed to know something, and after plying him liberally with the foul brew he favoured, I elicited the information that one of the pair might perhaps be a bruiser known by the soubriquet 'Chops', an *habitué* of yet another hostelry, where a friend of my drinking-companion's knew the landlord.

"At this final stop, the vilest yet, I found an interlocutor willing to divulge that Chops works with a colleague named 'Onions'. They match Probert's description of Bastion's putative murderers, Chops being the dark one and Onions the fair. They are known as a ruthless pair. Indeed, though I assumed at first that Chops gained his cognomen from his whiskers, it seems it derives from his use of a hatchet, and he grew the muttonchops to match it. His comrade's nickname came later as an ironical pairing. Though brutal by choice, they are willing to work to exacting specifications if the price is right. However, they have not been seen at their old haunts for some time, having, it is supposed, found gainful—if not beneficial—employment with a client who has retained their services on a lasting basis.

"And there my trail ran cold. It is unlikely that I shall return to the establishment in question, as the landlord took a dislike to my line of questioning, and I was forced to fight off several of his regulars in the alley outside before taking to my heels. They will, I fear, be more than usually suspicious of strangers for some little time."

I digested this new information alongside my kedgeree. "But does this really confirm Probert's story, Holmes? As you say, his description is a very vague one. Isn't it likely that if you looked hard enough you'd find a pair of roughs to match it, regardless of its truth?"

"An excellent point, Watson, and one we should not forget in our excitement. I fear, however, that I have learned little of use about Messrs Chops and Onions, whether they are our men or no, so the question may be moot for now. We must ask Hopkins whether he or his colleagues know of any criminals going by those names, though I fear the chances are small."

I read the newspaper while I finished my breakfast. By an interesting coincidence, there was a story about a brawl outside a tavern in Spitalfields, after which a man had been found savagely beaten to death. I said, "Did you see anything of this, Holmes? Apparently there was a killing outside a pub called the Butcher's Apron. It sounds like a very nasty business."

Holmes said, "The name is unfamiliar to me. Come, Watson, you must dress or we shall be late for our appointment with Hopkins."

I attired myself with haste, while Holmes summoned a cab to take us to Scotland Yard. There we were sent upstairs to meet Sergeant Douglass, who ushered us in to see his superior before retiring to his desk in the outer office.

Stanley Hopkins' own office was well appointed with modern furnishings, but overshadowed by nearby buildings, which gave it a gloomy look. We found him there with a like expression on his face, which became gloomier still when Holmes admitted how little headway he had made so far.

"The Commissioner isn't pleased with us," the young Inspector confided. "His view is that we have a perfectly satisfactory murderer in Probert, even if we have so far failed to determine his motive. He sees the man's statement as a transparent lie intended to shift the blame, though I pointed out that if he was trying to do that he could have concocted a story that would exonerate himself fully, rather than incriminating him as an accessory. Between ourselves, I think the Commissioner would be happier if we'd never discovered the evidence of Bastion's murder. A suicide would have been neater all around, and carried less risk of Lord Loomborough involving himself. The Commissioner can't complain at your intervention, of course, since it was decreed at the highest level, but he was most insistent that our efforts should not be wasted on what he called a wild goose chase."

"He will be pleased enough, I am sure, when we eventually present him with the goose," said Holmes, settling into one of the surprisingly comfortable chairs which faced Hopkins' desk. "Especially if it lays him a golden egg."

Hopkins rallied at the pleasantry, but became pensive once more as Holmes described his bootless search for "Chops" and "Onions". "They're not nicknames I recognise," said the Inspector, "though I'll ask around. I've not worked on crimes of common violence for a while."

"I had wondered whether they might have been in the late Mr Zimmerman's employ," Holmes suggested, "and have perhaps now transferred their loyalties to one of his associates."

Hopkins shrugged. "If so, I haven't come across them."

"I am also somewhat interested in the investigation preceding that which set you on to our friend Zimmerman," Holmes told Hopkins. "The spate of counterfeiting that you mentioned. There is some reason to suppose that it may have a bearing on the Bastion case."

Hopkins stared at him. "You're thinking of the note," he asked. "You suspect that it was forged, rather than exacted under duress? It would be difficult to do. Still, there are certainly some excellent forgers at large. We proved a handful of counterfeits, but had very little luck in finding those responsible for them."

"You surprise me, Hopkins," said Holmes, and I agreed. Hopkins was, as I have said, a fine detective and one of the Yard's most successful men. It was rare for him to fall short of prosecuting a case, especially since he could rely on Holmes' help on the occasions when he found himself baffled.

"It's remarkably difficult to do," Hopkins told us ruefully. "The mere existence of a forged document doesn't incriminate anyone in particular. In the case of a will, say, you can't arrest someone simply because they'd benefit from the forgery—not if there's no evidence they are responsible. In most cases there are a number of people who stand to gain, and often those who'd lose out are so embarrassed at being fooled that they'd prefer to avoid charges altogether. Finding out how and when a forgery entered circulation, when you can't necessarily trust any of your witnesses ... well, we had no luck, as I say. Eventually the Commissioner put a stop to that particular operation."

"You should have called on my services," Holmes told Hopkins, eschewing false modesty with his usual zeal. "I can think of several possible approaches to the problem."

"I would have done, but for the political ramifications. I'm deuced glad you were assigned this business from outside, in fact, rather than invited by me. The Commissioner can give my job to another inspector if he likes, one who'll be happy to stop at Probert, but he can hardly take you off the case."

"But why would he want to do such a thing?" I asked.

Hopkins sighed deeply. "Well, it's due to Lord Loomborough originally. He set out a list of the types of crime that were to take priority for my section—that is to say, those that are to be treated as the most serious and pervasive—and counterfeiting and other forms of fraud were ruled out. It was the first indication we had that he intended to be meddlesome, and is, I suppose, the reason why the Commissioner's so nervous now."

Holmes steepled his fingers. "It might be best to begin at the beginning, Hopkins."

"So you've often told me, sir," Hopkins smiled. "Very well. London has always had a smallish counterfeiting problem, as you know—banknotes, cheques, certificates and suchlike—but no more than should be expected in such a large city. Its escalation into a matter of unusual concern began a few years ago.

"We noticed that, while the supply of what you might call ordinary fakes remained about the same, the special cases increased sharply. A letter of recommendation here, a statement of provenance there, but their number increased, as did the quality. My team was asked to look into the matter.

"The Lesborne will was the first instance where we proved forgery. Suspicion was raised when it turned out that, on the date when his second will was supposedly made, Sir Lester Lesborne had been *en route* to Christiania aboard the SS *Incitatus*, and that the elderly butler and housekeeper who had supposedly witnessed it had not been with him. This was not something that could have been discovered without access to Sir Lester's personal diary and correspondence—and not very easily then, for he wasn't a methodical man. Indeed, it seemed more likely that he had made a mistake over the date, but then we tracked down the housekeeper. Her husband, the butler, had died, and she had gone to live with their grandson in Arbroath. She was adamant that they had witnessed only one will of Sir Lester's, the original that the one we held was supposed to have superseded."

"She could have been mistaken," Holmes pointed out, "or had some interest of her own in the matter."

"True enough," Hopkins agreed equably, "but a chemical analysis showed that, while the paper on which the new will was written appeared an exact match for that represented in Sir Lester's surviving correspondence of the time, it had in fact been manufactured more recently by the same company, who had changed their processes slightly in the interim. No paper of that precise type had been in existence until some time after one of the supposed witnesses had died.

"That clinched the matter, of course, and the second will was declared void, leaving the original to stand. Sir Lester's nephew, Dr Permenter of Camford University, professed himself astonished by the accuracy with which his uncle's handwriting had been reproduced."

"Would Dr Permenter have been a beneficiary of the forgery?" Holmes asked.

"No—his legacy was minor, and the second will did not change it substantially. The chief question was the division of Sir Lester's estate between his two daughters. The elder had married a man of whom the family disapproved, and the forged will was intended to look as if her father had disinherited her as a result. In fact, he had become rather fond of her husband since the marriage, and had intended no such thing."

"Presumably, then, the younger sister instigated the forgery," I suggested.

Hopkins shrugged. "She or her husband, or one of their sons or daughters, or anyone else who might have expected to benefit from her family's enrichment. There was no prosecution, though, and the families are well enough connected to have the matter hushed up."

"I am surprised that I had not heard of the case," Holmes observed. "It sounds a fascinating one."

"Oh, it was," Hopkins agreed enthusiastically. "It certainly piqued my interest. The next matter that came to our attention was a letter written to Lord Kerwinstone, purportedly by his late wife's sister. It introduced the bearer to him as a distant connexion by marriage, on which basis he was pleased to put the man up at Kerwin Hall. In fact there was no such relative, and the fellow cleared out Kerwinstone's safe and absconded with the family jewels the night after he arrived. The local police lost him long before anyone thought to involve us. Again, though, the facsimile of the sister-in-law's handwriting was held to be excellent.

"Then there was one you'll certainly have heard of, Mr Holmes—the inheritance of the Barraclagh earldom and its estate in Ireland. The title had been in abeyance for several generations before one Mr Leonard Griffon of Finchley discovered an old certificate of marriage between his great-grandmother and the third Earl of Barraclagh, suggesting that he was the legitimate heir. No other record of the union existed, but the Earl was notoriously eccentric, and it seemed plausible enough that he had told his friends nothing of the relationship. When he died the family holdings had gone to his brother, the fourth Earl, who then died without issue. The earldom was suspended, and the estates went to a distant cousin.

"Strictly speaking, we never disproved the story, but a thorough search of the estate itself eventually turned up the certification of an earlier, equally clandestine marriage, in a ruined stables where it is assumed that the Earl had secreted it for safekeeping. As there was no record of any divorce or annulment, and the woman in question was recorded as outliving the Earl, his marriage to Mr Griffon's great-grandmother was bigamous— if indeed it ever took place, which I personally doubt. That case was a popular curiosity for a while."

"I heard of it," Holmes agreed, "though your name was not mentioned. I did read, however, that the third Earl was terrified of horses, so the stables seemed an unlikely hiding place for him to have chosen."

"Perhaps. My theory was that the papers were stolen by an illiterate groom who hid them while he tried to work out the value of what he had." Hopkins grinned. "Since the Earl died in 1776, though, that was rather beyond the scope of our inquiries. But you're right, my name was never given out publicly in that case. There was some thought that all these forgeries might be linked, you see, and that this might tip someone off that we considered them so. We made nothing of that in the end, though, and I find it difficult to believe that they were the work of the same hand. The cases were tremendously diverse, as these things go, and unconnected as far as we could see.

"We looked into a number of other instances along similar lines. The one that troubles me most, though, has only happened quite recently. You have heard of Robert Foxon, the ivory importer who has been accused of massacring a native village when he was a sergeant during the Zulu War? That charge arose only recently, on the testimony of two soldiers who said he ordered their company to shoot forty Zulu women and children. The rest of the company had died since, and these two didn't want to take the guilt of it to their graves. The court-martial exonerated Foxon, and the men are to stand trial for perjury."

"I remember the case," I put in. I had been reading about it in the paper for the past several mornings. "Foxon's innocence was established by a signed affidavit from his lieutenant, placing him a good distance from the massacre."

Hopkins grimaced. "That's right. Major Macpherson, as he'd since become, had retired to India, and supposedly sent his testimony after hearing about the charges against Foxon. The Major died unexpectedly, though, in a shooting accident in the hills near Sind, before he could be asked to corroborate the story."

"A remarkable coincidence," Holmes observed sharply.

"And one I profoundly distrust," replied Hopkins, "especially as nobody has been able to locate the notary in Lahore who witnessed the affidavit. I firmly believe that it was another fake, and that Foxon's as guilty as sin. Furthermore, I believe he had Macpherson killed before the Major could reveal the imposture. Foxon's a rich man these days, and he has associates in India. The witnesses who tried to bring him to justice will likely die in gaol in his place."

"I agree, that is most troubling," Holmes said. "Especially since we may be dealing with another case that involves both forgery and murder. You made no headway in establishing the falsehood of the document?"

"Not after Lord Loomborough's edict arrived," said Hopkins, shaking his head. "It closed down the inquiry most effectively. Foxon maintains his innocence, and the court agreed. In most of the other cases, as I've said, we were stonewalled. Mr Griffon of Finchley, the Barraclagh claimant, disappeared, and he may well be dead too. To be sure he was in financial trouble like Bastion, but shortly before he vanished he expressed an interest in speaking to us on an urgent matter. We looked for him, but found nothing but dead ends, and now I'm too busy with the Zimmerman case to pursue it further."

Holmes tutted. "That is most unfortunate."

"Well, I'd be pleased to think that you were taking an interest in these cases, since I'm no longer permitted to," said the young Inspector. "I'm not sure that it helps us very much with Bastion, though."

"Perhaps not," said Holmes. "I gather, in any case, that the Commissioner would not look kindly upon your extending the scope of your investigation to include the question of forgery?"

"I wouldn't answer for his health or mine if he heard about it," Hopkins agreed cheerfully. "No, there's not a great deal I can do to help you on that side of things, officially at least. What I could do is send you to Dr Carson Graymare, one of the two graphologists who advised us on the letter Bastion wrote to Zimmerman. He's very well thought of, I understand, and has acted for the force as an expert witness in a number of cases."

"I know of his work," Holmes mused. "He has some modish theories, I believe, that have made him popular with the fashionable set. They show him their scrawl and he divines their character. I'd call it a cheap parlour trick, except that I believe they pay him rather well for the privilege. Still, I gather he has some professional credibility nevertheless, and if he comes also with your recommendation then it can do no harm for us to consult him."

He smiled, warmly and with no sign of the discomfort he had felt the night before over seeking the assistance of an expert. I wondered whether he had resigned himself to the expedient, or was merely putting on a show of good humour for our young friend. At times, Sherlock Holmes himself could be an excellent counterfeiter.

THE DAILY GAZETTE
14th June 1898
MAN MURDERED IN SPITALFIELDS

The police are searching for witnesses in the case of a man found dead behind a tavern in Spitalfields. The Butcher's Apron public house is well-known among the local denizens for its unruliness and violent altercations. A hapless witness who stumbled upon the body immediately summoned a beat constable, who took charge of the scene, but police say that there is no way to know how many earlier and less conscientious members of the public had passed without reporting the deceased's presence.

The body was of rough appearance, and was in all likelihood that of a petty criminal or prize-fighter, like so many of the inhabitants of this lawless and lamentably unsanitary region of our city. His corpse was bloody and he had been savagely beaten to death.

Inspector Athelney Jones of Scotland Yard is asking for public-spirited citizens who may have heard the brawl that doubtless led to the man's death, or who may be able to give information on the man's identity, to make themselves known to a police officer. He observed that, though violent loss of life is a routine event in the East End, the police must always take such killings seriously whenever they are brought to their attention.

A letter from Hopkins to Dr Graymare elicited a response, sent direct by messenger to Scotland Yard, inviting us to call on the eminent graphologist later that morning. Holmes examined the note intently, then showed it to me before placing it in his pocket. It appeared completely ordinary to me, and I was mystified by his interest.

First, though, Holmes had expressed a wish to speak to the famous Miss Adorée Felice, Bastion's mistress, in the luxurious rooms in Mayfair in which Bastion had installed her, and which, she told us shamelessly when we arrived, "still had two weeks to go on the rent, so why should I clear out and let someone else take them?"

Ungentlemanly though it may sound to say it, we found her exactly as vulgar as Mycroft had described, cheerfully admitting to playing Bastion for every penny she had been able to extract from him. I had been expecting a seductive temptress, worthy of prompting the fall from grace of a man such as Bastion. In fact her beauty was of a very ordinary kind, though she undoubtedly knew how to make the best of it. Had I not known her origin as Gillian McGuire, I would not have guessed that she was Irish, but the elaborate French accent she affected did little to disguise the London twang she had presumably acquired in adulthood.

Miss Felice had seemingly assumed that Bastion's resources were bottomless, and had been either oblivious or blithely indifferent to the possibility that her rapacity might bleed him dry, or that he might be forced to turn to unconventional sources in order to finance their life together.

"More fool me, I suppose," she said with a shrug. "But never such a fool as him." Asked about who she thought Bastion might in fact have turned to, whether she had met or heard of any dubious associates of his, or whether he had seemed to her the type of man to kill himself, she answered only with another shrug and some expression of indifference. When asked whether the name "Zimmerman" meant anything to her, she told us only that she knew of a pawnbroker in Soho of that name.

She was, however, able to supply us with a love-letter that Bastion had written to her, which there was every reason to suppose was genuine. She showed not a trace of remorse over her lover's demise.

"And so we reach another dead end, Watson," Holmes observed as we left her to plan her next conquest. "I had hoped, despite Mycroft's judgement of the matter, that she might prove to have some connexion with Zimmerman. If so, however, she is the most exceptional actress I have met, and should have been far more successful in her first choice of profession than she has been in her second." He had been filling his pipe as he spoke, and emphasised this last with a cloying rose-scented puff of his new tobacco blend.

I suspected that our visit to Dr Graymare would be equally a waste of time. It was a short walk to his offices in the smartest part of Bloomsbury, on the second floor of a townhouse whose lower floors housed a solicitor's and a medical practice whose income must have so far outstripped my own that I could but guess at it and marvel. The graphologist was a small man with a Van Dyke beard and pince-nez, turned out with excessive neatness, and exhibiting the self-importance with which I have noticed small men sometimes seek to compensate for their stature.

He greeted us warmly nevertheless. I wondered whether he expected to be paid for his time, and then remembered that Mycroft had instructed us to spare no expense. We would doubtless be forwarding him an invoice, care of the Diogenes Club.

Holmes continued to show little sign of unease at

approaching someone whose knowledge, albeit in a limited sphere, might exceed his own. Indeed he was affability itself. He observed immediately from the shape and development of the specialist's hands that he was ambidextrous, and congratulated him on having taken pains to improve the faculty.

"I have had little need, Mr Holmes," said Carson Graymare, with a quietly self-satisfied nod. "I have been equally proficient with both hands since infancy, and I was always encouraged by my tutors to take advantage of the gift."

Holmes nodded also, giving a convincing impression of being as absorbed by the details of the graphologist's early development as he evidently was himself. "Dr Graymare, I understand you have been of use to the police on more than one occasion?"

"That I have," Graymare agreed solemnly. "And if they consulted me more often, Mr Holmes, your friend Mr Hopkins might find himself less troubled by cases of fraudulent documents. From what he has told me, my judgement in those cases might have relieved him of the burden of some laborious detective work."

Holmes shook his head. "I fear, Dr Graymare, that our courts are not yet so enlightened that they would accept the unsupported word of a man of science in such a matter. The evidence Inspector Hopkins adduced would have been required as a supplement to even such an eminent authority as yourself."

Many would have suspected my friend, quite correctly, of flattery, but Graymare evidently shared the opinion of himself that Holmes was expressing, and preened himself visibly. For my own part, I was a little worried to find Holmes so conciliatory. Normally he reserved such insincerities for putting suspects at their ease. He continued, "I believe Inspector Hopkins spoke to you concerning a case of his quite recently?"

Graymare graciously acknowledged that this was so.

"You told him, I understand, that the author of a particular letter was who it was purported to be?"

"Excuse me, but I made no such judgement," Graymare replied pompously. "The question of *identification* is quite beyond my purview. I merely confirmed without a doubt that the two samples of writing he presented to me were products of the same hand."

"Of course," Holmes conceded. "Your adherence to the facts is to be admired. I wonder, though, whether you would be so good as to explain to Dr Watson and myself the thinking that led you to that conclusion."

"Of course, Mr Holmes, I should be delighted." Graymare cleared his throat, and began: "What many people fail to understand is that the mind and the body are inextricably linked, so utterly conjoined that the true man of science should disdain to distinguish them at all. A person's body expresses his character in its every behaviour and action."

I realised that this was a lecture he was well used to delivering, and settled myself for a long listen. Graymare continued, "A musician's instrumental technique, as practised in his mouth and lungs and fingers, is not simply a process for reproducing the correct sequence of notes; it is an expression of his very being—what, in a less enlightened age, would have been called his soul. The same is true of the actor, the athlete, the painter—in all cases, the performance of their craft through the action of their bodies is no mere production of technical competence, but a reflection of the workings of their mind.

"Yet these are merely the most crudely visible examples. In every one of us, our bodily behaviours are determined by the functioning of our brain, and thus by that same essential character. Though this is true of as mundane an action as shaking a hand or pouring a cup of tea, it comes through with especial depth and profundity in those actions specifically used for communicating—that is to say, in a person's speech and writing.

"The study of speech I leave to my colleagues in the field of phonetics. The study of handwriting I have made my own.

"Through painstaking study of innumerable examples, I have learned the tell-tale signs that show whether a man's disposition is nervous or stoical, sociable or reclusive, cheerful or prone to depression. All are expressed through his hands—not in the words he writes, in which I take no interest, but in the forms of the characters, the flow of the ink, the impression upon the paper. A man's words can easily deceive, but his hand, never. The true expert can discern the Romantic from the Cynic, the miser from the profligate, the saint from the Pharisee, all from the tiniest traces left by those traits in the strokes and circles and curlicues of ink upon a page."

This was not the end of his discourse, but it is as much of it as I care to reproduce. The man's self-importance was remarkable, and I had concluded long before he finished his monologue that we were wasting our time and Mycroft's money.

Holmes heard him out politely, nevertheless, before turning to the practical matter at hand. "And on this basis you concluded that the two samples of script that Hopkins showed you had been produced by the same individual?" he asked. I knew that Graymare had been shown the letter to Zimmerman alongside some departmental correspondence whose provenance was in no doubt.

Graymare nodded gravely. "The occasion for the writing may have been different, but the character behind it was exactly the same."

"And what was your assessment of that character?"

Graymare sat back in his chair and stared at his ceiling in an ostentatious act of recall. "The writer was a right-handed, well-educated professional man from a wealthy family, in good health for his late middle age. His ordinary habits are careful and restrained, but his letter-forms betray a wayward streak that may reveal itself in unpredictable ways. Most likely he is a womaniser, though he might perhaps be a gambler. In either case, the tendency will reveal itself only occasionally, when the passion is awoken in him, and the disruption to his mundane life may prove catastrophic, even fatal. In between times he will appear to be a stable, trustworthy man of exceptional acumen and considerable discretion. He may hold a position of trust, and for most of the time he will appear worthy of it. At root, however, he is wholly unreliable. If Mr Hopkins had been thinking of employing the writer, I would have advised him to avoid doing so at all costs." He returned his gaze to Holmes. "My full assessment was longer, of course, but the police will have the details."

At the beginning of this summary I had been impressed despite myself at the accuracy with which he reflected the character of Bastion as others had described him, but rather quickly I realised that much of it could have been guessed from simply reading the letters Hopkins gave him. I had seen music-hall fortune-tellers and false spirit-mediums carry off feats of apparent insight from far less obvious clues, and none of them could hold a candle to Holmes' ability to deduce hard facts from the knot of a man's tie or a smudge of dirt on his shirt-cuff. Since Graymare's clients would already have proven themselves willing to part with their scepticism along with their money, I was not surprised that his pronouncements so often impressed them.

"I have some further samples," said Holmes, "together with one of the first that you looked at. Would you do us the further kindness of giving your opinion as to whether these, too, are the product of the same hand?"

He placed on the table Bastion's letter to Zimmerman, together with the supposed suicide note, his letter to Miss Felice, a page from the appointment-book, and a further sheet which I did not recognise.

"A complete analysis would take several hours," the graphologist replied calmly. "But if you will grant me a few minutes, I shall essay a preliminary appraisal."

He took a jeweller's eye-glass from his desk and leaned in to examine them.

"The subject-matter is quite confidential," I warned him, worried lest we should find Bastion's suicide-note splashed across the front pages of the next day's newspapers, taking pride of place from the Shakespeare sonnet being sold by Boothby's.

Coldly he replied, "As I have told you, Dr Watson, I never concern myself with subject-matter. It is the hand that interests me, and the hand alone."

He fell silent for a quarter of an hour or so, contemplating the samples of script, before removing the eye-glass and sitting back with a smug sigh.

His voice betraying a faint trace of impatience now, Holmes asked him, "Well, Dr Graymare?"

"They are identical," said Graymare, "undoubtedly. I assure you that all of these samples are the work of the man we have been discussing."

Holmes frowned. "I am asking you now as an expert in forgery, Dr Graymare, not a guest at a society dinner-party. Have you no doubts upon this point? Could not a technically accomplished counterfeiter have reproduced the writing of one of the samples—the appointment-book, let us say—in one or all of the others?"

"A sufficiently capable forger might deceive a friend or relative of the writer," Graymare said dismissively. "Even a wife, if this author has one, though she is an unlucky woman if so. Such technical accomplishment is certainly possible. The technical perfection your explanation would call for is not. The divergences from the true hand might be minute, but they would be there. No counterfeiter could altogether eliminate the signs of his own character that would manifest themselves. The tiniest details of the lettering, the subtlest pressures of the pen upon the page, would betray the venality and dishonesty of any such enterprise."

Holmes said, "But let us say the counterfeiter's eye and knowledge were the equals of your own—no, sir, allow it, please, for argument's sake," he added as Graymare begged to differ. "Could not such an expert learn to compensate for these unconscious slips you mention—not perfectly, perhaps, I will accept that, but with such a nearness to perfection that even your practised eye was deceived into crediting it as identical with the original?"

Graymare was indignant. "No, sir."

"I find that very difficult to believe."

"Faced with one who has extended his study of graphology into true mastery, any such deception would inevitably fail. If this upsets your theories, sir, I am sorry for it, but in mine I am immutable."

Dr Graymare gazed at us with such serene self-admiration that I could not forbear a gasp of delight when Holmes replied, "I thank you for your opinion, Dr Graymare. For your information, three of these new samples are indeed attributed to Christopher Bastion, the supposed author of the first. The last of them I wrote myself, last night."

Graymare gaped at him like a gutted fish.

Holmes continued, "It appears to me, Doctor, that your theories are based in dogma, not in empirical investigation. You believe whatever is convenient for you, without an openness to learning new facts—a capital error for any person, but especially heinous in one with pretensions to the status of a scientist."

Graymare rallied a little. He said, "I do not believe you. You hope to trick me into admitting an error. Well, I remain unshakeable. As I have said, a man's words can lie, his hand never. All these documents are the work of the same writer, and you, sir, are a liar."

"When circumstances require it I have been a liar, I confess it," said Holmes unconcernedly. "On this occasion, it is only your own vanity that has misled you. Here—"

And, tearing a sheet of paper from Graymare's notepad, he wrote, in a neat and functional hand quite unlike his own: "I will be free at 11 o'clock and will be pleased to see Mr Holmes and Dr Watson then." He signed it, with a flourish, "Carson Graymare."

He then produced the note that Graymare had written to us, and threw it down next to his facsimile. The two were, as far as my untutored eye could tell, identical.

Holmes said, "You mentioned actors, Graymare—persons who subsume their own personalities in representing the life of another. It is a craft that deserves more respect than it receives, and so too, I begin to think, is forgery. Good day, sir." And so saying, he took his leave.

I followed him, leaving Graymare staring at the identical pieces of paper in confusion and dismay. So much, I thought, for the expertise of graphologists, and Mycroft Holmes echoed my thoughts, when we returned to the Diogenes Club to report on our progress so far.

"So, Graymare is a charlatan," he said. "Well, I am only a little surprised." The attendant Jennings had once again ushered us into the Stranger's Room, and as he led us in I had looked surreptitiously at the skin above his ears. The grooves that Holmes had mentioned were indeed there, and now that I saw them it was obvious that they had been left by spectacles, but they were so faint as to be almost invisible. Clearly I had some way to go before I could hope to match the Holmes brothers' powers of observation, let alone their unparalleled understanding of what they saw.

"That may be an overly harsh judgement," Sherlock conceded, with a hint of regret in his voice. "He appeared profoundly dismayed when I proved him wrong. The man may be quite sincere in his overgenerous assessment of his own abilities, which indeed may well be equal to the task he sets them, most of the time. That he is useless to us in our present investigation is perfectly apparent, however. I fear we must set aside his view concerning the authenticity of Bastion's purported letter to Zimmerman."

"Evidently so," Mycroft agreed, discontented. "There is, of course, the opinion of the other graphological expert to be considered, but if you are correct then a forgery good enough to deceive Graymare might have taken him in as well. No, don't trouble yourself to visit him and try the same trick—even if you were to fail, a better forger might still have succeeded. We should allow that there may be experts in *some* fields whose skills outstrip your own, Sherlock."

My friend did not acknowledge the witticism. "I need not tell you that this means we cannot trust the contents of either letter," he pointed out. "We may no more regard Bastion's betrayal as established fact than we can his suicide."

Mycroft waved this aside with a pudgy hand. "No more can we regard the converse as proven," he said. "We have, in fact, no evidence either way. All we have is the letter, and since we cannot yet discount the possibility that it is genuine, we must proceed as if the danger it implies is real, until we have definite information to the contrary."

Sherlock nodded. "Agreed. Indeed, one reason to forge such a letter might be to blackmail Bastion into turning traitor, if he was not one already."

His brother grunted, acknowledging the point. "These two men with the absurd culinary nicknames, though. They sound like a promising line of inquiry. Had they been sent as debt-collectors, as Probert assumed, it wouldn't have served their ends to kill their debtor."

"Not their immediate ends, perhaps," I put in, remembering past cases involving blackmail and extortion. "But if they were satisfied that Bastion couldn't pay, it would help to discourage others from defaulting if they knew they might end up dead."

Mycroft raised an eyebrow; Sherlock sighed. "I think not, Watson. If they intended Bastion's death to serve as an example, why go to the trouble of disguising it as a suicide?"

I felt profoundly foolish. He continued, "No, Mycroft is correct, although we cannot rule out some other, unrelated motive for the murder. However, just as we must proceed on the assumption that Bastion was indeed a traitor, we should assume that Chops and Onions are either in Zimmerman's employ or that of some confederate in his cause. I say 'employ," he added, "as from what I gather, their loyalty is unlikely to be motivated by considerations other than hard cash. I will continue to seek them, certainly, but at present I have no immediate hope of success there."

"So where has all this brought us?" Mycroft asked. "I can see that this forgery business has seized your interest, Sherlock, but it's hardly central to the question of how Bastion shared his knowledge."

I tended to agree with Mycroft on this point. Of all the crimes before us, from murder and coercion to espionage, the idea of a forged note, or even two forged notes, seemed to me the least serious and consequential.

The older Holmes continued, "For all we know, before these men killed Bastion he wrote out a detailed account of what he knew for them to take to their employers. I have to decide whether or not to trust his discretion prior to his death, and at present the risk of doing so looks far too great. To withdraw or otherwise protect the assets he could have betrayed will be costly, however, and carries its own risks, as well as closing down numerous highly promising operations. Lives and the interests of the Empire hang on the decision I make. I have said as much before, brother, but I repeat it now to focus your mind."

"Rest assured that Bastion remains the absolute crux of my investigations," Sherlock said. "If my inquiries seem to you more elliptical than such a focus would justify, then I fear that you must simply trust my methods. Why, incidentally, did Lord Loomborough seek to discourage the police from investigating cases of forgery?"

"He did not," said Mycroft heavily, "although your friend Hopkins may well see it that way. What he asked was that they should focus on crimes that seem to him, with some justification I might add, to be of greater concern to the public. I suppose he thought it would win votes for his party; in my experience that's generally why Ministers do things. If the Commissioner were a public servant worth his salt, mind you, he would have found a way to make the instruction serve his own purposes. Perhaps he felt that Hopkins was too ambitious, and sought to take him down a peg or two."

We left Mycroft Holmes in no better a temper than we had found him.

LETTER TO MISS ADORÉE FELICE

25th May 1898

My adored, felicitous, essential, incomparable Adorée –

Though it is only during the day that we must be apart, I long for you as, living, I have never longed. I yearn, with a yearning that never yields, to embrace you once again while you *da mi basia mille*, as the poet says.

In truth I should find your presence at my work most distracting, as, rather than advising my superiors, instructing my subordinates and making my reports, I should forever be enfolding you in my arms and raining passionate kisses upon your lips, your head, your shoulders and your arms – to say the least of it. (My colleagues would, I imagine, find this somewhat confounding also.)

Nevertheless, without you here I feel that some part of me, the most essential and most Christopherish part, is absent. Perhaps with that part missing I cannot, after all, serve my country with all my faculties. Perhaps, *pro bono publico*, I should hurry home to you and strive with all my conscientious sense of duty to complete myself, so that upon my return I may give my fullest attention to the essential matters of state that call upon it.

Adored one, you are the fount of all my fortune, the *sine qua non* of my serenity. I am completed by our every connection, and devastated by our every departure. I am –

Your own, your loving, your insufficient –
Christopher

That afternoon Stanley Hopkins sent us word that Probert's niece, Lucy Evans, whose safety the murderers had made their leverage against the unfortunate valet, had arrived in London by train. He had told us already that the housemaid had obtained her employers' permission to visit her uncle in prison and to answer the police's questions while she was in town. I had assumed that the interview would be of a routine nature, but to my surprise Holmes had asked to be present.

This time, though Sergeant Douglass was at his desk as before, it was Constable Fratelli who conducted us into Hopkins' office, where the Inspector asked about our visit to Graymare. When told Holmes' verdict on the man, Hopkins shook his head sorrowfully. "Do you know, that's what has concerned me most since that assignment. It seems that the technique of counterfeiting has developed to a point where exceptional skill is needed to detect such forgeries, and that at the same time people are becoming more willing to resort to them."

"You feel that our compatriots are becoming less honest and more gullible?" I sympathised. "I fear you may well be right."

Solemnly, Hopkins said, "Not as such, Doctor. In a way, that might be a preferable state of affairs. No, I worry that people are becoming less concerned with the question of Truth. Consider: if any document can be faked—any certificate, any sworn statement, any diary or account-book, even any historical record—then how can we establish a Truth that any of us can rely on? What is the practical value of a Truth that can never be definitively known? The boundary between fact and falsehood is crucial to the operation of the law, the sciences, Government itself, and it is that which is being eroded. If the very concept of evidence becomes discredited, then people will consider themselves free to believe whatever is most attractive or expedient to them, as you say Dr Graymare does, rather than what is borne out by the facts. With no consensus on which to build, society itself would begin to break apart."

"An alarming vision, Hopkins." Holmes smiled, a little indulgently. Hopkins was young, after all, and imaginative, and far more philosophically inclined than was healthy for a policeman. "But premature, I am pleased to say. Even with such an increase as you note, these forgeries can account for but a tiny fraction of the documents in circulation. And consider also that these cases might not even represent an increase. Perhaps such fakes have always existed, and it is our skill at discovering them that has improved. That would be a more hopeful development, would it not?"

At that point Fratelli ushered in Lucy Evans, a plump and rather plain girl bearing little resemblance to her rangy uncle.

"I'm glad you're here, Lucy," Stanley Hopkins said after we had all been introduced. His tone was kind and reassuring, without the patronising overtones I had heard from some of his colleagues when interviewing a domestic servant. "I need to ask you some questions about your uncle. As you know, he is in serious trouble, but you must understand that the only way you can help him is to tell the truth. It won't do any good if you try to guess what answers I might want to hear. Are we clear?"

"Of course, sir. I wouldn't lie, sir." The girl was quietly spoken, and to my ears very Welsh. Despite her concern when her uncle was mentioned, there was a firm clarity to her voice that made me feel that Hopkins was right to treat her with respect.

He asked, "When did you last see your uncle, Lucy?"

She replied, "It was back at New Year, sir. Mr Bastion gave him some time off to come and visit me and my Da in Cardiff. We don't see him very often, London being so far away and all."

"Of course," said Hopkins. "He's been with Mr Bastion for some time, I understand. Was he happy in his employ?"

"Oh yes, very fond of his master, he was. He said he was a kind man who treated his servants well, and paid well too. You can't ask for better than that, sir."

"I'm sure that's true," said Hopkins smoothly. I knew from some of our earlier conversations that the Inspector harboured certain Fabian sympathies that might have led him to differ from this sentiment, but he gave no sign of them now. "Did he give you any reason then to think there might have been a falling-out between them?"

Lucy shook her head definitely. "No, sir. Not then nor ever."

"Does he write to you often?"

"Not really." Lucy seemed to hesitate. "We're not really a family for correspondence." I saw Holmes nod thoughtfully to himself at this.

"Well, you lead busy lives," Hopkins said sagely. "So the news that came yesterday was the first that you had heard from your uncle since the New Year?"

"Yes, sir."

"Thank you." The Inspector made a careful note; more, I thought, to give Lucy the sense that her information was proving useful than because it really had been. "Let us turn to more recent times, then. As you were told yesterday, there had been a fear that you were in danger. Was there any truth to that idea at all?"

Lucy Evans shook her head vehemently. "No, sir, absolutely none. I've been going about my duties for Mrs Thornton, my employer, just as normal, with nothing any different until those policemen turned up yesterday. I was so shocked and confused when I heard they were asking after me. Mrs Thornton was quite dismayed, and as for Mrs Morgan, the housekeeper, I thought she'd have a fit. Well, sir, I'm sure I don't need to tell you what it looks like to them, or to the neighbours either, the police turning up on the front doorstep asking after the housemaid. I think they were glad to see the back of me today. I'll tell you frankly, I'll be lucky to keep my position, though of course it's selfish to be thinking of myself when poor Uncle Gilbert's in prison."

"I am sorry about that, Lucy." Hopkins looked annoyed. "The situation was an urgent one, but even so, the policemen should have known better than to use the front door. I'll write to Mrs Thornton and explain to her that no blame can possibly attach to you in this matter."

"That's very kind of you, sir." Lucy looked distinctly doubtful, though whether of Hopkins' promise or its likelihood of having any effect I could not tell.

The Inspector went on. "Had anybody else called around at all, before the policemen came? Anyone not known to the household?"

"Only the usual, sir, delivery boys and the like."

"Nobody asking for you who seemed at all suspicious?"

"No, sir. I don't know anyone of that sort, sir. Mrs Thornton would be quite right not to employ me if I did." Her lips pursed, and in that moment of moral judgement I caught an echo of a family resemblance. Probert had looked the same way when speculating about Bastion's debts.

Holmes leaned forward then. "Lucy. You spoke of delivery boys 'and the like'. Would that include salesmen?" I recalled that this was how Chops and Onions had introduced themselves to Probert, according to his story.

The girl's eyes widened. "Well, yes, sir. There was a man in the kitchen just last week, selling combs and ribbons and things. A new fellow who none of us had seen before. A few of us bought some things from him, but then Mrs Morgan came in and sent him packing."

"Combs and ribbons?" Stanley Hopkins repeated, obviously

catching Holmes' train of thought. "Did this man pay any special attention to your hair, Lucy?"

"My hair?" Lucy seemed even more dismayed. Her hair was nut-brown and curly, and certainly her best feature. "Well, I suppose so, sir. Not just mine, mind. He tried out his combs on all the girls, made a joke of complimenting us all on how nice our hair was."

"But he could have described yours to somebody else?" A thought struck Hopkins. "I don't suppose he asked you for a lock of it?"

"Certainly not, sir, and I wouldn't have put up with it if he had." Lucy seemed quite offended by the idea.

"I imagine he learned your name also," suggested Holmes.

"Well, yes, sir, we all told him our first names. Was that wrong, sir?" she added, a little plaintively. "I suppose it must have been from how you're saying it."

"You did nothing wrong, Lucy," said Hopkins quickly, with a warning glance at Holmes. "You've been very helpful indeed in telling us this, and I'm most grateful for your honesty."

But Holmes was not to be dissuaded. "But this flattering traveller in haircare accessories. Was he perhaps a big, burly fellow, his own hair either fair or dark with whiskers? Speaking perhaps with a London accent, and sporting a brown serge suit and a bowler hat?"

Lucy stared at him then smiled, a little wanly. "No, sir, not at all. A Welshman he was, from the Valleys by his accent, and quite a little fellow. He was fair-headed, mind, but he only had a little moustache."

"Of course. Well, there is no reason why they should not have engaged a local agent. A Londoner might have put you more on your guard."

"I don't understand all this about my hair, sirs," Lucy insisted, clearly expecting to be answered. When Hopkins explained to her about the lock of hair which Chops and Onions had shown to Probert to ensure his cooperation, her comment was, "But that could have been anybody's!"

We could only agree.

"They would have needed to be sure that it resembled yours sufficiently, however," Holmes explained, "and for that they needed somebody to describe it to them. Preferably one who had experience with hair. With a precise enough characterisation, obtaining a matching sample would be a trivial task."

"Yes, sir. Poor Uncle Gilbert. He's not a great thinker, you know," she added regretfully. "And he's ever so fond of me. I can just see how anxious and upset this would have made him."

"Well, Lucy, everything you've said makes it seem more likely that he has been telling us the truth," Hopkins said. "I won't deceive you—he's likely to go to prison, even so. But if he's lucky enough, you may have saved him from worse."

"Well, I'm glad of that, sir," Lucy said, as Fratelli began to lead her out. "Though I'd wish for better for him, of course."

"I'll write that letter while you're with your uncle," Hopkins promised her. "You can take it back to Cardiff with you for Mrs Thornton."

"Thank you," the girl replied, this time with a little more hope in her voice. She added, "He'll be wanting his cigarettes, poor man. I forgot to bring any."

"Here," I said, "take mine." I had a packet in my pocket that I had not yet opened.

I thought for a moment that she would refuse, but compassion for her uncle outweighed her pride, and she took them from my hand. "Thank you so much, sir," she said. "I know he'll be ever so grateful."

"One thing more, Lucy," Holmes said just as she was leaving.

"You will not read the letter that Inspector Hopkins gives you, will you?"

Lucy gaped, then looked offended again. "Certainly not, sir. It won't be addressed to me."

"I wonder, could you read me the name-plate on the office door there?"

For the first time, I thought that Lucy looked scared. She stared at Holmes, and then at the door. "It—it says Inspector Hopkins."

"The first name also?"

"S ... Stephen?" she ventured, then saw from our faces that her guess was wrong. "That's a cruel trick to play on a person!" she exclaimed, and then recalled her place. "I mean—if you don't mind my saying so, sir. You could have just asked me whether I could read."

"I have found that many servants stand on their pride when asked such questions," Holmes replied. "As you did just now, when you referred to not being 'a family for correspondence', and when you said that you would not read a letter not addressed to you. Can you read or write at all, Lucy?"

"I can puzzle out the letters if I have time," Lucy admitted defiantly. "I don't write, though, no. There's no call for it in my work. If I ever do get a letter, my friend Gwen usually reads it for me, and writes the reply."

"Thank you, Lucy," my friend said. Much to my surprise, he added, "And I apologise for tricking you. As the Inspector says, you have been most helpful."

After the housemaid left, Hopkins said, "She's right, I'm afraid. You didn't need to humiliate her like that. You're too used to dealing with people who have something to hide, Mr Holmes."

He was unwontedly indignant, and I found myself suppressing a fatherly smile, which would have been unlikely to improve his state of mind. I reminded myself that, while I might think of Stanley Hopkins as the ambitious young detective who had first sought to study with the master, he had now reached his thirties, and it was natural enough that he would begin to outgrow his tutelage.

"You are right, Hopkins, it was unnecessary," said Holmes, looking to his credit a little abashed. "I should have given her the opportunity to answer the direct question before putting the matter to the test. But we have established why a criminal capable of forging two letters should not have in this instance forged a third. A note in his niece's hand, pleading for Gilbert Probert to save her life, would have made for a far more compelling inducement to cooperate than what, as she observes, could have been many women's hair. But that was never an option if Lucy is illiterate."

"You're right, it is useful information," Hopkins conceded. "But the poor girl has been through enough distress already, and she's about to visit a beloved relative in prison. Some tact and sensitivity were called for."

"I have apologised to her, Hopkins," Holmes reminded him mildly, knowing that Hopkins was as aware as I of how rare an event this was.

"Well, so you have," the Inspector agreed. "If there's nothing else you were wanting to discuss at this point, though, I should write her employer that letter."

Our young friend's tone was dismissive, though his annoyance was reserved for Holmes, not myself. I gave him an embarrassed smile as we left.

I had arranged to meet Jerome Windward, Sir Hector's literarily inclined cousin, for a drink at the Criterion that evening, to return *The Assassins' Dagger* and give him my opinion of it. It was, I felt, the least I could do after he had done me the favour of allowing me to read it.

I found that he took my praise well, without false modesty but without attempting, as other aspiring writers have done, to take advantage of it to negotiate an introduction to my publishers or agent. "I'm still honing my craft, Dr Watson," he said. "I feel I can further it and myself yet. Of course, I lack your experience of the real world of crime, and must create my mysteries from the imagination. I would value your opinion of their realism, as well as their literary merit."

"I could find little fault on that side," I told him, "though you might benefit from speaking to some police officers about the details of their procedures. I suppose some of the descriptions could have been more vivid, for true verisimilitude. When one feels that one's life is really in danger, one's sensations become heightened in a way I am not sure you have succeeded in reflecting."

"Well, I lack your history of combat as well as of detective work," Windward acknowledged cheerfully. "I suppose I have time yet to make my own experiences, and you proud of me."

"Perhaps you could accompany Holmes and myself on a case," I suggested, and then, immediately realising that this might not be well received by Holmes, I added, "If he agrees, of course. I would need to discuss it with him first."

"Of course," Windward said. "I can imagine that he's a man who needs careful handling."

"One does not 'handle' Holmes," I replied. To my surprise, I found myself adding, "The man is quite ungovernable. Why, only this afternoon—" I stopped, conscious of my disloyalty. I hardly knew young Windward, and I certainly had no business confiding in him any concerns I might have had about my friend.

He said, "Don't worry, Doctor, I wouldn't occasion you discomfort by asking you for any indiscretion. Your friendship with Mr Holmes is a privileged calling, perhaps even a Sacred Duty. I am sure that you are sensible of that privilege, although

I suppose that, like all such duties, it can feel like a somewhat onerous honour at times."

"A little, perhaps," I admitted, "though I would not have it any other way."

Over the course of the evening, however, as my acquaintance with Windward deepened, and—truth to tell—I consumed rather more than I had intended of the Criterion's excellent Beaujolais, I found that the young author was an excellent listener, and that his sympathetic ear positively encouraged confidences. I told him how I bridled sometimes at Holmes' impatience with my slowness, and how his habit of showing off his astounding gifts could sometimes seem to be done at my expense. I said that there were times when he was moody, brusque and intolerant of others, while demanding extreme forbearance from those around him.

"None of which is to deny his most excellent qualities, of course," I insisted. "As well as his obvious intellect, his strength and fighting skills are outstanding. He is the bravest man I know, and the most faithful friend I have ever had. I just wish, sometimes, that he was a little easier to live with," I concluded, rather weakly.

"Of course," Windward said again.

"There was a time some years ago," I said, "when he filled our rooms with lumber and the bath with chemicals, all in the service of a case. Poor Mrs Hudson nearly evicted us ... but it is getting late," I realised, "and I have kept you talking for long enough already. It has been very good of you to listen to me, Mr Windward—"

"Please, Dr Watson, I would be honoured if you would call me Jerome."

"Jerome, then," I said, though in view of his tender age I did not invite him to call me John. "You must understand that I am not usually so garrulous. I have been troubled recently, that's all. Holmes has been ... well, more arrogant than usual, even for him. A little cruel, even, to those who did not deserve it. He has always been driven, when the hunt is on and he has the bit between his teeth …" I paused for a moment, conscious of confusing my animal metaphors terribly. "Even so, he does not usually forget his compassion for others."

"Ah, but he has you to remind him, Doctor," young Jerome smiled. "I am sure that that is why he keeps you always near him, and why you are as true a friend to him as he to you. You are his conscience, reminding him of what it means to be human. Without you he would be … something we have no name for. A superman, perhaps, or a demigod? Whatever one might call a being beyond our own sphere."

I stood up, suddenly uncomfortable at the turn of the conversation, and was alarmed to find myself a little unsteady on my feet. "I've drunk enough," I said. "It has been charming properly to make your acquaintance, Jerome. I shall expect a signed copy of your book when it is published, and I look forward very much to reading your future works."

I set out to walk home. Again it was a cool evening, though the day had once again been oppressively warm, and the air had the effect of somewhat clearing my head. I realised almost immediately that part of my unsteadiness was occasioned by having left my walking-cane at the bar along with my sobriety, but decided against returning for it. I had already embarrassed myself sufficiently for one evening.

Rather than return along Regent Street among the other strollers taking advantage of the bright evening light, I took the backstreets, hoping to be alone with my thoughts. With my instincts dulled by the red wine, it was a street or two before it occurred to me that I was being followed. One man was keeping pace behind me, with another lingering further back on the other side of the road. I quickened my pace a little, wincing at the ache from the old wound in my leg, and heard the footsteps behind me accelerate.

I am not a man to shrink from a fight, but I was outnumbered and, without my cane, would have nothing more to rely on than my fists. Gritting my teeth, I broke into a run, and headed towards Berkeley Square, where I was certain to find witnesses to my plight.

With the drink and the trouble from my leg, however, I was not at my speediest, and it was not long before I felt a hand on my arm and a rough voice said, "Hey, there. Dr Watson, ain't it?"

I turned and looked into the whiskered face of a well-built man in a serge suit and bowler hat. His equally bulky colleague came up quickly behind him, and I knew that I was facing the notorious Chops and Onions.

"How can I help you gentlemen?" I asked, still hoping, though with little expectation, that I might extract myself from the situation without violence.

"We've got a message for your Mr Holmes," said Chops—or was it Onions? I found I could no longer remember which was fair and which was dark, and under the circumstances it counted for little.

"I shall be glad to take it to him, if you tell it to me," I declared.

"We don't appreciate what happened at the Butcher's Apron," said the second man. "'Mugger' Maines was a friend of ours."

This meant nothing to me. "I'm sorry, I don't understand," I said, although I doubted that this would make any difference to the outcome.

"Yeah, never mind," said his colleague, flexing his fists as the first man tightened his grip upon my arms. "Anyway, it's not the sort of message you just tell."

I struggled to get free, but my captor grasped me ever more tightly and turned me to face his friend. "It's more the sort of message he's got to see," he snarled, cracking his knuckles.

Suddenly there was a cry of, "Hey, you men!" Both of them turned in alarm.

And Jerome Windward was there, carrying my cane. He brought it down with a crack on the fair head of the clean-shaven man—Onions, I recalled now—who recoiled with a cry and let go of my arms. His confederate aimed a punch at Windward, who ducked out of the way and swung the stick back to hit him in the legs.

"Come quickly, Doctor!" he cried, and grasped my arm. But this time I welcomed it, as he pulled me away and we ran, still pursued by the men, for the safety of the square. Glancing back I saw that Chops was now limping and Onions holding his head, and they fell behind before eventually giving up the pursuit altogether.

We arrived panting in the square, to the curious glances of the onlookers enjoying the evening cool among the greenery. With a flourish, Windward presented me with my cane. "You left this behind, Dr Watson," he announced. "I followed you to return it."

"It's extremely lucky you did," I admitted. "You saved me from a beating at the very least. Thank you, Jerome."

"Not in the least," he replied. "Anyone would have done the same. And I've now had just a taste of a real tangle with criminals."

"That you have," I agreed. "Those two are ruthless men, from what I am told. You were very brave to tackle them that way. I shall certainly recommend to Holmes that you join us on a case sometime soon."

"I could ask for no better repayment, Doctor," Windward replied. "And now I shall bid you goodnight."

I limped home with the cane, and found Holmes once again at work with his magnifying-glass. When I told him what had occurred, he evinced a touching concern for my wellbeing. "It was most fortunate that young Windward was there to assist you," he noted. "A plucky young man indeed. You were also somewhat lucky that Chops and Onions were unarmed. They must have had a gun or other weapon when they threatened Bastion, but evidently they did not bring it on this occasion. I would imagine that they intended to injure rather than to kill you, as a warning to me."

"Either way, I'm profoundly grateful that they didn't," I said.

"As am I, Watson, as am I."

Holmes showed me the lock of hair that he had been inspecting. "Probert has at last produced some material evidence to support his story," he said. "Or rather, the police have, in searching Bastion's pantry." The hair was curly and brown, a good match for Lucy Evans', and I could see how it had deceived her uncle. "Probert had set it aside in his distraction, and had then forgotten where he had put it—or so he says now. In any case, it corroborates his account as far as it goes."

"So Hopkins has stopped by?" I asked. I cursed myself for going out and enjoying myself—at least up to the point when I left the Criterion—when I could perhaps have brokered a reconciliation between the two men.

"Ah no, he sent Constable Fratelli. But he invites us to visit him again tomorrow."

"I'm glad to hear it," I said sincerely. "You really must develop more sensitivity to people's feelings, you know, Holmes. Not everyone is as practised as you in rising above them."

He gave me a chilly look. "I have my feelings, Watson. I am not some Analytical Engine of the kind the late Mr Babbage hoped to construct. I would have supposed that you, of all people, would have been aware of that."

"Of course," I said, embarrassed suddenly by my admonition, and ashamed at the recollection of all the indiscretions I had spilled to Windward. "I simply meant that your trained mind is able to set them aside when necessary. It is an admirable faculty that few of us share."

"Of that, Watson, I am all too painfully aware," Holmes replied coldly.

THE MORNING CHRONICLE
4th February 1898
BOOK REVIEW: *A STATESMAN'S LIFE*, VOLUME 3,
BY GEORGE, LORD LOOMBOROUGH

This volume of the noble Minister's reminiscences amply fulfils the promise of its predecessors: to wit, to provide the reader with entertaining anecdotes regarding the author's Westminster circle, carefully shorn of anything so vulgar as indiscretion, yet studiously witty at the expense of the political class as a whole, and of certain wholly anonymous members of it in particular.

That the author himself could scarcely be a more entrenched member of the class in question is one of the more enjoyable paradoxes encountered in these examples of the memoirist's art. The description given here of the events attendant upon the fall from favour of a former Minister not unconnected with fisheries (whose name, though sedulously unstated, will hold no mystery for any but the least politically alert of readers) is the most revealing we are likely to be graced with by one of those involved.

His Lordship's admirers often speak of his hard-headedness and willingness to take necessary decisions without too tender a concern for the feelings of others; qualities that, it is held, lend themselves commendably to his current eminence over the nation's upholders of the law. If the book has a fault, beyond its fondness for a few rather ostentatious figures of speech, it is that its zealousness in thus depicting its author may try the patience of those who are less in sympathy with such traits.

On the other hand, enthusiasts for the Minister's style, whether of prose or of government, will find much herein to please them.

The following days saw Holmes exerting himself in an urgent flurry of detective activity. That morning he and I revisited the street where I had been attacked, but found nothing to lead us any closer to Chops and Onions. "If this were one of Windward's crime stories," Holmes observed sardonically, "then one of them would have doubtless dropped a calling-card or laundry label that would have led us to him directly. I find that in reality things are rarely so convenient."

I considered this an unfair judgement on a work he had not even read, and said so. He raised his eyebrows slightly at my defence of the young author, but made no other comment.

"Holmes," I asked, remembering suddenly what one of my attackers had said, "do you know anybody going by the name 'Mugger Maines'?"

He shook his head gravely. "The name is unfamiliar to me," he said.

Holmes placed an advertisement in the newspapers asking for young women who had brown, curly hair and would be willing to donate a sample of it to come forward—with, of course, the aim of finding out from those willing whether they had been asked for such a thing before, and if so, by whom. For an entire afternoon a very motley collection of London's womanhood trooped through our chambers, ranging in age from childhood to advanced middle age, leaving behind them locks of every hair colour conceivable. It is surprising how many raven-haired women, redheads and even blondes are willing to represent themselves as brunettes if they judge that a monetary reward may result.

None of the women would admit to having donated the hair used by Chops and Onions, however, or even to having been asked, and so this line of inquiry also came to nothing.

Meanwhile, Hopkins' men had been making visits to chemists and apothecaries across London, in search of one who might have sold the prussic acid used to kill Christopher Bastion. Eventually one was identified in Holborn whose records showed such a bottle being sold, to a man using the name "John Smith", and answering Chops' description. It was concluded that Chops, if indeed it was he, had covered his tracks by travelling to acquire his murder weapon.

"It is, I suppose, conceivable that that is indeed his name," Holmes observed to Hopkins, with whom he was once again, to my relief, on civil if somewhat cooler terms, "but if so it is as good as an alias. We can hardly suspect every man in London who answers to it."

With his professional knowledge, Gilbert Probert's full description of the clothes worn by our suspects had been clearer than I could have managed, but he had not Holmes' fine attention to detail, and we had little hope of determining where they had been bought. Some diligent analysis on Holmes' part of the samples of charred rope had led him to the conclusion that it came from a particular chandler's in Lewisham, but our inquiries revealed that the purveyor sold many yards of it every day, and none of its staff had any special memories of a buyer resembling the men we sought.

"And," Holmes reminded me, "even if we were able to identify the gentlemen in question, and got so far as to locate and arrest them, we would still require their cooperation to tell us more of their employer and his aims. If they are loyal enough to him to keep their silence, or he canny enough to have concealed his identity from them, then we will have achieved little."

"We would have the actual murderers, Holmes," I pointed out to him. "The men who did the deed. That's something, surely?"

"Something, Watson, but not enough," he replied in

frustration. "And so, having exhausted all other avenues," he sighed, "we return to the question of forgery, where I begin to suspect that our attention should have been focused from the start. I am coming to believe that the question of the letter's authenticity may be central to that of Bastion's betrayal."

"How so?" I asked, sceptically. I admit that my friend's persistent interest in the matter of counterfeiting still seemed muddle-headed to me.

"If we can establish for certain, rather than merely suspecting, that the letter to Zimmerman is a lie, then we may have narrowed the possibilities considerably. If the document was forged to discredit him—perhaps, let us say, to deprive Sir Hector Askew of his chief assistant's services at a crucial time— then Bastion is absolved of any actual treachery. One need not fabricate evidence to incriminate a guilty man. If it was instead intended to blackmail him, then the possibility remains that it was unsuccessful."

"But how could we establish that?" I asked.

"I do not deny that it would be difficult. But Bastion strenuously denied disloyalty, while admitting his compromising affair of the heart. None of our efforts thus far have found any further evidence to suggest that he was a traitor. Even Mycroft will, I think, allow that the balance of probabilities lies in his favour."

"But in that case why have him killed?" I asked.

"As to that, we have equally little evidence linking Chops and Onions with Zimmerman. I said I could think of other reasons for murdering Bastion. If we can positively identify a forger, he may be able to tell us more about why both letters were fabricated, and at whose behest. That would certainly bring us closer to the instigator of the murder."

So Holmes threw himself into investigating, not only Bastion's notes, but all of the forged documents that had been dealt with by Hopkins' team of detectives. Of those the Inspector had mentioned, the letter to Lord Kerwinstone was held by his local police force, and Hopkins had promised to wire them and have it forwarded to his office. The third Earl of Barraclagh's marriage certificate had been taken to Ireland for evidence, while Major Macpherson's affidavit was kept in the Army records. The former would be inaccessible to us without a long wait or a sea-trip, while to avail ourselves of the latter we should require Mycroft's influence.

We did, however, speak to one Fitzalan Gerraghty, an Irish lawyer working in London, who had examined the Barraclagh certificate at an early stage in the case. Mr Gerraghty admitted that, were it not for the discovery of the original certificate, he would have argued strenuously in court that the estate should pass to the claimant.

He said, "It's still my view that both certifications were perfectly genuine, and the Earl a bigamist—not that that would do Mr Griffon any good, needless to say. I've seen a great many legal papers from around that place and time, and I'd swear that this was another of them. The paper's all dried out and crumbling, the ink's faded and the handwriting belongs to the period—as I say, I've seen its like many times before. If your Mr Hopkins is right and it's a fake, then all I can tell you is you're not just looking for an expert forger—you want someone who's an authority on legal history as well."

"If that is true, then it will narrow the field considerably," was Holmes' comment. He sounded sceptical, but I recalled that Sir Lester Lesborne's will had also been examined at the time by lawyers, who had found that, if real, it would have been legally valid in every particular.

That proven forgery was held in Scotland Yard's archives, to which Hopkins was easily able to obtain access for Holmes, alongside verified examples of Sir Lester's handwriting and a photographic copy of his real will. Once again, my friend became an appendage to his magnifying-glass, probing them all intently in search of clues to the false will's provenance. Eventually he sighed and declared it a consummate work of verisimilitude.

"The nature of forgery is such that the more successful it is, the fewer and subtler hallmarks it leaves," he told me, "and in this there are none that I can detect, at least without chemical analysis. I cannot tell at present whether it is the work of the same counterfeiter who created the Bastion letters, but I cannot imagine that there are many of such proficiency at work in England today."

I read the will myself, but it told me little that Hopkins had not already imparted to us. It claimed to be Sir Lester's final will and testament, superseding his previous will, and had supposedly been witnessed by his butler and housekeeper, Samuel and Jane Golightly. Sir Lester's wife having died many years before, the principal legatees were his daughters, Henrietta and Bernadette, and their families, and it was in the favour of the latter, younger, sister and her dependents that the new will had been made. She and her husband Sir James Minchcart were to receive Lesborne House and the lion's share of her father's fortune, with only a tenth part going to Henrietta and her husband, Mr Hunter. Minor legacies to more distant relatives, and to servants including the Golightlys, were altered sufficiently in detail to suggest a man whose thinking had changed somewhat in the intervening years, but not to any very material degree. Indeed, given how disorganised Sir Lester was reputed to have been in personal life, the high degree of correspondence between the documents was perhaps suspicious in itself.

There was no doubt that the Minehearts would have benefited most generously from the false will, but as Bernadette and Sir James had six children, four of whom had attained their majority at the time of their grandfather's death, and all eight would have received significant bequests, there was no way to know who had been sufficiently motivated to forge the will. Holmes made discreet inquiries about the family, but none was known to have criminal predilections, unusual money troubles, or any special expertise in calligraphy. He was naturally keen to interview the Mineheart family, but Hopkins could afford us no official support, and as Sir James was a private individual with few ties to the establishment, even Mycroft's influence was insufficient to overcome his intense aversion to the idea.

The elder Holmes was, however, able to arrange for us the loan of the Macpherson affidavit, though reluctantly and still disparaging his brother's misplaced priorities. It arrived with us by army messenger, the same morning as Constable Fratelli called with Lord Kerwinstone's letter, which had been sent down by train.

The Kerwinstone letter was brief, and interesting only in that it bore no resemblance to reality: purporting to come from Lord Kerwinstone's sister-in-law Mrs Edna Salisbury, it introduced the bearer as Percival Campion, her great-nephew, who hoped to stay for a while at Kerwin Hall before taking up his curacy. Since the letter had arrived with the thief, who had remained at the Hall for less than a day, Lord Kerwinstone would not have had any opportunity to consult his sister-in-law about it until it was far too late. Hopkins told us that Mrs Salisbury's only niece had died without issue, and no such person as Percival Campion had ever existed.

Major Macpherson's testimony was richer in narrative detail. It explained that Sergeant Foxon and two of his men had become separated from the rest of their company following the British Army's disastrous defeat at Isandlwana in Zululand in 1879, making their way across country and eventually regrouping with Lieutenant Macpherson's unit near the Boer town of Utrecht. Foxon had thus been many miles away, the document averred, when his remaining men, leaderless and lost, had taken possession of a Zulu village further down the Buffalo River, slaughtering the women and children while their menfolk were away fighting our forces. No blame for their crime, the document asserted, could possibly attach to him.

If, as Hopkins believed, this account was indeed another forgery, it must have drawn on a knowledge of the tactics used by the Army at this time and the deployment of troops on the battlefield, as the judges at the court-martial were senior officers who might be expected to have a good knowledge of such things, and might indeed have served in the same war. That Foxon had personally forged the letter, however, Holmes would not allow. The affidavit also noted that the Sergeant had lost two fingers from his right hand at Isandlwana, leading to his eventual discharge following the successful prosecution of the war; and such an injury would, Holmes assured us, preclude the degree of dexterity required for successful imitation of another man's handwriting.

"That Foxon is indeed missing the fingers in question we can scarcely doubt," he noted drily. "He appeared in person before the court-martial, and it would certainly have been noted if he had regrown them. I could only be wrong if he lopped them off after forging the letter, to throw us off the scent," he added, with a jocularity that seemed to me to overstep the boundaries of good taste.

In all the cases, however, his conclusions were similar. The proven forgeries—and the unproven, if they were indeed so— were meticulous, their attention to detail painstaking, their simulation of reality practically perfect. The paper stock used for the affidavit, for instance, was not only Indian but milled in Lahore, quite close to Macpherson's Punjabi retreat. The ink, too, was of the correct regional manufacture, not routinely sold in England, and while it would have been perfectly possible to import it, it would also have been costly and difficult.

"Was the document perhaps forged out there, and then sent over by packet mail as the court-martial was told it was?" I wondered. "Foxon must have had a man on the ground to kill Macpherson, if Hopkins' belief is correct."

"One would hardly send an expert counterfeiter to commit a common murder," Holmes replied. "I think it more likely that the agent, whoever it was, bought the supplies locally and sent them here for the forger's use." He set some inquiries in train with the manufacturers in question, but over such a distance it would be some time before we received any answer to his queries.

"If you could find a sample of the ink," I suggested, "you might find that its behaviour is affected by the climate. The temperature and humidity of the air in Lahore are quite different from those one finds anywhere in England."

"A fine suggestion, Watson," said Holmes, adding to my immediate disappointment, "but worthless, alas. If I could simulate the conditions of an Indian climate for the sake of such an experiment, the forger might equally recreate them for his own purposes, and we can be sure that he would try. It seems to be a point of professional pride to make the imitation as close as humanly possible—though it is hardly likely that Lord Kerwinstone, for instance, would have suspected foul play had his sister-in-law written to him on uncharacteristic notepaper. Such excessive, I might almost say obsessive, zeal for verisimilitude is perhaps our principal reason to suppose that the same forger is operating in each case."

I said, "If only Dr Graymare's theories were correct, and fraudulent intention could be deduced from the outpouring of the forger's innermost soul onto the page."

Holmes said, "Proof of insincerity would not in itself be sufficient. Mrs Salisbury might have been exaggerating her great-nephew's virtues to rid herself of his company, for instance. More to the point, however, Graymare would have had us believe that the author himself, or herself, might be infallibly identified by such scrutiny. While it gave me some small satisfaction to prove his theories were wrong, I confess it would be far more convenient for our purposes had they been correct."

I said, "In reality, the hypothetical problem you put to him has stymied us. If one man, whether it be Graymare or yourself, can become so expert in handwriting, and in the behaviours of ink and paper, that he can detect any forgery, then cannot another man, equally expert, learn the exact errors to avoid in order to deceive him? Is this not the age-old paradox of the unstoppable force and the immovable object?"

Holmes shook his head. "Fortunately, Watson, neither of those philosophical absolutes is workable in reality. The relationship between the detective and the criminal more closely resembles that between predator and prey. The gazelles that are able to outrun the cheetah are those that live to breed, and thus their next generation will be in the main faster. And yet the cheetahs who survive are those who run fast enough to catch the gazelles, and so generation by generation both species increase in speed. Gazelles continue to succumb to cheetahs, however, and by the same token detectives continue to catch criminals."

"But how, in a case such as this?"

"There are always limits to what is practically possible. In the case of the Lesborne will, for instance, the correct paper stock was no longer available and had to be approximated. The forger knew what was needed for perfect accuracy, but was unable to obtain it. Between theoretical understanding and practical workability is where we must look for any such failure."

On the second day of Holmes' work on the manuscripts, a letter arrived from Dr Graymare, addressed to me. I recognised the fussily neat hand that Holmes had so effectively imitated, and the terse style, still so uninterested in the actual words of a communication. It read: "We must meet, to discuss a matter of the utmost urgency and concern to yourself. I ask you please not to discuss this with Mr Holmes." It named a day and time, and suggested a particular bench in Hyde Park, overlooking the Serpentine.

The message was delivered while Holmes was out, and shortly after I had read another mention in the newspaper of the altercation at the tavern in Spitalfields which was, I now recalled, the context in which I had first heard the "Butcher's Apron" mentioned. Apparently the man who had been found dead in the aftermath of the fight at this hostelry was one Daniel Maines— presumably the "Mugger Maines" of Chops and Onion's message to Holmes. His killer was still being sought.

I remembered that Holmes had denied hearing either name, and in identical terms. I trusted his word, of course, and had no reason to give a moment's credence to that of the two thugs, but their unexplained reference to the incident discomfited me.

This uneasy feeling had just settled upon me when Graymare's message arrived, and at first I was indignant at the effrontery of his request. Almost immediately, though, I found myself curious as to what the graphologist had to say to me that he did not consider fit for Holmes' ears. I had assumed our business definitively closed after his humiliation at my friend's hands, but evidently he felt otherwise.

After some consideration, I opted not to tell Holmes of the note and its contents, instead committing the latter to memory and burning the former in the grate. I remained ambivalent for the moment on whether to attend the meeting as Graymare proposed.

Shortly after Holmes' return, Stanley Hopkins arrived at

our rooms in Baker Street, bringing with him the loyal Sergeant Douglass and a hollow-cheeked, bespectacled man in a top hat and opera cloak. He looked like a respectable undertaker, an impression quickly modified when he removed his hat to release a disorderly mane of grey hair.

Excitedly, the Inspector introduced him. "This is Dr Hadrian Permenter, the Shakespearean scholar. He's come to me with rather an interesting idea. I can't be involved in an official capacity, for reasons you're familiar with already, but nobody could object to my putting him in touch with you."

I thought the man's name seemed familiar, but the recollection failed to arrive as I shook his hand and invited him and the policemen to sit.

Holmes set aside a manual of papermaking, on which he had been making careful notes. He had some idea that a forger might wish to create his own paper stock to customised specifications, and was considering how far this might be feasible. I had an idea that any practical experiment to confirm this would involve some kind of liquid suspension, and had caught Holmes speculatively eyeing our bath that morning, so I was happy to have him distracted.

As naturally as if continuing a conversation, my friend said, "Dr Permenter, are you certain that your suspicions are not informed by your own family's recent embarrassment? It would be understandable if you were overcautious, especially with your professional reputation at stake."

The don peered in confusion between Holmes and Hopkins, as if trying to remember to which of them he had already confided the suspicions Holmes had mentioned, whatever those might be.

I sighed and said, "My friend likes to demonstrate his mental acuity, Dr Permenter. Many of our clients find it reassuring, as they know that he will bring the same deductive faculty to their case as he does to their first acquaintance. Holmes, since I'm apparently the only person in the room who is unaware of Dr Permenter's purpose here, will you allow him to state it aloud?"

"Of course," Holmes agreed, and then immediately launched into his own explanation. "I recognised your name, of course— 'My nephew Hadrian Permenter, of Prince's College, Camford,' as both your uncle's real and false wills had it." I recognised now where I had encountered the scholar's name before, and recently at that: he was Sir Lester Lesborne's nephew. So this was to be yet more of the forgery question, I thought.

Holmes went on, "Since you went to Inspector Hopkins, whom you doubtless knew from the case of Sir Lester's contested legacy, and since he mentioned the obstacles to his official involvement in such cases, it is clear that your concern relates to forgery. Given your area of specialism, the object of that concern was obvious at once. The manuscript attributed to Shakespeare that is due for auction at Boothby's has been in the newspapers enough of late that even I, taking as I do scant interest in poetry, could hardly fail to have become aware of it, and of the dispute concerning its authenticity. I ask again, are you quite sure that your view of the matter is not coloured by your experiences in that earlier case?"

I too remembered this story, now that Holmes mentioned it. As he said, the newspapers had taken a keen interest. The single yellowing folio page had been found tucked into an antique ledger that had lain undisturbed for generations in the library of an old manor house. It was inscribed with a sonnet in what some at least believed to be the Bard's own hand. The delighted owner of the house and ledger had had more use for cash than literature, and so had put the discovery up for auction, taking care to remain anonymous to prevent fortune-hunters from descending on the house where it had been found. American millionaires and foreign royalty were reputed to be interested, and the lot was expected to fetch an extravagant sum.

Dr Permenter spoke, in a somewhat distant and dusty voice. "As you have said, Mr Holmes, my academic reputation is involved, and I take it very seriously. I have urged caution concerning the manuscript because I firmly believe it to be inauthentic."

"Yet others disagree, do they not?"

Permenter said sharply, "If they do, then it is hardly my fault. The facts are there before them as they are before me. If the likes of Professor Rames take a different view, then it is their own foolishness that they demonstrate, not mine. Rames is a very slipshod scholar, I am sorry to say, and prone to the most outlandish theories. He also hopes, I understand, to acquire the page for the Camford University Museum, of which he is a trustee, so you may believe him every bit as likely to be swayed by partiality as I am myself."

"Oh, I do," Holmes agreed blithely.

The don gave him an aggrieved frown, but conceded the point. "Very well, then. If you will allow me …?" He withdrew from his pocket a typed sheet of paper, evidently a transcription of the sonnet, which he read to us.

SONNET ATTRIBUTED TO SHAKESPEARE

Love that is feigned is but the shade of Love,
And shades will oft dissemble and deceive.
Their natures ill, such spectres' falsehoods prove.
Yet also walk, unrestful, those we grieve,
At labour still to expiate their Sin,
And honest—if they were so—as before.
Some ghosts occasion Fortune for their kin,
And others from Misfortune keep them sure.
Thus Truth persists, though Falsehood may be rife.
The dead may walk, and at the end shall rise,
And those once shades shall win unending Life;
'Tis so with Love. Though it begin in lies,
What lies must rise and quicken, as we see,
And live in Truth and Perpetuity.

When the scholar had finished, Holmes said, "A somewhat spurious sentiment, if I may say so. From what I have observed a false emotion seldom becomes real through imitation."

Permenter tutted. "The speaker of Shakespeare's sonnets is often a constructed character who does not represent the author's own views. But that is hardly the point."

"Then pray elucidate your argument for us, Dr Permenter. I readily admit that Shakespearean scholarship is an area of human inquiry in which I am far from all-knowing."

Permenter nodded and collected his thoughts. "As you will have observed, this manuscript presents the appearance of a poem in the fourteen-line sonnet form, written in language approximating that of Shakespeare's time, and using his customary scheme of rhyme and metre. There are no signature, marginalia or other annotations that might identify it further. This much is uncontested, and on this basis some have rushed to the conclusion that the page represents a hitherto unknown work by the poet.

"Now, when we refer to 'Shakespeare's sonnets', we normally mean the complete cycle of one hundred and fifty-four poems that were gathered together in a printing of 1609. His only writings in this verse form that fall outside the collection appear within the texts of his plays—three in *Romeo and Juliet*, one in *Henry V*, and two in *Love's Labour's Lost*. The last case is unusual, in that these two sonnets are presented in dialogue as having been composed by persons in the play. As you doubtless recall," said Permenter—though his optimism on this point seemed to me radically misplaced, given the limitations of Holmes' knowledge outside his own criminological sphere—"that play ends unsatisfactorily, with the main characters being given a year and a day to prove the truth of their love. Contemporary records exist of a play by Shakespeare named *Love's Labour's Won*, now lost to us, which some have surmised to be a sequel to this earlier work.

"Now, on this basis, the supposed discovery of a sonnet not among those collected in the 1609 quarto, which forms part of the text of no known play, deals specifically with the question of authenticity as applied to Love, and incorporates the words *labour* and *win* as well as *love*, has caused some quite excitable comment. The speculation has inevitably arisen that this sonnet was written for inclusion in *Love's Labour's Won*, and thus that it forms the only surviving fragment of the text of this missing Shakespeare play.

"The fact that these lines lend themselves to such a sensational interpretation strongly suggests to me that they are not merely inauthentic but a deliberate hoax, aimed either at embarrassing the academic establishment or, as I admit seems more probable, garnering what we may expect to be a very substantial monetary reward."

"So you don't believe that that explanation is likely?" I asked.

"Frankly, Dr Watson, I doubt the entire existence of *Love's Labour's Won*, especially as a sequel to the earlier play."

This, I confess, surprised me. While I am certainly no literary scholar, even I had heard of the legendary lost play of that title. Permenter continued, "There is, to be sure, a list of Shakespeare's comedies compiled in 1598 that includes one given that name. However, there is every possibility that the compiler was mistaken or misled, or that he was thinking of a play that we know by a different appellation, since the titles of such works were far from fixed in Shakespeare's day.

"Even if a play by that name existed and has since been lost, the idea of a sequel is grossly improbable. No playwright of Shakespeare's era is known to have written a sequel to a comedy—or to a tragedy, for that matter. Serial dramatisation was reserved for history plays, where it was naturally understood that the events depicted were followed by others. Comedies were usually complete stories in themselves, and ordinarily finished with all the *dramatis personae* receiving their just deserts."

"Forgive me, though, Dr Permenter," put in Hopkins a little diffidently, "but from what you just said that doesn't happen in *Love's Labour's Lost*, does it? The characters are all sent away to prove their love. That sounds like a situation where a sequel might follow naturally, and surely *Love's Labour's Won* would be the obvious thing to call it."

Permenter grunted impatiently, as I suppose anyone might on finding a younger man intruding on their own area of specialism. "That is the argument that has often been made, not least by Professor Jonathan Rames. I can only reiterate that it is profoundly unlikely. To expect the inattentive Elizabethan audience to remember the events of a play performed previously, when not founded in known historical events, would be foolishly hopeful.

"That has not, of course, stopped Rames from publishing a fatuous article in one of the less reputable journals of literary criticism, speculating as to which of the characters from the earlier play might speak the new sonnet in the dialogue of *Love's Labour's Won*, and what it tells us about the sequel's plot and themes. It primarily tells *me* that Rames is a crackpot, willing to embrace the most absurd theories in the interest—"

"Excuse me, Dr Permenter," said Holmes, rather hurriedly. "But I find that academic discourse like this is invariably best summed up in writing, and I have no doubt that you can supply us with articles to its effect. At present I am more interested in the specifics of the manuscript at Boothby's. What can you tell us about it? Do the physical materials used appear to be of Shakespeare's time, for instance?"

Reluctantly, Permenter seemed to accept that this was not an opportunity to expound upon his academic hobbyhorses. "Did they not, I would hope that even my most misguided colleagues would refuse to accept it as authentic. The paper, ink and handwriting are all consistent with that period, as far as that goes, but all could have been acquired or reproduced by a sufficiently knowledgeable forger in modern times, or indeed at any point over the past four hundred years.

"Quill pens are simple to make, for instance, and the chemical composition of ink has barely changed since the Middle Ages. The paper would be difficult to manufacture, but this folio shows signs of the practice, common at the time, of erasing the writing on a superseded document to approximate a blank sheet, and many documents from the era still exist which might even now be treated in this way. Fresh ink may be aged with prolonged exposure to bright sunlight, at least so far as would be consistent with the page's preservation within a ledger."

"And the handwriting?" Holmes asked. "Does it match Shakespeare's?"

Dr Permenter sighed. "Alas, we have very little handwriting of Shakespeare's to compare it with. There are five signatures in the cursive style known as 'secretary hand', all somewhat different from one another, which are widely accepted as his own. All other samples are contested, but from what I know, the writing on the page is sufficiently consistent with them all. But you must know as well as I that such things may be falsified. My own uncle's will—"

"Quite so," said Holmes, impatient in turn now that he was being addressed on his own specialism. "But do you mean that your grounds for suspecting forgery in the case of this page are simply theoretical? You believe it unlikely that this play existed, and so you reject *a priori* this apparent demonstration of it?"

"Such circular thinking would ill befit a scholar." Permenter's grey voice became somewhat more animated. "It would not exclude the possibility that this is an authentic sonnet by Shakespeare that was omitted from the quarto collection. It could have been composed after 1609, for instance; or written for a different play, also lost; or rejected as unworthy of inclusion. It might even have been written for a play named *Love's Labour's Won* that shared nothing with *Love's Labour's Lost* but the titular similarity.

"But I can accept none of these alternatives. I do not believe that the poem is written in the authentic Shakespearean style."

"But I understood you to say that the hand—" Holmes began, but was interrupted in turn.

"I am speaking of his *literary* style, Mr Holmes. The words themselves are not those Shakespeare would have chosen. Oh, there has been some effort to reproduce the technique of the sonnets, but it is hollow and unconvincing. If the poem is authentically Elizabethan, which I do not allow, then it must have been written by a contemporary imitator of Shakespeare, not by the man himself. If that were true it would have historical interest, of course, but hardly the value that is claimed for it.

"The sonnet form requires a change of mood—the *volta*—between the initial octave and the sestet that follows, yet here the ninth line acts as a summary of what comes before. The repetition of *shades* and *walk* is dull, and the rhymes are contrived—'as we see' being particularly trite. Shakespeare's rhymes and his wordplay are subtler, less obvious. The pun on *lies* near the end is nearer to what I should expect. Then there is the vocabulary. The word *unending*, mundane though it may seem to the modern reader, does not occur elsewhere in Shakespeare's work, nor is it attested in English until some time after his death. Shakespeare uses both *unrest* and *restful*, but not *unrestful*. And while he writes often of ghosts, he never describes them as *spectres*."

"You checked the *Complete Works* for those specific words?" I said. "Good heavens." The extract had sounded Shakespearean enough to me, but then my literary sensibility runs little deeper than Wilkie Collins.

Permenter gave a dry laugh. "I have students for such work, Dr Watson," he said, "but I am confident of their conclusions. There is also the zeugma in the final line—"

"I'm sorry, sir, the what?" asked Hopkins, lost. I thought that Holmes looked rather relieved to have been spared the indignity of asking the question himself.

"A zeugma or syllepsis is a rhetorical device," the academic explained, a little wearily, "a form of wordplay. It is seen when a single word is used to govern two or more other words, but with different senses in each case. The word is taken from the Greek for 'yoke', by analogy with oxen. The example most frequently cited is found in Mr Dickens' work: 'She went straight home, in a flood of tears and a sedan-chair.' To be *in tears* requires a different understanding of the word *in* from being *in a sedan-chair,* yet the same instance of *in* governs both. The last line in the passage I read just now is similar: *to live in truth* means truly to live, yet *to live in perpetuity* means to live for ever. Again, the preposition functions differently in each case. Though zeugma is not altogether absent from Shakespeare's work, it is a device he very rarely uses in this form."

Holmes was looking disappointed. "Forgive me, Dr Permenter," he said again, "but these seem rather nebulous grounds upon which to conclude that the poem is a hoax. Perhaps to an academic they may seem substantial enough, but to a court of law—and, I admit, to myself—they could hardly be said to constitute proof of forgery."

Permenter's disappointment mirrored Holmes' own. "Sir, I am aware that you consider yourself a man of science rather than of scholarship, but I can assure you that these are facts, as certain as the magnitude of gravity or the atomic weight of nitrogen. As a recognised authority in the field, I assure you that the poem is spurious. You may of course seek material proof that will satisfy you, but for my own part I have staked my reputation upon it."

"I, too, respect your reputation, Dr Permenter," Holmes replied, "and yet I have found experts to be unreliable on more than one occasion. I must assume that, were I to put the points that you have made to Professor Rames, he would produce counterarguments that seem to him equally persuasive—since he, too, is a recognised authority in the field."

"Well, if you wish to satisfy yourself upon *that* score then you must speak to him," replied Permenter sourly.

"I shall indeed," Holmes agreed at once. "But I thank you for bringing this matter to my attention, Dr Permenter. It may well bear some investigation."

It seemed that Permenter intended to stay in London until the auction, in the hope of convincing the potential buyers that they were being sold a pig in a poke. Douglass offered to accompany him back to his hotel while Hopkins stayed behind, but Holmes' scepticism had put the don in an ill temper and he declined the offer. The sergeant merely found a cab for him before returning to us.

Meanwhile, we passed around the typed transcript, which Permenter had agreed to turn over to our use. Of course, the words alone told us little.

"Even if the sonnet is counterfeit," Hopkins observed, "I'm afraid there's no guarantee that its maker is the same man who forged the Lesborne will. I'm not sure that the thought has even occurred to Dr Permenter—he just thinks that his experiences have made him more canny about such things. But if all the other work is really that of one person, then he's shown himself versatile enough to try his hand at something like this. At worst, I suppose, by looking into it we might learn something about new counterfeiting techniques, or the current market for forgeries. Or rather, you might, for of course I must stay out of it for now."

"We must certainly view the page itself, at least," Holmes agreed. "I think that Boothby's will agree to it. I have done them certain favours in the past. Not every theft that occurs in London comes to the attention of your people, Hopkins, especially when the victims have a reputation like Boothby's to consider."

It seemed that the auctioneers were allowing limited viewings by prospective buyers, and they were happy enough to accommodate us within their schedule. Accordingly, the next day, Holmes and I were admitted to the secure vault where the sonnet was on display. An attendant stood conspicuously by while Holmes did his best, through the glass case in which the page was held, to reach a verdict on its penmanship and grade of ink. Despite the favours the company owed him— and I knew them to be considerable—Boothby's had refused to countenance his touching such a precious artifact, let alone removing samples for analysis.

I was tempted to some expression of awe at finding myself in the presence of a paper that the Bard himself had handled, but in view of Dr Permenter's comments I would not permit myself the embarrassment that I should feel were this to be proven incorrect. I comforted myself with the knowledge that, if this did prove to be Shakespeare's own authentic script, I could still tell others that I had seen it. I suspected that there would be scant opportunity for that in future, if it ended up in the collection of some Austrian princeling or American oil prospector.

Holmes lingered for as long as the attendant would allow him, and we were preparing ourselves to leave the vault when the door was opened and a second attendant came in, followed by a rotund, monkish man in a grey suit, whose resemblance to Friar Tuck was emphasised by a large bald patch on his crown.

He did not share the Merry Man's jovial good temper, however. "I beg your pardon," he said in dismay upon seeing us. "I suppose I am a little early."

"Not in the least," Holmes assured him easily. "On the contrary, you have arrived at a most opportune time, Professor Jonathan Rames of Ascension College."

On this occasion I was unawed by Holmes' preternatural knowledge. I had looked at the visitors' appointment list on the way in, and rather suspected that he had requested this particular time as an opportunity to speak to Dr Permenter's rival.

Professor Rames seemed equally unimpressed. "And who might you be, sir?" he asked testily.

The two of us introduced ourselves, and Holmes explained that in addition to his better-known interests he was a keen amateur Shakespearean scholar, and had prevailed upon his friends at Boothby's to let him view the sonnet for curiosity's sake. Rames, who had been taken aback at hearing my friend's name, seemed marginally reassured by this claim. While he had clearly heard of Holmes, his credulousness on this point suggested that he had not read very closely my descriptions of his character.

"Professor," Holmes asked, "I wonder whether we might prevail upon you to share a little of your knowledge with us? I understand that there has been some contention about the authenticity of this work. What, if anything, is your opinion of the question?"

Rames looked as if he was about to snap at us, but the temptation to display his erudition won through. He sounded irritable, however, as he replied, "I can quite assure you, Mr Holmes, there is no such question. The sonnet is entirely worthy of the Bard, and quite in keeping with his style. The handwriting, too, is his, insofar as we can ascertain such a thing."

"So you have no thought that this might be a forgery?"

"My dear sir, you may set your mind at ease about that," Rames scoffed. "Oh, to be sure there have been forgeries of Shakespeare. A hundred years ago a number of prominent figures, including Sheridan and Boswell, were lamentably taken in by a hoax perpetrated by a man named Ireland. But it was quickly discovered. His plays, if we can dignify them with the description, were riddled with anachronistic words, invented spellings and other historical inaccuracies. The sheer number of works that was supposedly discovered was also quite implausible. In reality, it seems sadly optimistic even to hope that we might recover more of this play. The manor house in which it was found is being scoured from top to bottom, naturally, but thus far nothing further has turned up."

"That indeed is suggestive," Holmes agreed. "Rarity has its own value, and one might expect the price of any future discoveries to be set by what is paid for this one."

Rames looked annoyed once more, and I stepped in with a more academic point, in the hope that it might soothe him.

"If I may, though, Professor Rames," I said, "you spoke of anachronistic words. Isn't the word *unending* from a later time than Shakespeare's?"

The professor scowled at me. "Just barely," he said. "It is first found less than a lifetime later, and the lack of written attestation before then does not mean that it was not in use. Besides, it is a perfectly obvious compound of the verb *to end*. Any author might have coined it independently at any time."

"And *spectre* and ..." I struggled to remember.

His scowl deepened. "Have you been talking to Permenter? I see you have. Well, I should not be surprised—he seems determined to denigrate my judgement across the capital. The man is obsessed with these textual minutiae, with a pedantry that altogether blinds him to the beauty and poetry of the Bard's work as a whole.

"The fact is that both *spectre* and *unrestful* were in use in Shakespeare's time, and it would be ludicrous to assume that he was unfamiliar with them simply because he does not himself use them elsewhere. Indeed, there are a number of words that the Bard used only once in his works—some of which no other author has ever used, except in reference to him. *Love's Labour's Lost* contains the word *honorificabilitudinitatibus*, for instance, though that is used for jocular effect. *Hamlet* contains a reference to a poison named *hebenon*, which—"

Holmes interrupted him, perhaps the only time that I have known him to decline a discussion of poisons. "That is fascinating indeed, Professor. Speaking of *Love's Labour's Lost*, however, I understand that you have argued for this sonnet as a fragment of the missing play *Love's Labour's Won*. Might I ask your view of Dr Permenter's contention that for an Elizabethan playwright to pen a sequel to a comedy would be so unconventional as to be incredible?"

Rames actually snorted. "Really, the man's lack of imagination is prodigious. Of course, it would be unconventional. The Bard was never a conventional author; why, the very ending of *Love's Labour's Lost* rejects convention outright. No other Elizabethan playwright made an invented character from a history play the hero of a comedy either, and yet Falstaff plays that role in *The Merry Wives of Windsor*. Nor did any of Shakespeare's contemporaries depart from the conventional genres of Comedy, Tragedy and History as far as he did in his final plays. The Bard was unique, an author wholly *sui generis*. We can hardly set rules for his behaviour by observing that of others."

"And so you have no misgivings at all about the manuscript?" Holmes asked him.

"As I have said," Rames retorted stubbornly, "I am quite satisfied that it is genuine, and I fully anticipate that there is much to be gleaned from it about the Bard's early career. Now, if you will forgive me, my appointment here is of limited duration and I intend to use it to the full. Good day, sir."

"One final question, Professor Rames, if you will indulge me," said Holmes. "If it were to be proven beyond doubt that this page were a forgery, what would that lead you to conclude about the forger?"

Rames glared. "I would conclude that he was an expert in Shakespeare's writings, with a consummate degree of depth and understanding, and moreover a poet of considerable skill in his own right. Neither are traits that any sane man would credit finding in a common criminal."

Holmes nodded. "That is what I thought. Good day to you, Professor, and I am sorry to have trespassed so impudently upon your time.

"And so we leave little the wiser, Watson," he continued, as our attendant conducted us out of the heavy steel doors of the vault, "except perhaps for a surer understanding of the depth and rancour of these academic quarrels. One of our experts insists, on what seem to us perfectly trivial grounds, that the sonnet is a transparent forgery, the other that it is not merely authentic but a work of profound literary merit. Each insists that the opinion of the other is worthless. And thus the two cancel one another out and evaporate, like your unstoppable force and immovable object."

We passed through several further doors, the attendant locking each behind us as we went in a manner that reminded me of the many prisons I had visited since meeting Holmes, until at last we stepped out of the building, blinking, into the bright sunshine of a hot London Summer.

"I am in the mood for fresh air after that vault," Holmes suggested, adding with a regretful sigh, "or at least, the freshest that London is able to offer us at present." He began to fill his pipe once more. "Will you walk with me back to Baker Street, Watson?"

We strolled companionably together, Holmes' pipe-smoke reeking of his new Turkish Delight blend—though that was at least preferable to the unadulterated stench of the streets. We had not gone more than a few streets before he proposed taking a shortcut he professed to know among the back-alleys. I was a little puzzled as to where it could lead, but since Holmes' knowledge of the topography of the capital was unrivalled by any man I had ever met, I agreed at once.

As we entered the alley, however, much to my surprise, he murmured, "Have you your revolver, Watson?"

"No, I am afraid not," I replied. I had considered bringing it along, in view of the recent assault upon my person, but had concluded that if there were anywhere it would be altogether superfluous, it would be inside a secure vault. "Why ever do you ask?"

"A pity, but not to be helped. We have been followed since Boothby's," he told me calmly, "by two men."

"Chops and Onions?" I gasped.

"The very same. The first I observed loitering across the street as we emerged, and recognised him from the descriptions I have been giving out across half of London. His colleague has been loping along at a greater distance, and I imagine will have circled around ahead of us when he saw us entering this passage. Ah!" he cried delightedly, as the blond man who had attacked me rounded the corner ahead of us. "Mr Onions, I presume. And I can only suppose that your friend Mr Chops is close upon our tail."

I glanced back and saw the muttonchopped figure of my other erstwhile assailant approaching from the far end of the alley, a wicked-looking hatchet in his hand.

"Yeah, we heard you'd been asking about us," said Onions, pulling out a Bowie knife from his belt. "Haven't found us yet though, have you?"

Holmes frowned in theatrical puzzlement. "It might appear that I have," he argued, "for here you are."

"Nah," said Chops. "We found you. It's different. Mostly because of who comes out worst."

"You'll thank us, though," Onions supplied, and I had the sense that during their career together their threats had developed into a practised routine. "Because of how we're going to make sure no-one ever finds you again."

"Really? That sounds most inconvenient," said Holmes. "My address is well known, gentlemen. You could have asked for me there at any time."

During this sinister banter, the men had been steadily advancing on us from both ends of the alley, and were now within striking distance. The adjoining walls were too high to scale and there were no doors or even windows into the buildings to allow for our escape that way. Plainly, we would have to stand our ground and fight. Grimly, I hefted my walking-stick.

With an oath Chops essayed the first blow, swiping his hatchet viciously at Holmes' face. Holmes sidestepped, blocking the blade with his own walking-stick. The axe embedded itself in the wood, but Holmes' stick had been bored through with a core of iron for just such an occasion, and it held. He tried to twist the chopper from the whiskered man's hand, but Chops was too strong and wrested it away.

I had little leisure to observe Holmes' battle further, however, for by now Onions was upon me, thrusting with his knife. I am not so quick as Holmes, and he nicked my arm, but I got a good hard blow in with my stick on the side of his head as I ducked away. Both bleeding now, we circled each other, he stabbing his blade at me here and there with surprising litheness for such a big man, I doing my best to parry his jabs as they came. As we orbited one another, I was able to glance at Holmes, who had dropped his stick and was wrestling with Chops for control of the hatchet. I deeply regretted, with what little leisure my predicament allowed me, my missing revolver.

But Onions feinted with the knife, and when I moved my stick to fend him off, he kicked me hard in the shin. Though I had been expecting some dirty fighting, anticipation could do little to quell the pain that burst through my injured leg, and I fell back, crying out. Onions pressed his advantage, slashing at my midriff so that I had to stumble backward once more, landing up with my back to the wall.

The fair-headed man gave an evil smile and lunged at me, but this time I was able to lurch aside, and the Bowie knife scraped against the brickwork. I stepped further away, and stumbled awkwardly over some object on the alley floor. And, as I struggled to arrest my fall, I saw that it was Holmes' discarded walking-stick. I gripped it hastily and swung it upwards, as Onions dived towards me. It caught him full in the stomach and he doubled over, winded.

My own opponent being temporarily incommoded, I risked another look at Holmes, who had deprived Chops of his weapon and tossed that, too, away. He was putting his *baritsu* training to effective use, raining a series of precise and skilful blows on Chops, who was responding with sallies of his own, fuelled by brute strength. My friend seemed to be getting the better of the fight, though. And so I turned back to Onions, who had recovered enough to slash his knife wildly at my face.

I had two sticks now, however, and was thus able to attack him from two angles. With one I beat away his knife hand, while with the other I beset him about the head and shoulders. He was soon bleeding heavily from his forehead, wiping the mess out of his eyes. After a particularly successful buffet of mine cracked across his skull, he cried out in pain and backed away, raising his hand to ward me off. He glanced behind me and, seeing how things were going for his comrade, turned and ran.

At once I turned to Holmes, who was reeling from a lucky blow from one of Chops' heavy fists. I called his name and threw him his walking-stick, shortly thereafter bringing my own down on Chops' head. I was weakened and panting, however, and this had less effect than I would have hoped.

But Holmes was now enraged. Now that he had his cane again he began to batter his unarmed assailant mercilessly. Chops flailed wildly at him, but the heavy cane was a formidable weapon, and I could see how each blow hurt its recipient. The whiskered man turned to run like his comrade, but Holmes swung the stick low, tripping him, and the thug went down. Holmes hit him again on the back, and the man rolled over, his hands up now in a begging motion.

"Oh no, my man," my friend said, "that won't do at all. You found me, remember? And now we must learn which one of us comes out the worse."

And he raised his stick again, and brought it crashing down on the man's upraised hands. Chops yowled in pain, rolled again, and scrambled to his knees. "Please," he said. "No more." Holmes hit him again and again, until he managed to scrabble to his feet and run away, shrieking imprecations down on both our heads.

The afternoon was hot even in this shady alleyway, and my friend was out of breath. He mopped his brow. "There," he said. "I fancy that that will discourage them from seeking us out with further messages." He picked up the departed man's hatchet from the alley floor.

"Really, Holmes," I expostulated. "Was such a beating quite necessary? The man was begging for mercy."

"I imagine that the late Christopher Bastion did likewise, Watson," Holmes noted coldly, "and received precious little from our Mr Chops."

"But even so … this savagery is quite unlike you, old man." I was altogether most concerned, not only about my friend's state of mind but also about the damage he might have done. From what I had been able to see Chops was in no immediate danger, but I could not rule out internal bleeding that might, if left untreated, lead to his death. I would shed few tears for such a man, but I knew full well that despite the services that Holmes had rendered the constabulary, he could expect no favour from them should it come to a murder charge. Indeed, there were officers who smarted so from the humiliations he had dealt them over the years that they might perform their duty, in such a case, with exceptional relish.

He sighed. "I am sorry—you're right, Watson. It was unwonted, and uncalled for. To tell the truth, I felt immoderately angry with the fellow for his recent attack on you, and with myself for not having prevented it. I confess, I may for once have let my temper get the better of me."

I shook my head in bafflement and confusion. The battle had been brutal but quick, and it could scarcely have been more than ten minutes since Holmes and I had stood trading niceties about Shakespeare with a Camford don. My arm smarted, and I rubbed absently at the place where Onions' blow had landed.

"But Watson, you're bleeding," Holmes said, and at once was all solicitude, although in truth the cut to my arm was shallow and I was more annoyed by the damage to my jacket. He insisted on binding the wound with my handkerchief nevertheless, and quickly hailed us a cab, one of the new electric "Hummingbird" models introduced by Mr Bersey, for our return to Baker Street.

"Well, my dear fellow," he said as the cabman started the motor, the vehicle whirred gently away and we settled back into our seats, "I think we can conclude from this that Chops' and Onions' employer is displeased with us. This tells us that, however frustrating our investigation may appear from our own point of view, there must be something that we have been doing properly. I wish I could divine what it is."

But in the meantime I had been going through my pockets. "Bother," I said. "I seem to have dropped my notebook. I had intended to write up an account of this altercation, while it was still fresh in my mind." I glanced back towards the alley, but I found that I was quite exhausted. The idea of returning to search for the lost item was too dispiriting to contemplate.

"I shall very gladly buy you a new one, Watson," he promised me, and though his tone was pleasant I was haunted by the look of guilty contrition in his eyes.

LETTER TO LORD KERWINSTONE

Grovedown-on-Sea
28th July 1897

Dear Frederick

I suppose you will be surprised to hear from me, as it has been so long since we last corresponded, and you have, I suspect, imagined me quite the invalid these days. In truth I have not been well, and have rarely had the energy to write.

I write now, however, with pleasure — and the fountain-pen which dear Edith gave me for my 70th birthday — to introduce a distant connexion of hers, and thus of yours: my great-nephew, Percival Campion.

It is likely that you have not heard of him before now — he has lived with his family in Pembrokeshire, and my illness has prevented my having much communication with him, as it has with you — but he has recently been staying with me, and has quickly shown himself a most kind and attentive guest. Having completed his studies in Divinity at Camford, he intends in the Autumn to take up his dog-collar and a position as a curate in Wells.

In the meantime he hopes to spend some time birdwatching on the coast, and on my recommendation hopes that you will allow him to make Kerwin Hall his base. So confident am I that you will accommodate my wishes and him that I am sending him this letter to bring with him as his introduction to you.

I am confident that you will find him to be an agreeable houseguest, of quiet and studious habits, and a polite, if rather single-minded, conversationalist.

Your affectionate sister-in-law
Edna Salisbury

The next day was the date decreed by Dr Graymare for our clandestine appointment in Hyde Park. I had considered the matter carefully, and decided that, given the open situation in which he had suggested we should meet, there was no harm in my attending, even—for the time being, at least—without Holmes' knowledge. Holmes had received a message from Mycroft that morning, informing him that Lord Loomborough insisted on meeting us urgently at the Diogenes Club, and I arranged to catch up with him there.

This time, I did take with me my service revolver, and was careful to follow the main streets, with no shortcuts. Though I had no reason to suspect that Carson Graymare was capable of physical violence, Holmes had given the graphologist ample reason to resent him, and I was by now on my guard against ambush from even the most unlikely quarter.

I found Dr Graymare sitting at the bench that he had indicated. He was engaged in fastidiously tearing slices of bread into exactly equal squares and feeding them to the ducks. He looked up when he saw me, his pince-nez glinting in the bright sunshine. "Ah, Dr Watson," he said, easily enough. "I am grateful to you for coming. I realise that it was presumptuous of me to ask you for discretion, but I must seek your assurance on this point: have you told Mr Holmes that you were meeting me?"

"I have not," I told him, "though you are right that it was a presumptuous request. Might I inquire what matter is of such urgency and concern that it may be imparted only to my ears, and requires both his absence and his ignorance?"

"Please, sit," said Graymare, patting the bench next to him. In truth, my leg had been paining me since the altercation with

Chops and Onions, so rather than stand on either it or my dignity, I did as he suggested.

Graymare was fussily dismembering another slice of bread. The ducks were grateful enough, flapping around him and quacking excitedly, but my own patience was limited. "Please, Dr Graymare, come to the point," I said. "Or I shall be leaving directly."

The little man threw the last of his breadcrumbs to a plump white bird, then shooed the flock away. "Very well," he said. "I understand your curiosity. The fact is that I *am* concerned, and so should you be. Indeed, you should fear for your safety, Dr Watson."

I thought again of Chops and Onions. "That much has become apparent to me over the past few days," I informed him. "May I ask, though, how it is that you are aware of it?"

He looked at me with surprise. "Really? So he is becoming violent, then?"

I frowned. "Who do you mean, man? Stop beating about the bush and tell me what you know."

"Why, Mr Holmes, of course. His disorder has begun to show itself in his behaviour?" He gazed at me intently, gauging my reaction, which was an incredulous one. "I see that it has not. You have been experiencing violence from some other quarter. I suppose I should have guessed that that must be routine in your adopted profession."

"What are you talking about?" I replied stoutly, though I confess to some unease. "Holmes, violent? Whatever can you mean?"

Graymare shook his head, and gazed sorrowfully after the departed ducks, who were now being fed by an equally plump child at the behest of its nanny. He said, "I can quite believe that Mr Holmes is unique. He has proven that to us both, as well as to many others in London. But I believe that, because of that, he is also very dangerous."

"Dangerous?" I repeated, and again I felt a tension scrabbling at my spine. Holmes behaviour the previous day had been without precedent. His brutal beating of Chops—whom he had, after all, lured into the alleyway after us—was quite unlike the man I knew who, while perfectly capable of fisticuffs and even armed combat when the situation called for it, was habitually just and merciful, and unfailingly in control of himself. I wondered once again, with a greater depth of unease than before, just what had been the truth surrounding the death of Daniel "Mugger" Maines at the Butcher's Apron tavern in Spitalfields, which Chops and Onions had been so ready to lay at my friend's door.

Nevertheless, I continued, "You're talking about my friend and colleague, and one of the most respected upholders of the law in London. He's no more capable of unwarranted violence than I am—less so, indeed," I added, conscious that I might be protesting too much.

Graymare shook his head. "You think you know his character, but his handwriting tells me otherwise."

"His handwriting!" I said, scornfully. Here, at least, I felt that I was on safe ground. Holmes had conclusively proved that Graymare's technique of handwriting analysis could no more be relied upon than could a drunken cabbie.

Calmly, Graymare said, "Yes, Dr Watson, his handwriting. I can well understand how you might view my methods as discredited, in light of Mr Holmes' demonstration of the other day. I can only repeat that they have proven efficacious in every other situation to which I have applied them. Holmes is the first to confound my expectations to any extent at all, let alone so completely. I still cannot fully understand how he achieved it, technically speaking. But I do know what it tells me."

"And what is that?" I scoffed.

"As I have said, a person's script betrays his personality. You think that you know your friend's character, but a man who can falsify his handwriting to such a degree has no character. He spoke of actors and their ability to take on another person's identity at will. I believe that he was speaking of himself. I believe that the Sherlock Holmes you know, and have presented to the world in your accounts, is no more than a mask he wears. It is a mask that fits him well, no doubt, and one he feels comfortable wearing—but it is one that he can remove at will, as he did in my office when he forged my own hand. You think you know Sherlock Holmes, and in a sense you do, but in a truer sense there *is* no Sherlock Holmes.

"And I believe that you are beginning to realise this," Graymare added. He had been watching my face closely as he spoke, and though I had done my best to hide my dismay at what he was telling me I have never had much skill at dissembling. I, at least, would have been a miserable failure as an actor.

Holmes, on the other hand … I remembered all the times when he had surprised me by revealing himself, having engaged me in conversation in an assumed disguise. A little old road-sweeper, a provincial parson, a charwoman … the people he seemed capable of becoming were limited only by his physique, and even that was remarkably flexible. He had always taken delight in his ability to deceive, and though he was not a man to crow over others, I knew from remarks that he had made that he also rejoiced quietly in the superiority of his intellect.

I knew, too—better than I had ever recorded for my reading public—his dark, sour moods, and the strangeness of certain of his habits. And I had conscientiously read everything that I could find about the effects that the long-term use of cocaine could have upon a man's psyche, and had been disquieted by it. If nothing else, his focus on the forgery aspect of our current case was beginning to show the hallmarks of a monomania.

But Graymare, being Graymare, was still speaking. "I suppose that your life has been in danger on many occasions,

Doctor," he said, "and perhaps my warning will be of little interest to you. But if you have been relying on your friend to support you in such danger, or to protect you from harm ... well, I expect that he will, so long as it suits him. But once that ceases to be true, he will shrug off your friendship as easily as doffing his hat, and with as little compunction. You are not safe with him, and if your interests ever begin to conflict with his, or if exceptional events occur to throw him off his habitual equilibrium, then you will not be safe *from* him either.

"I feel it my public duty to warn you of this," he concluded, priggishly. Seeing the obstinacy in my face, he added, "You may, of course, ignore it as you please. My conscience in the matter will be clear. But if you consider the matter dispassionately, I believe that you will see the truth in what I have told you."

I stood. Stiffly, I said, "You have said your piece, Dr Graymare. I thank you for your concern. I do not expect that we will meet again. Good day."

He nodded shortly, lips pursed, and turned his face back towards his aquatic friends.

As I approached the exit from the park, deep in thought, I almost walked into a diminutive figure standing in my path. As I apologised, I realised that this small person was familiar to me. "Sneaky?" I said, recognising one of the street urchins who acted as Holmes' Irregulars. "Sneaky" was a lad of indeterminate age and baptismal name, who was known for his stealth and had been employed by Holmes on eavesdropping missions on more than one occasion. He was loitering near the park gates, with the innocent air of a child who would no more think of stealing a wallet from a passer-by than he would of making off with the statue of Achilles.

"Afternoon, Dr Watson," Sneaky said cheerfully, handing back my wallet with a cheeky grin. "Nice day, isn't it?"

I agreed that it was, but having no wish to engage in further conversation in my current state of mind, I bade him good day. I was about to move on when a thought struck me. "Sneaky," I said, "when Mr Holmes goes out in his disguises, do you Irregulars know where he goes?"

"Oh," Sneaky said nonchalantly, "there's always a few of us keeps tabs on him. He never knows when he might need us, and he likes to have us near to 'and for if he needs to send a message, like. He can disguise himself how he likes, we've seen them all before."

I said, "Would you be able to find out where he was on a particular night?"

Sneaky looked confused. "If I was you I'd ask him yourself, Doctor. It wouldn't be like Mr 'Olmes to forget, would it?"

I agreed that it would not. Inspired by a sudden fit of invention, however, I added, "But he's set me a challenge. I said I hoped one day to be a detective like him, and he bet me that I couldn't find out where he was five nights ago. There was a particular tavern, he said, where he got into some trouble. Would you be able to tell me which one it was?"

"Oh, that's easy," Sneaky said. "We knows all about that. It was the Butcher's Apron over in Spitalfields. Sammy and Molly seen him taking on three coves by himself and giving them all a good walloping. They told us all about it the next day."

Very troubled, I said, "How did the fight end, do you know?"

"Nah," said Sneaky, evidently not a regular reader of the newspapers, "Sam and Moll got spotted by some of the coves' pals and 'opped it. I bet he gave them all a proper licking, though. Mr 'Olmes is an arty scrapper with his dabs."

Absently passing Sneaky a few pennies for his trouble, I dawdled my way to St James', doing my best to keep a wary eye out for any watchers or followers, but sorely distracted by the uneasiness in my mind.

I found Holmes outside the door of the Diogenes Club, holding his pocket-watch and pacing impatiently. "Ah, Watson," he snapped. "Your errands have overrun, I fear. Had Lord Loomborough not asked particularly for the presence of us both, I should have gone in without you."

Inside we were met by the same attendant as before, who looked far from delighted to see us. Hastily he ushered us into the Stranger's Room, keeping a stern eye on Holmes as we passed the glass wall behind which the club's members sat on display.

Mycroft Holmes was awaiting us in the room, tapping impatiently at his own watch. I realised that it was the twin of Sherlock's, and wondered whether they had been given to the brothers by the same relative, but as I knew almost nothing of the Holmes family beyond Sherlock and Mycroft, I could speculate no further.

"You are late," Mycroft reminded us heavily as we entered, "and Lord Loomborough is not a man for patience. Fortunately he too has been detained, by urgent business at his Ministry, though I understand that he will be with us shortly. When he arrives I shall effect the introductions, but I shall not linger. I am not your keeper, Sherlock, though men such as Loomborough may hold me responsible for you."

"We must both be grateful for that, to be sure," said Sherlock with a sly smile.

Mycroft snorted. He said, "You cannot expect any very comfortable reception from Loomborough, I fear. I am told that he resents your derailment of Scotland Yard's investigation into the Bastion affair with these irrelevant inquiries into putative forgeries." I wondered whether Loomborough's authority would finally be enough to dissuade his brother from his preoccupation with the counterfeiting issue, although in honesty I had rarely known him to be dissuaded from any course he chose to pursue.

Mycroft continued, "Though your friend Inspector Hopkins may not credit it, Loomborough also takes quite an interest in his career, regarding him as one of the sharpest tools at the constabulary's disposal. It was for that reason that he had him removed from investigating such trivialities in the first place, and placed in charge of the more exceptional crimes that come into the Yard's orbit. The Minister is, I am told, displeased. Ah, Jennings," he added as the attendant returned. "Is His Lordship here?"

Jennings nodded silently, and I realised that I had never yet heard the man, or any of the other attendants at the Diogenes, speak. Without a word he ushered in a man as tall and imposing as Mycroft was massive, with an authority and gravity to match the older Holmes' own. Sherlock and I stood politely as we took the measure of him.

Lord Loomborough was a handsome man of vigorous middle age, his dark hair ungreying despite the deep creases in his face. He bore a passing similarity to the late President Lincoln, a resemblance that he accentuated by wearing a Shenandoah beard. I knew that this was a deliberate homage because it had been mentioned in a volume of his memoirs, and while I had never read the books in question I had seen this titbit discussed with interest in reviews. The memoirs had been well received in the press: they were considered both informative and lively, and said to have been written with considerable wit.

Loomborough was a careful cultivator of his public image, the species of politician who gains consent for government through popular acceptance of his authority, rather than imposing it majestically from above. Paradoxically, he had achieved this by emphasising, in his memoirs, his speeches and elsewhere, a supposed ruthlessness that set him apart from his peers and led his colleagues, and the public, to feel that they would prefer him on their side rather than otherwise.

I knew also, from reading about his career in the papers, that his rise to power had been accompanied by a string of scandals involving his rivals. A junior Minister for Fisheries had exchanged compromising letters with a notorious adventuress; a Whip was found to be the author of an anonymous article criticising the leader of his party; while the former Minister for Policing had, as it turned out, been taking illicit payments, and had foolishly issued receipts for the money. On each occasion, Loomborough had been on hand to take advantage of his colleague's discomfiture, calling for each man's resignation or dismissal and then, after the minimum decent interval, stepping into the vacuum caused by his departure.

In this way, His Lordship had worked his way up to his current eminence. Though Minister for Policing was not, to be sure, one of the great offices of state, it was a position of immense practical importance and commanded considerable respect. He had a great many political allies—their numbers doubtless bolstered by the propensity of those who opposed him to fall into ignominy—and it was widely expected that he was destined before long for greater things.

For his part, Mycroft Holmes had not risen when Loomborough entered. Evidently he, at least, felt secure enough in his position that the Minister could not cow him. As he had promised, he introduced us and then rose to his feet, huffing and blowing like the walrus he so notably resembled, before withdrawing discreetly and leaving us with the statesman.

"Lord Loomborough," Holmes began, respectfully enough. "This is indeed an honour. While I have worked in both official and private capacities for clients at the highest echelons of power, I do not believe that any Minister of State has hitherto taken such an interest as your own in an ordinary collaboration between myself and the police."

Lord Loomborough sat, and bade us do likewise. He said, "Naturally I am interested, Mr Holmes. I am sure it cannot have escaped you that Christopher Bastion and I were at school together. We were close at that time, though not in recent years, and I must confess that his death has brought me a share of pain. It would pain me all the more to have to believe in his treachery."

"Do you mean that you do not?" I blurted out, and cursed myself for my loose tongue. This was a man whom Holmes and I could not afford to alienate, assuming that we had not done so before this meeting even started. My conversation with Graymare had evidently shaken my equilibrium more than I had realised.

But Loomborough accepted the question with equanimity. "It is natural enough that you should ask, Dr Watson. The evidence, even at this stage, seems somewhat damning, and I accept that it may yet turn out to be true. I am undecided upon the matter; I merely observe that if it is indeed proven that Christopher Bastion was a traitor to his country, then that knowledge will occasion me almost as much distress as his death. He is a man I would have relied upon absolutely, just as Sir Hector and his predecessors have."

"It is an opinion that is widely shared, sir," Holmes commented. "And one that may prove to be warranted, though I cannot for now regard the question as settled. You mentioned that you and Mr Bastion had not been close friends of late. May I inquire how often you had seen one another?"

"Very little, I am afraid." Loomborough shook his head with obvious regret. "We met at social occasions only, perhaps a few times a year, and while our relations were cordial enough, I had little thought of enjoying his companionship to the full while it lasted. Had I but known ... but of course such foreknowledge is given to none of us, whatever earthly authority we may attain."

"I suppose there would be some delicacy surrounding a

friendship between a minister and a senior civil servant," Holmes suggested. "A certain distance would need to be maintained."

"Quite so, Mr Holmes. Or so I told myself. The consideration seems a foolish one now." Loomborough shook his head again sadly.

"What were your thoughts when the scandal involving Mr Bastion broke?" Holmes asked. "You must have been among the first to hear of it."

Lord Loomborough inclined his head. "I was shocked, naturally, quite shocked. At first I was absolutely convinced that it must be a mistake, but in the face of the evidence—the evidence that you have now begun to call into question—I could only lament how low my old schoolfriend had fallen. And when I received news of his suicide, well …" He bowed his head further in sorrow.

Holmes continued with his questioning. We had not expected to find His Lordship so congenial and accommodating, and it was natural for my friend to take the opportunity to speak to one of Bastion's oldest acquaintances. "Did that suicide seem plausible to you, before it was established that it was in fact a murder?"

Loomborough sighed. "As with his betrayal, I could believe nothing else, given what seemed to be the evidence of his own words. I suppose that it appeared in keeping to me, given the shocking departure of the betrayal itself, that he should feel he had left himself no other recourse. I concluded that either I had not known him as well as I believed, or that he had changed more than I had realised since our youth together. In either case, I bitterly regretted it."

"And now, sir?" Holmes asked, quite gently.

"Now that you have shown him to have been killed by another hand," said the Minister with passion, "and that that hand may have extinguished others also, I can but urge you to do everything in your power to find the parties responsible. Traitor or no, Christopher Bastion was my friend. If he betrayed his country, then he was brought to that point by the action of others, and I would see them punished as well; but for his murderers, I *must* have Justice." His words were passionate, but his voice was stern and resolute.

Pensively, Holmes asked, "And do you have any recommendations, sir, as to how we should go about that?"

Loomborough shook his head decisively. "You are the expert in these matters, Mr Holmes. I may be the minister in charge of policing, and naturally I have been thoroughly briefed upon the case, but I have no experience of investigative work. Your inquiry must take the course it will, provided that it leads you to Bastion's killers. That must be the end you keep in mind, gentlemen, but how you may best achieve it you, not I, are best placed to judge."

Holmes asked, "It does not trouble you, then, that at present our investigation is concerned with answering the questions of who forged Bastion's suicide note, whether they also forged the letter establishing his espionage, and whether they might not be responsible for certain other forgeries which you asked Inspector Hopkins to leave alone, but that he has been good enough, at my insistence and without compromising his own duties, to bring to our attention?"

Loomborough raised his eyebrows. "I admit that the relevance of such matters seems to me tangential at best, but if you feel that this is the avenue that will best serve to lead you to the guilty parties, then that is wholly a matter for your judgement. Your reputation is such that I should be foolish to question your methods, let alone seek to direct them."

"You take a very understanding view of the matter, Lord Loomborough," said Holmes, "and I thank you for it."

"The only thing that will upset me," said Lord Loomborough, suddenly stern, "will be if your efforts fail. That should displease me greatly. But I am assured by your brother, among many others who stand, as you say, at the highest echelons of power, that I may absolutely rely upon your abilities."

The words concerned me, recalling as they did those he had used of Bastion, who had proven—whatever the truth of his relations with Zimmerman—to have been sadly fallible. But Holmes had no such misgivings.

"I can assure you," he said smoothly, "that we shall do all within our power. That does not guarantee success, I am afraid, but in my experience it places the balance of probability strongly in its favour."

We emerged from the Diogenes Club, satisfied that we were not in fact defying ministerial wishes with our investigations, but had every official support for them. "This case succeeds in surprising me at every turn," Holmes admitted, which again was quite unlike him.

I did not share with Holmes my own disquiet. Lord Loomborough had been described and presented to me as a martinet, yet had proven in person to be kind and even genial. Before him, Carson Graymare, who I had assumed to have no especial interest in my welfare, had expressed concern for the safety of my person. Both men I had believed to be of one character, yet had revealed themselves as of quite another.

Could I be equally deceived in my view of my friend Holmes, as Graymare had suggested? Was it possible that he, too, would turn out to be wholly unlike the person I had believed in?

I could not credit it, yet the seed of doubt had been planted within me. And it is in the nature of seeds to grow.

THE MORNING CHRONICLE
20th June 1898
LOVE'S LABOUR'S WON NO LONGER LOST:
SENSATIONAL DISCOVERY AT MANOR HOUSE

Scholars have announced the discovery of the legendary missing Shakespeare play *Love's Labour's Won*, at the private home where recently the manuscript of a hitherto unknown poem by the Bard was also found.

The previous discovery, a sonnet now on sale at Boothby's Auction House, has attracted much attention from the academic world and from wealthy collectors. However, the fame of this more substantial work, a full five-act play, will undoubtedly eclipse that of the poem, which is a mere 14 lines long.

The manor house, whose name and location have been kept strictly private to spare the owner and his family from the depredations of amateur fortune-seekers, has been subject to a rigorous search by scholars of the most reputable probity, who finally discovered the unbound manuscript in a locked sea-chest in the attic. It is thought that an earlier owner of the house, a contemporary of Shakespeare, was presented with the manuscript by the Bard himself, perhaps in gratitude for some gift of money or other act of patronage.

Naturally there has been unkind speculation that this new find is a forgery. For instance, Dr Hadrian Permenter of Prince's College, Camford, who has previously cast doubt on the authenticity of the sonnet, now asks why, if that poem is authentic and a part of this play, it was separated from the manuscript? Such trivialities are unlikely to trouble the serious Shakespearean enthusiast.

Professor Jonathan Rames of Ascension College told our reporter that the new manuscript is undoubtedly Shakespeare's original manuscript of *Love's Labour's Won*, the sequel to his popular *Love's Labour's Lost*, and that it will be of incalculable value in casting light on the poet's work and his career.

Dr Rames informs our reporter that he will treat the subject at length in a forthcoming monograph, to be published by Camford University Press, and that he expects to be exploring this new frontier in Shakespeare scholarship for a great many years to come.

"I trust that you have information of some exceptional significance to impart, Sherlock," Mycroft Holmes admonished his brother from our best armchair. "You know that I do not care to have my routine interrupted." He sipped lightly at a cup of Mrs Hudson's best Darjeeling, and delicately helped himself to half the biscuits that she had provided for our gathering.

"Forgive me, brother," said Sherlock Holmes, "but you will perhaps allow that, of all the establishments of its kind in London, the Diogenes Club is the least well suited to hosting conferences. I felt it best to hold a conclave between the four of us here in my rooms."

For Stanley Hopkins was also in attendance, sitting upright in a straight-backed chair and gripping his cup of tea with unnecessary firmness. He was clearly ill at ease at finding himself in the presence of an official of Mycroft's seniority, though not being of the older Holmes' immediate circle he was ignorant of the full scope of his activities and authority.

Mycroft conceded his brother's point with a short nod. "I hope, at least, that what you have to tell us relates to the final days of the late Christopher Bastion."

"It does indeed," said Holmes, "although the scope of its implications is far greater." He had spent the past day and night at his desk, surrounded by cooling cups of tea, forgoing sleep and pausing only grudgingly for meals, poring minutely over the many documents this case had accumulated and taking reams of notes that meant nothing to me. This was, he had informed us all, a symposium to present his findings.

"In other words, this is more about the counterfeiting business," Mycroft observed caustically. "You know how I respect your talents, brother, and if you are persuaded that you have found forged documents then I am altogether prepared to believe you. But unless you can demonstrate that they affect my areas of concern, then they are nothing to me but an interesting fact that I can store against the day when it may, Fate willing, become useful. Meanwhile, I must prioritise. I have an Empire to ... serve," he concluded, modifying his statement in deference to Hopkins' presence.

"I must crave your indulgence," Sherlock told him, "since my investigation of the forgeries has now convinced me that Bastion was not a traitor. My particular grounds for thinking this I shall share with you, if you will allow me."

Grumpily, Mycroft subsided further into his chair. It creaked like a galleon in a strong headwind, but held.

With a nervous glance at the older Holmes, Inspector Hopkins ventured, "I'm very happy to assist in any way I can, gentlemen, but I must repeat that I'm here purely as a private citizen, not a representative of the Yard."

"That is understood, Hopkins," said Sherlock, "and my brother will certainly vouch for the fact with your Commissioner, if he or Lord Loomborough continue to cause you difficulties. I suspect, however, that by the time this case is concluded your superiors will have little alternative but to take an interest."

"So what is it you have to tell us, Sherlock?" Mycroft repeated impatiently. "My time has a certain value, you know."

"And I shall not trespass too inveterately upon it," his brother promised. "As you know, this case—for I shall, for now, treat the multiple instances of counterfeiting as a single case—revolves around the difficulty of proving forgery where no physical evidence is available. Of our known false documents, one was shown to be unreliable by circumstance alone. The letter from Mrs Salisbury to introduce Percival Campion to Lord Kerwinstone was certainly spurious, since the bearer was not, in fact, Campion. There is still doubt as to whether the Barraclagh marriage certificate was false at all, though the convenience of its discovery, and the disappearance of the discoverer, weigh heavily against it. In neither case could Hopkins and his men, the Yard's best and brightest, discover any material evidence of fraud.

"Only in the case of the Lesborne will did happenstance come to Hopkins' aid. First, it transpired that Sir Lester Lesborne had been absent at the time when the will was supposedly made, a fact that could only have been known to those with intimate knowledge of his life. Secondly, there was the discontinuation of a particular paper stock, a matter beyond the control of any criminal, and for which ours did his utmost to compensate, falling only somewhat short of complete success. But for these two historical accidents, we would have no evidence of forgery in any of these cases that was not purely circumstantial.

"From the fact that at least two of these documents have been falsified, however, we can deduce that there have been in operation in England one or more forgers who create facsimiles of the very highest standard that is practically and technically achievable, and that these are, barring rare strokes of luck, virtually impossible to distinguish from real documents."

Hopkins had been nodding along to this, his interest now fully engaged. With no trace of his earlier diffidence, he said, "That's what my team concluded, to be sure, before our work was put a stop to. What we couldn't establish was whether this was all the work of one man. It would be most disconcerting to think that multiple forgers of that calibre were at work in our bailiwick, but in the nature of things, the more perfect a fake the less trace the forger leaves. And these were so close to perfect that we had little hope of finding such traces."

Holmes nodded. "Indeed. For a while I, too, was tempted to despair on that point. However, these facsimiles are not in every respect perfect. There is one practical limitation that the forger has failed to take into account, and with it I can demonstrate that not only the letter and the will, but also the testimony from Major Macpherson exonerating Robert Foxon, Christopher Bastion's suicide letter, and—crucially to your concerns, Mycroft—his letter offering his services to Zimmerman, originate from the same source."

I could see now that Mycroft's interest had also been piqued. "Pray go on," he told his brother, as he took another biscuit.

"I was given the idea by Dr Permenter," said Holmes. "He had been interested in the supposed Shakespearean sonnet held by Boothby's, and the question of its authenticity. He alerted me to an analytical approach that had previously eluded me, pertaining as it does to an area of academia whose contributions to criminology I have previously considered insignificant. This is the analysis of writing style. At the time I dismissed it as of little evidential value, but on consideration I realised that the facts it discovered should be taken into account like any others."

"But Holmes," I said, "the documents are all written in different styles. A will, a witness statement, a certification of marriage, a letter between family members—those all read quite differently, and nothing like a suicide note."

Holmes agreed. "Superficially, that is quite true. The documents are written with differing degrees of formality, complexity and adherence to formula. Even the documents that one might expect to be similar are disparate. Sir Lester's purported will is a dry read, in keeping with his real one, whereas the Macpherson affidavit is rather chatty for a legal document. A man who was fabricating such diverse pages would certainly do his utmost to suit his writing style to the situation.

"However, after further consultation with Dr Permenter, I am persuaded that his conscious effort to achieve this would not be enough. We each have habits of speech and writing of which we are not wholly aware, and which slip by in everything we say and do. Were I to match my actions to yours, Watson, and write an account of one of our adventures, I am sure that my work would be clearly distinguishable from your own. Perhaps I shall do it some day. It would be an instructive exercise.

"In any case, this was the approach that Dr Permenter has been attempting to use to discredit the supposed Shakespeare sonnet. Setting aside the Barraclagh marriage certificate, whose wording was dictated by legal formulae, I applied it accordingly to our two known forgeries, to establish which linguistic elements they might have in common that were *not* those of the documentary style in which they were composed. I was able to find several."

"Good Heavens," said Hopkins mildly. "I didn't think of that for a moment. I've always been eager to listen to what the universities can tell us about police work, but it didn't occur to me that I should extend that to literary criticism."

"You are not alone in overlooking the possibility," said Holmes. "I confess that, had I taken the care to familiarise myself with scholarly methods of textual analysis, this case would have begun to make itself clear to me much sooner. It seems that what Dr Graymare told us was true of handwriting—that it is all but impossible to disguise in a way that can deceive one armed with techniques of expert analysis—may be more correctly applied to verbal style. In any case, I now have a list of the characteristics that our particular writer—for I am now convinced that all the documents were composed, at least, by one mind—brings unbidden to his writing.

"One is his use of *occasion* as a verb, meaning *to cause*. It is not exceptionally rare, but most people, I dare say, have occasion to employ it rarely. It is used far more often, as I did just then, as a noun. Our writer's employment of it in a verbal sense is habitual.

"He also has a somewhat archaic habit of occasionally capitalising abstract nouns, particularly those that seem to him to be of exceptional significance. He rarely uses parentheses, preferring to surround the tangential observations of which he is rather fond with a long dash. He is prone to beginning sentences with a conjunction such as *And* or *But*, though that is a common enough grammatical solecism. And he invariably spells *connexion* with an *x*, rather than the more common *ct.*"

Well, I thought, that at least was unexceptional. I did the same myself, though my editor would invariably amend my spelling to his own preference.

"Most telling of all, however, is his use of zeugma—the rhetorical device which Dr Permenter was good enough to explain to us, Hopkins."

"I recall it," said Hopkins, and Mycroft, who unlike Sherlock had absorbed most of his classical education, nodded impatiently. For my part it took me a moment to recall that this was the trick whereby one word was used to join two others, like a pair of oxen in a yoke.

Holmes said, "There are two instances of zeugma in Sir Lester's false will, and none in his real one. The letter from Mrs Salisbury to Lord Kerwinstone includes a sentence beginning 'I write now, however, with pleasure—and the fountain-pen which dear Edith gave me for my 70th birthday—to introduce ...'

"Having discovered these verbal quirks, I sought them in the Macpherson affidavit. I found several instances. The Zulus *occasioned* the British Army some inconvenience, it seems. Foxon abandoned his position along with his hopes of *Victory*, though never his *Duty*. The author does his best to write in the unpolished style that one might expect of a military man—" Here Holmes broke off and, with a quick smile at me, added, "—I should say that of a man who has remained in the military rather than succumbing to the temptations of a literary career—but he cannot hide these customary turns of phrase."

Holmes looked more serious now. "So now we turn to the Bastion letters. Here, in the suicide note, we find *Duty* capitalised once again as well as *Family*, two instances of *occasion* as a verb, and a parenthetical remark enclosed by dashes. And here, a reference to 'the action I am about to take, along with my life and my leave of it.' A zeugma, a very palpable zeugma."

We had known, of course, or at least considered it very probable, that the suicide note was a forgery. Mycroft said softly, "And the letter to Zimmerman, Sherlock?"

Sherlock read aloud, and with emphasis:

"'But I can assure you that nothing could be further from the Truth. The time has come to show my true colours along with my hand—for however I might phrase the disgrace I now contemplate, it occasions me no greater sense of satisfaction—and you, if you are willing to review them, certain particulars of my work in connexion with the service of Government that I have been, and remain, under a solemn oath to keep concealed.'"

"Good Lord," said Hopkins, astounded. "I believe that's a royal flush."

I would not have taken our young friend for a card player, and having said this he flushed slightly himself. "The men play during quiet times at work," he added defensively. "It's easy to pick up the jargon."

Mycroft said, "This is most intriguing news, Sherlock. You have, I suppose, examined Bastion's other writings, to account for the possibility that he himself was the forger?"

His brother looked affronted. "Naturally so. His love-letter to Miss Adorée Felice, for instance, which we must believe to be as sincere as she is otherwise, waxes poetical yet makes use of quite different rhetorical devices. There is an excess of alliteration, and a reliance on Latin tags. Bastion's official reports are not altogether averse to *occasioning* from time to time, but otherwise he demonstrates none of these distinguishing traits. He even spells *connection* with a *ct*. The same author composed the letter of betrayal as the suicide note, the Macpherson affidavit and the two established forgeries—and that author was certainly not Bastion."

Hopkins said, "Does this mean that the Shakespeare sonnet is forged as well?" He consulted the meticulous copy he had taken of Permenter's transcript. "That has a zeugma, of course, as Dr Permenter pointed out. But there's also an *occasion*, and a number of capitals for abstract nouns—though as you say, that's not so unusual in an older document."

"It seems a great deal more likely than not," Holmes agreed. "Especially since Permenter tells me that Shakespeare did not use *occasion* as a verb, and normally only capitalised concepts which he also personified. I dare say Boothby's could be induced to put us in touch with the anonymous seller, but there seems no greater likelihood of their cooperating with our investigation than did the Mineheart family, or Mr Griffon of Finchley—especially now that a new manuscript, a complete play no less, has been conveniently 'discovered' under the same provenance. I may say that, despite the unwitting consistency that he displays—which is forgivable enough, as Dr Permenter assures me that all of us in our own ways do the same—the fellow is a literary genius who is quite wasted on criminal work."

"This is quite astounding." Hopkins shook his head warily. "But I doubt it would stand up in a court of law, even so. You could get Permenter to testify, I presume, and probably other specialists in the subject, but a good defence counsel would call men like Rames in response, and make their arguments sound like so much hot air. This is all very abstruse stuff for the average British jury."

Holmes shrugged. "Well, that is moot for the moment, since

we have no suspect for the forgeries, and the charge of espionage against Bastion will never come before a court. On that point I need only persuade you, Mycroft."

Mycroft said, "I am now quite satisfied that Bastion did not willingly surrender his secrets to Zimmerman, and I thank you for that. I cannot, however, be fully confident that he was not induced to do so before his death. Your violent acquaintances evidently assumed that they could not compel him to write his own suicide note, but we have no evidence that they did not force compliance from him in other respects."

Holmes shook his head decisively. "They could not risk that. Their plan relied on disguising the murder as a suicide, and that would never stand if there were evidence of physical abuse. To be sure, the threat of violence alone might have been sufficient, but they could hardly rely on it. Besides, there is little reason to suppose that the murderers were affiliated with Zimmerman. They may not even have been working with the forger, since others have clearly contracted his services on an occasional basis. Perhaps their employer did the same."

"And perhaps that employer was Zimmerman," Mycroft observed. "You cannot say that you have altogether ruled it out, Sherlock."

Sherlock sighed with exasperation, but I could see that Mycroft's point was well taken. The big man rose to his feet and shook himself like a mammoth, shedding biscuit crumbs over the carpet. He took out his red silk handkerchief and brushed the last of them off himself, saying, "You have made progress, Sherlock, and I admit that I am impressed. I was wrong to suppose that you had become preoccupied with running up a blind alley. There is still some work to be done before this case is fully resolved, but I have every confidence that I will hear from you shortly."

With that the older Holmes took his leave, his younger

brother gazing coolly and thoughtfully after him.

Stanley Hopkins, who had been taking careful notes throughout (for, as he stressed, his personal use alone) became visibly more at ease. He said, "I didn't like to say this in front of your brother, Mr Holmes, but there is an objection to your theory. We know our man to be a master forger, the best in the business. Very well, I've no difficulty accepting that. But to fake the Macpherson testimony he'd need a good enough knowledge of the Zulu War to fool men who were there—Foxon could have helped him, of course, but as a Sergeant he wouldn't have had the strategic view that would be apparent to a senior officer. To forge the Barraclagh certification, the forger would have needed to know all about eighteenth-century legal documents. And the sonnet must have been composed by someone who knew enough about Shakespeare to pass muster with Professor Rames and his colleagues. How likely is it that the same man would happen to be a legal and military historian *and* a Shakespeare expert, while still finding time to practise his skill as the best counterfeiter we've ever encountered?"

I said, "A man can have a number of careers, I suppose, especially over a long life. I've been a medic, a soldier and a writer, and I'm not in my dotage yet."

Holmes smiled. "I think you have earned by now the right to call yourself a detective also, Watson. But no, it beggars belief that the same individual would have at his fingertips the knowledge to carry out all of these jobs alone. He must have some means, whether through bribery, blackmail or coercion, of calling on the assistance of experts in multiple fields. We are looking at a single master forger, but multiple accomplices."

"What we're looking at," said Hopkins, "is a bespoke and probably very expensive counterfeiting service, guaranteed all but undetectable and drawing on the very best knowledge in some very esoteric areas. My God," he said, with sudden passion, "but I wish I was allowed to investigate this properly! I can't, of course. But all these clients must have paid handsomely for such work—though perhaps some of them offered a share of the proceeds instead. Mr Griffon, the Barraclagh claimant, was hard up at the time, but if he'd come into the estate he could easily have spared a large part of the money that came with it."

I said, "Presumably Lord Kerwinstone's burglar, the false Percival Campion, made a similar arrangement."

"We can only assume so," agreed Holmes. "As for the Shakespeare finds, the cumulative proceeds from the sale of the sonnet and the play will be incalculable. In that respect, I imagine that the sonnet is intended as bait: they will wait to see who buys it for a fortune at auction, and then offer them direct sale of the full play for a king's ransom."

We all paused to consider for a moment the amount of money that such a transaction might bring in. It would buy the fraudsters a small country.

"I must say, though, that we've found nothing to suggest that Zimmerman had anything like this going on," said Hopkins. "He did own an ordinary volume of Shakespeare, of course, but so might anyone. I don't think he's our man for this business, though as you say he may have contracted the real forger's services. That letter must have found its way to him somehow, though. I say, do you think someone else was trying to bring the two of them into contact? Perhaps a rival spy helped to get Zimmerman caught."

"It is true enough that the advantages to an espionage agency of a bespoke service such as you describe would be substantial," Holmes replied, once again staring queerly at the door through which his brother had left. "But I think it likely that our forger and his friends knew of Zimmerman already. Perhaps indeed they sent him the letter, but it seems to me to have been aimed at discrediting Bastion—an end in which it succeeded beyond what they could have hoped."

I said, "Beyond what they could have hoped? Do you think, then, that the forgers were serving their own ends this time, rather than working to a commission?"

Holmes looked surprised. "How perceptive, Watson. Yes, my tongue betrayed me there. As you know, I prefer not to reveal my working theories until I can confirm them, but in this instance, perhaps it is only fair. My hypothesis at present is that Bastion proved himself a threat to the forger's organisation. He may have come across some evidence of substance to incriminate them— relating perhaps to a transaction between them and a client. I think he may have been in a position to reveal what he knew. They used the false letter in an attempt to threaten him into silence, but it failed. After his disgrace he was more determined than ever to clear his name. Perhaps he threatened to go to the police, or the press. In any case, they realised that they had to silence him decisively, and permanently."

Hopkins and I considered this. Eventually the Inspector said, "But the letter would do no good if only Zimmerman saw it. Whoever sent it to him must have known that it would be discovered. But that can only mean that they knew in advance that he would be arrested."

"Indeed," said my friend gravely. "That is an undeniable complication, and one whose implications I cannot at present fully elucidate. But it opens up a number of possibilities, none of them reassuring."

At that point there came an urgent hammering on the door of our rooms, and Sergeant Douglass entered, a little breathless.

"It's Probert," the man said, without pausing to greet us. "Bastion's manservant. He's gone and hung himself in his cell!"

THE CAMFORD JOURNAL OF LITERATURE
Pentecost Term 1894

Dear Sirs –

The vexed question of the date of composition of Shakespeare's *Much Ado About Nothing* may be closer to a full and satisfactory resolution, thanks to a letter by an undistinguished contemporary woollen-merchant named Jonah Sammael, recently forwarded to St Osyth's College by an alumnus who discovered it in a private collection.

The letter, which I am seeking permission to publish in full, was written to Sammael's sister Hannah Greete, and deals primarily with gossip concerning their family and mutual acquaintances. However, it contains a gratifyingly detailed account of his attendance at a performance of the play, identified by its title, and dateable with precision to the 29th of September 1598. This is two years before it was entered into the Stationers' Register, and some fourteen before the earliest performance of which we have previously held a definite record, during the nuptial celebrations of Princess Elizabeth and Frederick V, Elector of Palatine.

The letter bears the date of the 10th of October, and though the year is not given, Sammael (evidently something of an aficionado of the theatre) mentions, as a recent event, "a diuel fought at Hog's-down Fields betwixt the play-wrighter Mr. Jonson and one Spenser, on accounte of whose decease Jonson now stands arraigned." Ben Jonson's fatal duel with Gabriel Spenser, following which Jonson was indicted for manslaughter, took place in Hoxton on 22nd September 1598.

A week later Sammael was in the audience for Shakespeare's play. The name of the theatre where the performance was staged is, alas, not given, but the epistolary informs us that:

"At Michael-mass, I with Thos. Bridges saw the Lord Chamberlain's Men plaie their new Comedie of *Much Adoe about Nothing*, wherein Mr. Kempe the Clown occasioned us much merriment as Dog-berrie, a Constable. The plaie is writ by the same actor, Mr. Shake-shafte, whose *Comedie of Errors* so amused you and Greete when you staied with us after Mary's birth. And I warrant that this Loue Storie of Betriss and Benedick will please you also, for both are perverse and wittie and stubborne and at first refute their Connexion with contumelious wordes, but later are reconciled."

We may hope that Mrs Greete followed her brother's recommendation, and took the trouble to seek out a performance of this most delightful of Shakespeare's comedies.

Yours faithfully
Prof. A. Treverson
St Osyth's College, Camford

Gilbert Probert had been in custody in Scotland Yard's own facilities while the investigation into Bastion's death continued, on the basis that he might be needed for further interviews at a moment's notice—if, for instance, Chops or Onions were taken into custody, and he were needed to identify them as the men who had arranged to call unbidden upon his employer.

It was here that the manservant had been found hanged while Stanley Hopkins was with Holmes, Mycroft and myself at Baker Street. Anticipating their Inspector's instructions, his men had insisted that the cell be left untouched, with Probert still dangling grimly where he had been found, until it had been thoroughly examined.

When Douglass led us to the cell we found Constable Kean stationed at the door to ensure that any evidence remained untampered with. "No one's been in, sirs," he said. "Not since he was found. Not that there's much doubt to be had, in our view, but that's what we all thought about Mr Bastion, too."

All the immediate indications were with him upon this point, however. It appeared that Probert had twisted his bedsheet into a rope, attached it to a protruding nail above the barred window, and stumbled from the bed to a painfully suspended death. A Bible, a wooden cup and plate had been arranged on the bare mattress, as if Probert had intended to make things easier for whoever cleaned up the cell. Only an ash-tray, lying spilled beneath the window sill, marred this impression of neatness.

I essayed a brief examination of the manservant's body, whose purplish face and protruding tongue confirmed the expected diagnosis of death by strangulation, then Kean and Douglass cut him down and sent him away to the morgue. His stockinged feet protruded pathetically from beneath the blanket covering him as the men carried the stretcher away.

Holmes had been waiting impatiently throughout this, his eyes roving around the room. Hopkins was watching him curiously, hoping as ever to learn from the master.

"I don't think we're going to find many clues here," I hazarded. Already, though, Holmes had seized the wooden cup and was peering into it. Carefully he removed an empty, crumpled cigarette packet, which I recognised as the one I had given to Lucy Evans to pass on to her uncle, and a book of matches, about half full. The room smelled of tobacco smoke, and I was glad to know that my gift had at least provided the poor fellow with some solace in his final hours.

Holmes knelt to inspect the pile of grey soot lying beneath the window. After a moment, he straightened. "You say that nobody has entered, Douglass?" he asked the sergeant.

"No, sir," the man replied stoutly.

"Then this is homicide," he said decisively. "And the roster of potential suspects is distinctly limited. You have a murderer in the building, Hopkins, and unless they had some personal grudge against Probert, they were acting on behalf of those who killed his master. Once again we have proof that the objects of our investigation are feeling threatened."

"A little slower, sir, if you please," asked Hopkins, his face pale. Behind him, Douglass looked equally confounded. "Would you mind explaining the basis for your conclusion?"

Holmes tutted, exasperated anew. "Really, Hopkins," he said. "You know my methods; apply them. Meanwhile, Watson and I have an appointment with Dr Permenter at the Athenaeum."

More than a little annoyed, Hopkins said, "I understand your interest in the forgeries, Mr Holmes—indeed, I share it, as you know—but you've just informed me that there's a murderer at loose in Scotland Yard! Not to mention a victim," he added bitterly, "who was under our protection and had every right to suppose that we would keep him safe. Surely that must take priority over a meeting with an expert witness?"

"Not on this occasion, I fear," said Holmes. "I have been charged with determining the truth of Christopher Bastion's loyalties, and I am within sight of that goal. A death such as poor Probert's, regrettable though it is, presents but trivial difficulties, and falls well within your own considerable capabilities, Inspector. Will you accompany me, Watson?"

I gave Hopkins an apologetic shrug and made to follow Holmes, but he stopped in his tracks almost at once. "Mr Griffon of Finchley," he declared. "He disappeared, I believe?"

"The false Barraclagh claimant?" Hopkins' voice was still irked. "He did, yes. We had hopes of getting him to talk, but he went missing instead. We haven't found a trace of him since."

"I assume there is a case file relating to the matter. Would you have it sent over to Baker Street?" demanded Holmes.

Embarrassed by my friend's behaviour (and, to be frank, not relishing the prospect of another hour of being lectured on Shakespearean stylistics) I told him, "I'll catch up with you shortly, Holmes. Perhaps we can look into this together, Hopkins."

"Very well," said Holmes, and left without another word.

I was mortified at his rudeness. But Hopkins was already turning his attention to the evidence—his professional pride dented, but his attention, once engaged, as dogged as a terrier's. Following Holmes' earlier actions, he inspected both the cigarette packet and the matches ("I slipped him those myself," he noted), then bent to stare at the patch of ash beneath the window.

I said, "Probert was an orderly man by nature, as one would expect of a valet. But he can hardly be considered responsible for mess created in his death-throes."

"It's not that," Hopkins told me, grimly. "There's a partial boot-print."

"A boot?" I repeated. We both stared at the dead man's shoes, left neatly beside the door. I said, "I can't imagine how they thought Holmes would miss that."

"Well, it's probable they weren't thinking very clearly," Hopkins said. "Most criminals don't, in my experience, and I'm afraid it's often true of policemen also. That boot's police issue, you see. I recognise the tread pattern. My God, poor Probert!" He shook his head sadly. "He was a sorry sort, but he deserved better than this."

"A policeman killed him?" I repeated, aghast. "That's a terrible betrayal."

Hopkins said gravely, "If so, then the implications are very severe. As Mr Holmes says, this must have been done to silence Probert. Our investigation has obviously been compromised."

I said, "Well, we already knew the forgers had advanced warning of Zimmerman's arrest. Perhaps this simply narrows the field."

"It already consisted of men I trusted," said Hopkins dolefully. "No wonder Mr Holmes doesn't want to confide in me."

I patted the Inspector on the shoulder. "It's nothing personal, old man," I assured him. "He's always like this in the final stages of a case. I've seen him be equally rude to everyone from farmhands to royalty." Yet again, though, and even after all that we had discovered, I could not help wondering whether Holmes' priorities in this case were altogether proportionate.

We went to Hopkins' office, where I waited for Constable Vincent to retrieve the folder on the Griffon disappearance. "Though there's little enough in there," Hopkins told me gloomily. "We never found a trace of him."

Hopkins lent me a briefcase and I headed with it to the

Athenaeum Club, where Dr Hadrian Permenter was staying while in London.

I found the academic with Holmes in the morning-room, taking tea. "Ah, Watson," Holmes said, all congeniality now. "Please sit with us. Will you have some tea? No? As you wish; I shall." He gestured to a nearby waiter. "Dr Permenter has some very interesting news to impart to us about this newly discovered Shakespeare play."

"Oh, good," I replied. Despite my best efforts, I had evidently only missed the preface to their conversation.

Permenter cleared his throat. In his dusty voice, he said, "Mr Holmes asked me to use my College's influence to acquire a transcript of this new manuscript, Dr Watson, and to examine it for elements that might, if it were to be accepted as authentic, alter our perception of Shakespeare. He was particularly keen to hear about anything that could be taken as bearing out certain eccentric theories that have, on the basis of the evidence available to us thus far, seemed thoroughly unlikely."

"And you have found something to the point, naturally," Holmes beamed.

"Naturally." Permenter returned his smile, without humour. "I should observe that amateur Shakespearean scholarship accretes absurd and outlandish speculation, and its proponents are capable of finding purported evidence in almost anything. You will be familiar, no doubt, with the highly dubious idea that another author, Sir Francis Bacon, wrote the plays, and had them performed and published under Shakespeare's name, for reasons doubtless best known to himself. The supposed evidence for this includes the contention that the texts are built around cryptogrammatic codes announcing Bacon's authorship, their attainment of some of the most exquisite poetry created in the English language being, I suppose, quite incidental to this crucial end. I am pleased to say that few reputable scholars would give such nonsense the time of day, but there are other conjectures that in my view are equally unlikely, but which have garnered some more serious attention.

"Some of these relate to the years between 1585 and 1592, during which time we have no record of Shakespeare's whereabouts. It is usually supposed that he spent the period as a schoolmaster in the countryside, but less plausible ideas abound. One such is that he travelled widely in Europe, something that is not thought to have happened at any other period of his life. Some have suggested that he did so as a spy, a capacity in which his fellow playwright Marlowe is known to have been employed. His plays, of course, are set in many places, from Egypt to Denmark, but Shakespeare shows no great knowledge of their geography, as anyone who has scoured a map for the seacoast of Bohemia could tell you. There is no reason to suppose that he was any more personally familiar with Venice or Verona than with Troy or Fairyland. However, this is the idea that has been proposed.

"Now, *Love's Labour's Lost* occurs, as you have doubtless learned by now, in the kingdom of Navarre, now part of Spain, and this spurious *Love's Labour's Won* uses the same setting.

"Early in Act Two a Spanish messenger enters, who before he details his news insists on recounting the travels that have brought him to Navarre from Seville. I can read his speech to you now ..."

He took up his typescript copy of the text, but Holmes hastily interposed. "There is no pressing need for us to hear it read aloud, Dr Permenter. Your exegesis will be sufficient for our purposes."

Permenter sniffed. "Very well. It is not a very poetical passage, being largely a list of places in Iberia through which the messenger has passed—Toledo, Madrid, Saragossa and the like. However, he does mention how many days he rode between each destination on his itinerary. Bearing in mind your most intriguing suggestion, I checked these figures against contemporary maps held at the British Museum. In every case the number given is a perfectly valid, though not unassailable, estimate of the duration of travel between them in Shakespeare's day.

"I need not observe again how much at odds this is with Shakespeare's habitual haphazard approach to geography. I would have expected him to work from a broad general knowledge, and to add distances, if he felt them necessary at all, to the correct number of syllables to fit the scansion of the line. Such accuracy is so far from what would be expected that, were the play to be accepted as genuine, I dare say that it would have taken some time before this surprising fact came to light.

"However, once explicated, it would lend considerable credence to the idea that Shakespeare himself, or at least a source of his, had not only travelled the regions in question but taken careful notes along the way. This would greatly enhance the reputation of those scholars who have espoused the theory of the widely travelled playwright, and of one in particular who is known to be working on a dual study of Shakespeare and Miguel de Cervantes, the Spanish author of *Don Quixote*, predicated upon the bizarre idea that the two men met occasionally as spies in the employ of their respective Crowns."

During this recital Holmes had leaned far back in his chair, steepled his fingers and half-closed his eyes. Without stirring, he said now, "And the author of the work espousing this outlandish hypothesis would be …?"

Permenter smiled with the malicious satisfaction of an academic who is creating a great deal of trouble for a rival. "Why, Professor Jonathan Rames. Who, as I discovered from speaking to the staff at the Museum, had sight some months ago of the very maps that I have consulted today."

At once, Holmes was on his feet and calling for his hat and coat. "Then we must pay a visit to Professor Rames at once. Come, Watson! I am once again indebted to you for your assistance, Dr Permenter." He made as if to leave in a great bustle, then became completely still once more. He said, "I do not suppose that you are able to furnish us with the Professor's address in town?"

"I took the liberty of writing it down for you," said Permenter coolly, handing me a piece of paper.

It seemed that Rames' nephew-in-law and niece maintained a townhouse in Kensington, of which the Professor had been given the use while the family was away, and so it was there that we hastened by cab. During our journey, between puffs of pungent rose-scented smoke, Holmes explained to me the reasoning behind the research topic he had given Dr Permenter.

He said, "It was Rames himself who alerted me to the possibility that the fabricated Shakespeare works might support some of his more unlikely ideas. He said of the sonnet, 'I fully anticipate that there is much to be gleaned from it about the Bard's early career,' and he is reported in the *Morning Chronicle* as having made a similar comment in relation to this newly discovered play.

"He was not, of course, the instigator of this particular fraud—that will be our anonymous seller—but he is evidently the Shakespearean expert brought in by the forger to lend both play and sonnet the maximum possible credibility. Evidently our man reckoned without academic self-interest, for Rames compromised this end by inserting evidence vindicating his own pet theory. Inevitably he has been among the most vocal advocates of the authenticity of these works, since he has every interest in their being accepted as genuine by the academic establishment."

On arrival at the address Permenter had given us, we found Professor Rames at home, and far from delighted to see us. At first he tried to have the butler forbid us entry, but Holmes blustered his way in and a moment later was confronting the little round academic in the house's drawing-room. At Rames' despairing gesture of dismissal, the servant withdrew—not, I hoped, to call the police, for that would be a bothersome complication.

"Professor Rames," Holmes said without preamble. "We know that the page of Shakespeare held by Boothby's is fake, as is the newly discovered play manuscript. Furthermore, we know that the reason you have been so vocal in asserting otherwise is that you were intimately involved in their creation. No," he added, holding up a hand to forestall the man's inevitable protests, "we have as yet no positive proof of this, but that is not important at present. The point is that we know. Either you may deny it, and I shall continue to pursue that knowledge until I have uncovered the proof in question—an endeavour in which you may be assured that I shall succeed—or you may tell us everything you know at once, and I shall do all in my power to keep your name out of the matter. I fear it is no exaggeration to say that not merely your academic reputation but your life as a free man may depend upon what you say to me next."

Rames went quite white, and sat down in a chair as if Holmes had punched him in the stomach. "Oh my," he said weakly.

After a few deep breaths he rallied, rang for a footman, and called for brandy. As the servant left he said, "Mr Holmes, I can see that you believe what you say, but you are mistaken, I am afraid, quite mistaken. I can only state that I … I believe the work to be genuine, and that if … if by some terrible mischance it is not, then I had nothing whatsoever to do with it!" His voice had cracked and he was close to sobbing.

We waited while the footman returned and poured the Professor his drink. Politely the man offered Holmes and myself a glass each, but we demurred. At Rames' bidding he left the decanter behind.

Holmes waited until the servant had left and then said, "So be it, Professor. I outlined your alternatives. You have chosen denial, and my response is as I stated before."

He turned to go, but (as I am quite sure he had expected) Rames cried, "Wait, Mr Holmes! Please, wait!"

Holmes turned, stern and majestic as any Shakespearean Duke passing judgement. "What for, pray? For more spurious self-vindication? I do not care to hear it, sir."

"No, no," said Rames, truly sobbing now. He took a fortifying gulp of the brandy, and poured himself some more. Breathing deeply, he recovered himself sufficiently to speak.

He said, "You have the truth of it, Mr Holmes, but I cannot cooperate with you. I simply cannot. If I do not I may lose everything and go to prison, but if I do then he will kill me, I am certain of it."

"I can assure you that the police will protect you," said Holmes, projecting a confidence he can hardly have felt, given where we had found ourselves less than an hour before.

Rames shook his head convulsively. "Certainly not. His reach runs everywhere. My only hope is to send you away without a shred of information about his identity, and to trust to your honour that you will not assert that I have done otherwise. I … I have, I suppose, been extremely foolish. I did not intend to get in so deep."

He took another glass of brandy. Knowing his moment, Holmes kept his silence.

Rames said, "This is not the first time he has drawn upon my assistance in such a matter. The first time was while I was writing an earlier book of mine, a new outline of the chronology of Shakespeare's plays. I was convinced, indeed I remain morally certain still, that *Much Ado About Nothing* was performed at least two years before the earliest record of its existence, but I had been able to find no historical confirmation of this. It was essential to my argument that I should have something conclusive. The fact that no actual account of an earlier staging had survived was the purest historical accident—there should, in justice to my thesis, have been something.

"I heard from an alumnus of my College that there was a person who, for a price, could arrange for an appropriate evidence to be discovered, and I … availed myself of his services. He had no special knowledge of the subject, but I specified exactly how to make it perfectly convincing. The price was high, but well spent for my purposes.

"But I had made an idiotic mistake. The fact that this person could prove the record fabricated, and that I had been instrumental in fabricating it, gave him power over me. When he approached me for help in the far more serious and culpable matter of concocting these new works, I could not afford to turn him down. Especially when he told me what would happen if I went to the police."

Rames swallowed, though he had taken no drink this time. "I do not know whether you have encountered his associates, Mr Holmes. I have never met such violent men. I will do nothing that might incur a second visit, even if it costs me my livelihood and my liberty."

Coolly, Holmes said, "I have come across worse men than Mr Chops and Mr Onions, Professor, and I do not habitually move within the cut-throat world of academia."

"You are pleased to joke," Rames muttered bitterly.

"For now, perhaps," said Holmes grimly, "but I must warn you not to test my good humour. I, too, am capable of violence, Professor Rames, when I am not given what I need."

"Steady on, Holmes," I expostulated, recalling with dismay the brutal beating he had handed out to Chops when their paths had crossed—as well as the unresolved question of the passing of "Mugger" Maines at the Butcher's Apron. Rames was dishonest, evidently, and a coward, but he was no thug to be browbeaten with such threats. I placed a hand on his arm, but he shrugged it off.

It seemed, however, that Rames was not to be cowed. He said, "I repeat that I am not willing to defy these men. You must not think me wholly selfish, Mr Holmes. I have relatives—my niece and her little boys, my elderly mother—who do not deserve to suffer for my errors. And suffer they would, if I were to betray these people; I was left in no doubt upon that score."

"And I repeat," said Holmes, refusing to back down, "that if you cooperate I shall keep your name out of it." Again, I was dubious about his ability to keep this promise, and almost said as much. His behaviour now had strayed so far from that of the man I had known for so long that I began to doubt my loyalty to his cause, which I had always believed to be that of Justice. I understood his urgency to catch Bastion's murderer, and to see halted an operation that could create miscarriages like the exoneration of Robert Foxon, but surely it could not be worth this wretched man's life, let alone those of his family? There must be another way.

Holmes said, "A name is all I need. You need not tell me how you heard it, or who from. You were given this man's name, I presume?"

Rames nodded. "But I could not possibly—"

Holmes said, "I do not ask you to inform, merely to confirm. You will be giving away nothing I do not know already."

This was news to me, and I shot him a questioning glance, but he was staring resolutely at Professor Rames. He said, "If you do this then I shall leave, and I shall see that this investigation does not trouble you again. Or, if you prefer, I could arrange for a police guard outside this house." Rames shook his head in alarm.

"Very well," said Holmes. "Answer me this, then, Professor Rames. A yea or nay will be sufficient. The name you heard spoken of as masterminding this convenient counterfeiting service. Was it perchance the name of Mr Mycroft Holmes?"

Mutely, Rames nodded.

Sherlock Holmes gave a grunt of satisfaction, spun on his heel, and left the room, leaving me utterly dumbfounded.

LETTER TO PROFESSOR ANDREW TREVERSON

London
20th June 1898

Dear Treverson

I have no doubt that you will have seen the news concerning *Love's Labour's Won*. Thanks to my work on the "Love that is feigned" sonnet, I have been afforded the opportunity to examine the manuscript, and I can attest beyond a doubt that it is the second part of the narrative begun in *Love's Labour's Lost*, the two forming as much a dramatic unity as *Henry IV* Parts One and Two.

Beyond some variations in the spellings of names, which as you know is quite characteristic of the Bard, the characters and settings are the same. The former are shown returning to the latter, to report upon the success or otherwise of their endeavours to remain true to their love for a year and a day, and are at length, after some amusing misunderstandings, permitted the happy unity that was deferred for them at the end of the prior play.

I take some small satisfaction in noting that a somewhat revised form of "Love that is feigned" is presented to Rosalind by Berowne in Act II, exactly as I predicted in my article for the *CTL*. Evidently the folio currently on sale represents an earlier draft of the poem.

I shall of course endeavour to procure this new manuscript for the University Museum, as I retain every hope of doing with the sonnet. Although the concomitant expenditure will naturally be vastly greater, I have no doubt that the generosity of our donors will provide. In the meantime I am ensuring that transcriptions of the manuscript are available to all who request to study them, without prejudice, and I write to invite you to avail yourself of a copy.

You may be entertained to learn that one of the first and most eager enquirers extended this courtesy has been Dr Hadrian Permenter. You may also think that he might well be keen to study the play, given his previous opinion, so forthrightly and so often expressed, that it has no business existing whatsoever.

I shall naturally refrain from any expression of triumph at the vindication of my alternative theory, and I shall derive no pleasure whatsoever from the humiliation that it will doubtless provoke for Permenter, along with Highbury, Cheeseman and the rest of their covey of pedantic naysayers. A simple apology from each of them, published in any of the reputable journals, will be all I shall expect.

Please pass my most cordial regards to Starkley, Cotswold and the rest of your fellows in St Osyth's SCR.

Yours as ever

J. Rames

Holmes was silent all the way back to Baker Street. He took out his pipe but failed to fill it, instead tapping it against his teeth and exhaling explosively. Despite the depth of my own mental turmoil, I refrained from provoking him by interrupting his cogitations until our arrival back at Number 221B, when the necessity of disembarking and paying the driver provided its own distraction.

I had intended to question my friend closely once we had returned to our rooms, but in the event there was no need. The moment our door was closed against the outside world, he began pacing wildly back and forth across the room like a caged bear, from window to fireplace to door to window, giving flow to a cascade of words. I could not have dammed such a torrent even had I wished his silence.

"I said that the advantages to intelligence agents of such expert counterfeiting must be considerable," he said, "and so they must. False credentials, identification papers, incriminating documents, letters sowing dissent between allies ... all of these would be invaluable to the profession, provided they stood up to the most exacting scrutiny. If such a forger were indeed active in London, then surely Mycroft with his myriad informers would not only be aware of his work, but would have made use of it himself from time to time. Why, then, has he given no hint of such knowledge during all the time that you and I have been pursuing this affair? He has contented himself with trying to dissuade me from following this line of inquiry, although he must have realised its potential contribution to the end he sought.

"The obvious conclusion is that Mycroft not only knows of this counterfeiting service, but is himself involved. After all, if such a business, with its evident utility to him, did not exist, then it would be to his great advantage to create it. Present company not excepted, there is no man in London more gifted or more polymathic in his own right than Mycroft, nor with a greater directory of contacts to augment his own compendious knowledge with the expertise of others. If he does not produce the forgeries, he is certainly the paymaster and principal of whoever does. But I think it likely he does. He is at least as capable of it as I."

"But, Holmes—" I attempted desperately to interject, but he was not to be diverted.

He waved a hand dismissively. "Oh, no doubt at first this unique consultancy existed purely to further the work of Her Majesty's intelligence services, in the ways I have suggested. In time, however, its usefulness beyond that sphere would have become apparent. As we have seen, private individuals are willing to pay extravagant sums for documents of unquestionable provenance, whether to establish them in a fortune like Mr Griffon, save them from gaol like Sergeant Foxon or even, in the case of Professor Rames, confirm their academic prejudices. And espionage work needs always to be funded. Mycroft has no special wealth of his own. Rich dinners and membership of a club like the Diogenes do not come cheaply, and though he conceals it well, I have long suspected that he harbours a discreet gambling habit.

"I do not say that he has used this operation to enrich himself (though that may yet prove to be the case), merely that he has no personal fortune to call upon when his agents are in urgent need of funds, and the coffers of Government have run dry. Indeed, it would not wholly surprise me if there were no other client in the case of the Shakespeare manuscript, which will undoubtedly prove their most lucrative fraud yet. In all probability, the anonymous seller is one of Mycroft's agents, and the tale of the manor house a convenient fiction.

"All this being the case, it would be a short step, and one that my brother would be more than willing to take, to protect his investment, by violent means if necessary. The disappearance of Leonard Griffon may have been the first such incident. The murder of Probert is merely the most recent. If the knowledge of such a conspiracy were to be made public, as Hopkins said, no document would be considered trustworthy—certainly not by any rival intelligence agencies. The careful preservation of the secret is necessary if it is to continue to be useful."

"But—" I said again, but once more Holmes overrode me.

"Enter, then, the Honourable Christopher Bastion. He was high in the confidences of many in government, and saw much that happened under the auspices of the Foreign Office. He seems to have been, despite his manifest weaknesses, a man deserving the virtue of his title. If he stumbled upon some scrap of evidence that Mycroft's people had failed to eradicate, then it might well have led him directly to Mycroft, and that would lead Mycroft to exposure. My brother could not risk such information reaching the ears of any government minister. Sir Hector Askew is honest also, I think, though weak, and while Lord Loomborough may not be scrupulous he is certainly ambitious, and may covet the power that Mycroft wields.

"Therefore Mycroft arranged for Bastion's disgrace, and when it seemed that that would not be sufficient to silence him, for his demise. In both cases he used the resources available to him—a man placed in Hopkins' team of officers, the services of Chops and Onions, and of course the skills of his pet forger."

"Then why—" I essayed again. This time Holmes deigned to respond, in his own fashion, to the objection I would have raised.

"Why did Mycroft ask me to establish whether Christopher Bastion was a traitor, thus risking the discovery that he had been instrumental in fabricating the only evidence that suggested it? Because it is not himself whom Mycroft needs to satisfy on this point. His nominal superiors in government—superior in rank, that is, though not in reach or capability—cannot know of this clandestine business of his. Ministers come and go, and not all would be prepared to wink at such illegality. At least some of our politicians are surely sufficiently conscientious that the deliberate murder of civilians would give them pause. Mycroft came to me, his brother, for help, in the hope that I would prove Bastion's innocence—since he is indeed innocent—through other means, but trusting that if I did uncover his involvement, he could rely on family loyalty to assure my silence."

And with that word, Holmes did finally fall silent, leaving me reeling mentally from the impact of this verbal barrage. It took me a few minutes to gather my thoughts.

Mycroft was not an easy man to like (any more, some would say, than his brother was), but it had never occurred to me to question his integrity. Apart from anything else, Sherlock had vouched for him, and they had shown what, according to their peculiar fashion, might have been called brotherly affection. He was, I had been assured, a servant of the Empire, a force for order and a power of good in the world. I understood, of course, that spying sometimes necessitated conduct that would be considered dishonourable in ordinary life, but surely that excuse could never account for the deep deceit and casual slaughter of which we had learned.

If Mycroft believed that his brother's loyalty would buy my silence by proxy, then he was quite mistaken. It was Sherlock to whom I owed my friendship, not him. Quietly, I asked Holmes, "What shall you do now?"

"That, Watson, is a question upon which I must cogitate. With this new information, I have the advantage. My brother is on the back foot now, and my next move must be crucial and decisive. He has challenged me to play this game—for it was no doing of mine, I am sure—and I shall play it to the bitter end."

"Game?" I repeated, aghast. "Holmes, two men to our certain knowledge have been killed. This is no *game*."

"Oh, this was always a game, Watson," Holmes replied grimly. "It is one in which the stakes are perilously high, that is all."

The time had come to ask the question that had been so preying on my mind. "Holmes, what happened at the Butcher's Apron in Spitalfields? I know that you were there, though you have denied it. You told me you had been in a fight that night. Who killed 'Mugger' Maines?"

"It is not a matter that I care to discuss, Watson," said Holmes with finality. He threw himself into his armchair and lit his pipe, sinking into an ever-deepening fug of his favoured Turkish Delight tobacco-smoke as he refused to be drawn further, or even to acknowledge my increasingly agitated questions. Eventually, dazed and frantic, I took myself outside for a walk, to clear my head in the early evening sunshine. After wandering around in confusion for some little time I found myself back in Hyde Park, staring across the Serpentine at the very bench where I had had my rendezvous with Dr Carson Graymare.

To say that I was deeply troubled would be a ludicrous understatement. For some time now I had been concerned by my friend's statements and behaviour. My meeting with Graymare, and my discovery that Holmes had lied to me about the death of Maines, had brought all my fears to the surface. If, as the graphologist had suggested, my good friend was nothing more than a character assumed by a consummate actor, and the real Sherlock Holmes was an impostor, cold and calculating (or "reptilian", as he had once described the late Professor Moriarty to me), rather than the unconventional but good-hearted champion of Justice whom I had believed I knew … well, then, the world was a far less comforting place than I had imagined.

I tried to remind myself of all the times that Holmes had saved my life, and the lives of others, championing the innocent and vulnerable against those who sought to victimise, exploit or destroy them, but the events of the day kept intruding upon my mind. His callousness in the face of Probert's death, and his dismissal of Hopkins' self-recrimination as an irrelevance; his collusion with Dr Permenter against the latter's academic rival; most of all, his threats of violence against the terrified Professor Rames; all spread themselves in my mind like tree-roots, undermining the foundations of my faith in my friend. Even before today, his savagery in the alleyway, and the cruel trick that he had played on Lucy Evans, had given me pause, though I had set those concerns aside at the time.

Now they returned, and I was finally forced to confront the question of whether Holmes' egomania, aggravated by his addiction to cocaine, had grown altogether out of control.

Indeed, I grew less easy still as I recalled his words on the morning when we had been entrusted by Mycroft with looking into Bastion's death: "He loves to have me dance to his tune, Watson, but how invigorating the measure is!" I had thought then of a puppet twitching on its strings, but had Holmes been seeing this case, even then, as a contest between himself and his brother?

I tried to calm myself, so that I might reason as the Holmes I knew would have: to summarise the facts at my disposal and, crucially, to assess how reliable they might be. The truth was, though, that most of what troubled me was what I had seen at first hand. This whole case turned on issues of authenticity, and now the genuineness of our very friendship was in question.

If Holmes could not truly be trusted, as Graymare had implied, then how far might I rely on all that I had believed until now? There were many events experienced by Holmes alone for which I had had only his word, which I had set out faithfully in my narratives of his adventures. Had I misled my readers, again and again, on his behalf?

Like Shakespeare, Holmes had had his Missing Years—those following his fateful duel with that same Professor Moriarty at the Reichenbach Falls, when I and everyone else in England (except, apparently, his brother) had believed him dead. I wondered, could that incident also have been what Holmes had called "a convenient fiction"? I had been wholly absent for the climactic events, having been called away by—I recalled with a sudden cold shock—a forged letter. I had but glimpsed a man whom I believed afterwards to have been Moriarty, as a distant figure walking rapidly through the Swiss countryside; everything else I knew of him came from Holmes. "I know every move of your game," Holmes had reported his enemy as telling him—and in that case my friend, too, had referred several times to their contest in those terms.

It was, I realised, something of a habit with him. "The game is afoot," indeed.

Holmes, like his brother, was a man apart, his exceptional intellect giving him a unique perspective on humanity. It was hard to imagine that this had had no effect on his morality. Unlike Mycroft, whose affinity with the collective hermitage that was the Diogenes Club betrayed the superficial nature of his many professional connexions, Sherlock had friends who cared for him—myself, Mrs Hudson, young Hopkins, even Inspector Lestrade. But I was well aware that the long-term effects of cocaine use could include a loss of interest in friendship, along with the irritability and restlessness that Holmes so often evinced. The drug could also induce panic attacks and psychosis, as well as a belief that others were trying to harm one. Such effects might, in time, become just as damaging to a man as Mycroft's social isolation.

In my mind's eye I saw the brothers, each so convinced of his superiority to the generality of mankind, setting himself above his fellows and taking control of them, as an author dictates the actions of his characters—manoeuvring them about a game-board like the noblemen of France playing human chess before the Revolution, to stave off the unbearable depredations of the boredom that so eternally threatened.

I wondered—and though the thought appalled me, I forced myself to face it resolutely—whether there had ever really been a Moriarty. Had he existed at all—a supposition for which, if Holmes' word were not to be trusted, I had little evidence? Or was *Moriarty* just another name for *Mycroft*? If so, the disguise was a superficial one. The Moriarty whom Sherlock described may have been thin where Mycroft was huge, ascetic where Mycroft was self-indulgent, but he had represented each as a man of exceptional intellect, sitting at the centre of a web of knowledge and influence.

And that game, too, had had "perilously high stakes", as Sherlock had discovered at the Falls ... but perhaps they were not the ones I had assumed. Could my friend (if indeed I might now call him friend at all) perhaps have spent those lost years travelling as one of Mycroft's agents, just as Rames and his fellow eccentric Shakespeareans believed the young playwright had been spying for the Tudor Crown? If Holmes had lost his game with "Moriarty," perhaps his forfeit was to set off on his wanderings, working at his brother's behest until at last the latter allowed him to come home.

These were deep waters indeed, I found myself thinking, as Holmes had remarked to me during more than one of our cases— and again I realised with a pang how far I had come to rely upon him, and how much his ways of thinking had informed my own.

If I had been mistaken in him all this time, what did that say for our association, and my future? Who would John Watson be, without Sherlock Holmes?

My digressions had brought me within sight of the Wellington Arch, and its exit from the Park. Disturbed beyond imagining, I hastened back to Baker Street, to have it out with Holmes once and for all. If our relationship were to survive, there must be honesty between us; and if I was mistaken in my suspicions—as I steadfastly hoped that I was—then the only way I could be certain was to confront Holmes with them.

I found him gone. He had left behind him a room full of cloying smoke, and a note on the table: "Gone to the Diogenes. Do not follow. When I return I will tell you what to do. S.H." Again, he assumed that he could pull my strings and I would dance for him.

I wondered what I would in fact do if, when he returned, he told me that his brother had convinced him to keep silent and allow the counterfeiting operation, with its benefits to the intelligence services of the nation as well as its wealthy criminals, to continue, and that his instructions to me were to do the same.

But no—I knew very well what I would do. The question was, how would Holmes react when I told him? Would I, too, be seen as a necessary casualty of Mycroft's need for secrecy?

I retired to my room and began writing up the notes I had been taking throughout the case, into the manuscript you now hold in your hands. I have been writing in a feverish frenzy, but even so, it has taken me hours, and I expect Holmes to return at any moment.

I think, perhaps, that I should hide this document before Holmes does return. I think, perhaps, that it should be available to speak for me, if—for some reason I dare not name—I am no longer capable of doing so.

For while I have been writing a further point has occurred to me, and it is one that occasions me perhaps more disquiet than any of the others. Somebody forged Christopher Bastion's purported letter to Zimmerman, and arranged for it to be found at the spy's address when he was arrested—somebody who Holmes would have me believe was Mycroft. To be sure, this tactic served the immediate end of Bastion's fall from grace, but it has proven inconvenient to Mycroft thereafter, since it has led to Sherlock's discovery of his conspiracy.

That letter displayed the idiosyncrasies of style that Holmes has found in all the other forgeries. The obvious conclusion is that, as Holmes has asserted, it had the same author; but that is not the only possible conclusion. The possibility has not been eliminated that it was instead forged by someone with an awareness of those idiosyncrasies and how to mimic them.

Any such person must have been observing the forgery investigation from the beginning, have already seen the pertinent documents, and have drawn upon a very adequate working knowledge of the techniques of textual analysis to determine their shared features. Such a person would, of course, be responsible for the disgrace of Christopher Bastion, and thus would bear considerable responsibility for what came afterwards, including the deaths of both Bastion and Probert, whoever actually ordered or enacted those deaths.

I know that Sherlock Holmes is a capable imitator of others' handwriting. I know that he follows Stanley Hopkins' career with interest. And I know that he has many friends in the lower ranks of the police force.

I also know that it has often been his habit to pretend to know less than he does, so that he may dazzle with his knowledge once it is displayed.

But how if, in this instance, he chose not to show it? How if—to be quite clear what I am proposing—Sherlock Holmes himself forged the Bastion letter, and had a sympathetic policeman "discover" it at Zimmerman's house, occasioning all the events that followed, up to the revelation of Mycroft's connexion with the counterfeiting ring—all to place himself at the advantage in their Great Game, and his brother on the back foot?

I remember how, that day at breakfast, he seemed to have anticipated Mycroft's summons before it arrived. He said, "I have heard this morning of a death that is likely to interest him." *How did he know of Bastion's death?*

It seems that I must put this question to him also—and with it, my life into his hands.

THE DAILY GAZETTE
20th June 1898
SPITALFIELDS KILLER REMAINS AT LARGE

The police continue to be frustrated in their search for the killer of an East End "tough" who was found dead behind a Spitalfields hostelry. The deceased has been identified by neighbours as Daniel Maines, a well-known brawler and petty criminal who was an *habitué* of the Butcher's Apron, a locale that is known to be no stranger to violence.

Witnesses attest to the sounds of a scuffle emerging from behind the inn earlier in the evening, but nobody will admit to knowing the pretext, who was involved, or what the outcome may have been, beyond that it seemingly resulted in Maines' death.

Asked how far the loss of such a man was truly to be regretted, Inspector Jones reminded our reporter that the presence of a murderer on the loose in the capital ought to be a cause of concern to all. He cautions the public to remember that whatever the deceased's shortcomings, he was an Englishman and a Christian, and asks again that anybody with information relating to the murder should contact the police at once.

Asked whether the police had any plans to retain the services of a freelance agent with a proven record of apprehending like killers, such as the celebrated Mr Sherlock Holmes of Baker Street, Inspector Jones firmly declined to comment.

In the meantime, the culprit continues to elude the able men of Scotland Yard.

NARRATIVE OF
JOHN H. WATSON, M.D.

CHAPTER ONE

I awoke in the small hours, convinced that somebody was in my bedroom. The sun had not yet risen and the window was dark. From where I lay, I could see only the familiar shadows of my shelves and wardrobe, but the sense of an intruder was irresistible, and as I came fully to myself I realised that the door to Holmes's rooms lay open.

"Holmes?" I whispered. "Is that you?"

One of the shadows disgorged a patch of darkness in human shape, which came at me with an abrupt rush. At once I was very much awake.

I rolled out of the bed, taking the covers with me, and pitched myself to the floor, my flimsy bedside table splintering beneath my body. My attacker tried to turn in his headlong dash, but was too late to correct his course and fell awkwardly, half on and half off the bed. I rolled further away, cursing my haste. I had been sleeping with my revolver underneath my pillow, but had not thought to seize it in my abrupt egress from the bed. I could only hope that my assailant did not discover it.

I was, moreover, tangled up in my bedclothes, which seriously impeded my movement. I had at least my arms free, so I grasped the nearest item of furniture, my gramophone, and began to pull myself upright.

At this point another black shape detached itself from the shadows and charged me, the profile of a hatchet in its hand, and I realised that I was, not for the first time, facing two attackers. Desperately, I steadied myself and pushed my very expensive gramophone over into the second man's path. It fell with a huge crash, and the man tumbled over onto me with a violent curse, losing hold of his axe.

My first assailant was regaining his feet now, and I did my best to deflect the falling man in his direction, but his weight was considerable and I succeeded only in freeing myself from beneath him. I had at least worked myself loose from the bedclothes, and quickly I gathered them up and threw them over the heads of the men, who were again approaching me.

They were between me and the bed where my Enfield lay, but there were other weapons in the room, and I knew its inventory and floor plan far better than these strangers. Ducking away around the bed, while they swore and struggled to free themselves from my sheets, I made for the cabinet where I kept the souvenirs of my service in Afghanistan. These included a Pashtun spear, which I conjectured might be of some use in my current predicament.

Holmes was absent, I could only presume, though it was a late hour for him to be still at the Diogenes Club. It seemed he had chosen a most inconvenient time to embark upon one of his nocturnal research expeditions. My pistol was still beneath my pillow, I assumed, but one of the men had his head free now and was turning to face me. The gun was within his reach as well as mine, and if I went to retrieve it, it could provoke an ugly struggle between us for possession of the weapon – one that I should be sure to lose, as soon as his compatriot came to his aid.

Instead, to draw them away from the bed and avert the danger of one of them discovering the firearm on his own, I gave vent to a wordless war-cry, and pulled the Pashtun spear away from its mounting on the wall. I also seized a round hide shield, of the kind used by the Pathan tribesmen.

I thrust the spear at the nearer man and he stepped backwards in alarm, treading on the toes of his fellow. Both men were clear of the blanket now, and in the dimness I saw the further of the two stoop to recover his lost axe.

The connection to Holmes's room was behind me, and I retreated inside, slamming it quickly. The room was cold, as an empty room can be at night in high summer, and again I felt sure that my friend had never returned from his errand. I dived for the other door, the one leading through to the sitting-room, but it had an infuriating tendency to stick, and in my panic it took me several moments to force it open. By then the man with the hatchet was in the outer room, blocking my way, while his fellow tore open the connecting door between the bedrooms. I found myself cornered.

"Shame, that," one of them said, in a coarse voice. "I was hoping as you'd have locked it, so's I could break it down with my chopper."

"Keep back!" I cried, as menacingly as I could. I threw the shield at the man in the sitting-room, who ducked but still suffered a glancing blow to the forehead. I transferred the spear to my left hand, jabbing it again at the fellow in the connecting doorway, who wielded a wicked-looking army knife, and seized the nearest object I could find on Holmes's shelves, to use again as a projectile.

It was a wooden cross, and for an absurd moment I was put in mind of Mr Stoker's lurid Gothic tales, before I remembered seeing it around Holmes's neck in one of his guises as a Roman priest. However, the fantastical image of his using it to ward away a creature of the night gave me a desperate idea. Trusting in the murk to support me in a risky bluff, I held the wooden shape by one of its arms, and raised it with the foot towards the man in the sitting-room door. "Keep back!" I repeated. "I've got Holmes's gun!"

"Gun, is it?" said the man at the door of my room. He sounded sceptical.

"Yes," I insisted, "and you may be sure he keeps it fully loaded." In fact I doubted this very much. I had no idea where Holmes habitually kept his Webley, but I was quite certain he would not leave it, loaded or no, within the reach of any intruder who had penetrated this far into his sanctum unmolested. I could only bargain on these men's ignorance of my friend's character, and their natural caution.

A spark flared, and as I blinked away the brightness I saw that the man with the knife had lit a match. "No, it ain't," he said curtly, and his fellow dived towards me with his hatchet.

It was too late to turn my spear in his direction. I desperately blocked him with the cross, which sheared in two under the blade, and ducked away. His friend was coming towards me now as well, tossing aside the match. It fell on Holmes's bed, where it began to smoulder.

I leaped back, hurling Holmes's make-up table to the ground between us. It scattered pots and jars of ointment across the wooden floor, and its great silvered mirror shattered into sharp fragments. One flew up to slice the hatchetman's hand, and he cursed me again.

Now, though, I was trapped between Holmes's bed and the wall. I took up his punching-ball, staggering a little from the lead that weighed it down, and swung the heavy base at the nearer man, who stepped away and seized it from me. I jabbed with the Pashtun spear at his fellow, who made a grab at the weapon with his free hand, but I twisted it free and thrust again. With a powerful blow of his axe he severed the blade from the shaft, leaving me holding nothing more useful than a long stick.

Both men had rounded the bed now, and were advancing towards me once more. Part of the counterpane was alight where the match had fallen, and in the dim glare I recognised, as if there had been any doubt in the matter, the faces of the pair of roughs who had attacked Holmes and myself in an alleyway a few days previously. I tore at the burning bedding and threw it at them, but they were not to be caught that way twice. One beat the bundle aside and it fell, still flickering, to the floor, while his comrade barely paused in his approach.

I swept my arm across the nearest shelves, pitching the keepsakes of a dozen successful cases under their feet, but this did not slow them in the slightest. I turned the decapitated spear and used it like a quarterstaff to push back against them both, but their combined weight quickly forced me into the very corner of the room, my face full of their reeking breath.

"This is it for you," said the man with the hatchet, and I was appalled at the indifference in his tone. This was, after all, the kind of task he carried out on a routine basis, as part of his job; though it could mean the end of everything for me, to him it was simply his bread and butter.

I pushed for one final time with the Afghan spear, then let it drop to the floor. "So be it, then," I said. If I was to perish here and now, then I would perish like an Englishman.

I saw the hatchetman nod curtly in the dim light, and he raised his axe.

Then there was a thudding sound, he gave a sudden groan, and he fell to the floor with a noise like a heavy log of wood being dropped. His comrade looked around in alarm, and then he, too, received a ringing blow about the head with what could only have been the iron poker from our fireplace.

"Holmes!" I gasped at the figure silhouetted in the dancing flames. "Thank God you're here!"

The man left standing looked from me to the newcomer to his fallen comrade, calculated his odds shortly, vaulted the bed and ran back into my room. I heard the sound of breaking glass and, I assumed, the sound of him leaping or dropping from my window down to the street below.

The figure standing before me gave a little moan. Letting the poker fall to the floor with a loud clatter, it sat down suddenly on the bare bed. It said, "Lord, Dr Watson, you mustn't give me a fright like that again."

"Mrs Hudson?" I gasped. I fumbled on Holmes's shelves until I found a candle and some matches. Lighting it revealed our valiant landlady in her nightgown, looking very flushed and fanning herself with one hand. Hastily, I took Holmes's pillow and smothered the burning bedclothes on the floor. If I allowed the house to burn down on top of everything else that had happened tonight, I thought to myself a little hysterically, there was a strong chance I might be evicted.

The immediate danger past, I examined the prone body of the whiskered hatchetman. Mrs Hudson's poker had landed a lucky strike on the occiput, from which he was bleeding profusely. He was quite unconscious. Satisfying myself that neither this wound nor his others were serious, I confiscated his vicious weapon, staunched the flow of blood, then gathered up the bedclothes from the floor and tore them into strips. "They were already ruined, I'm afraid," I told the protesting Mrs Hudson as I tied the man up.

"What was he doing here, Doctor?" she asked me. "Do you know who he is?"

"We haven't been formally introduced," I told her grimly,

"but from what I gather those who know him call him Chops. He and his friend Onions attacked Holmes and me in an alley the other day. It seems that they came back to finish the job."

"That's more excitement than I've seen in some time, Doctor," she told me, "even living with Mr Holmes. I'm not sure that I'd care to see it again."

"Mrs Hudson," I said with absolute sincerity, "I must apologise, and thank you. You are a brave and resourceful woman, and my accounts of Holmes's adventures have, I regret to say, undervalued your worth."

"Well," she said shrewdly, "I dare say that's why these ruffians thought nothing of coming into the house while I was here. Those bedsheets are coming out of your rent, though, that's all I can say."

"I shall buy you a whole new set of linen," I promised her.

Together we manoeuvred the inert intruder onto Holmes's bed, to which I secured him with further knots, using my own sheets for ropes. "I must send for Inspector Hopkins at once," I said. "Dash it all, though, I wonder where Holmes has got to?"

Mrs Hudson had gone back through to the sitting-room, and was lighting the lamps. "I think that we could both do with some tea while we wait for the Inspector," she said.

"I wouldn't dream of asking you for any such thing, Mrs Hudson," I assured her, as I kicked the fallen Pathan shield back into my bedroom.

She sat down in my favourite armchair and said, a little sharply, "I was hoping that you might make it, Doctor, just this once." Remembering my manners at last, I found a jacket of mine and placed it around her shoulders, fetching my own dressing-gown while I was about it.

"I believe I can do better than tea," I said, carrying over the brandy decanter and two glasses. "Hello, though, what's this?"

A calfskin document-wallet was sitting on the coffee-table.

It was not mine nor, as far as I knew, Holmes's, and it had certainly not been there when I had gone to bed. I put down the tray and picked it up to examine it. If our nocturnal visitors had left it behind, then it was of better quality than I would have expected from them.

Distracted now, I opened it up while Mrs Hudson, with a faint sigh, poured drinks for us both.

The first thing that I found was a note, reading, "Gone to the Diogenes. Do not follow. When I return I will tell you what to do. S.H."

"Whatever is this?" I wondered. The writing was Holmes's, that was clear at once, but I did not recognise this example of it. "Why would he leave a note unaddressed inside a folder like this? And why tell me he's gone to the Diogenes Club? I know full well he went there earlier – did he come back and then leave again? And what do you suppose the rest of this can be?"

I pulled out the rest of the wallet's contents – a thick sheaf of papers covered in handwriting. This time, astonished, I recognised the script as my own.

I took the pile closer to the lamp, sat down next to my landlady, and read the first few lines.

The manuscript began:

> "'I must agree with you, Watson,' said my friend Sherlock Holmes, breaking a half-hour's silence. 'General Gordon would not have shared such reservations. He would have been glad of anything that promoted present peace between the countries he loved, with the Future a secondary consideration.'"

I stared at Mrs Hudson in absolute bewilderment.

"I didn't write this," I protested. "Who on earth did?"

CHAPTER TWO

"But it's your handwriting, Doctor," Mrs Hudson pointed out sensibly. "I'd recognise it anywhere, though that's not to say I can always read it. It's proper doctor's writing, as they say."

"It's not, though," I repeated feebly.

Certainly, however, it was an impeccable imitation. Mrs Hudson was correct to suggest that I was not the neatest of scribes, and I would have been the first to admit that my lettering can be a little idiosyncratic, but everything I saw was quite as I should have expected, had I written this myself. Even the paper was the same, down to the watermark, as that which I habitually used for the manuscripts I sent to my publisher.

Had it not been for the most recent case in which Holmes and I had been involved, I would have been forced to conclude that I had indeed written this account, and had forgotten the matter in a bout of amnesia brought on by my recent struggle with the intruders.

As it was I said, "The fact is, Mrs Hudson, that Holmes and I have been looking into a complicated matter of forgery. Very complicated, and exceptionally sophisticated. I already knew that these people could produce facsimiles that would fool even the most careful observer, but to see it done in one's own hand, and even in one's own words … well, it's quite uncanny."

Uncanny was the right word, I thought. It was eerie, and even frightening, to see deeds that I had never done, words I had not spoken, and sentiments that would never have occurred to me, expressed so eloquently in my own voice.

"Why have they done it, though?" she asked, as baffled as I. "Why would anyone want to forge one of your old stories?"

"It's not an old story at all," I said, choosing to ignore her disparaging tone as I leafed through the manuscript. "It's an account of this latest case of ours, but … not at all a correct one. Parts of it seem to be accurate enough, but others are entirely fabricated."

Shaking her head, she asked again, "But why would anybody do that?"

"It could be for any number of reasons," I told her. "If there's one thing I've learned over the past week, it's the varied uses an ingenious criminal can find for forgery."

I felt that I owed it to her, after her precipitate and disagreeable involvement in the case, to explain it as best I could. I briefly outlined our recent involvement in the legacy of Scotland Yard's investigation into counterfeiting, at first as it touched the death of the Honourable Christopher Bastion, the senior civil servant and putative traitor, and the arrest of his supposed spymaster, the late Zimmerman, but later as a crime that warranted attention for its own sake, threatening as it did to invalidate honest men's wills, exculpate murderers, introduce criminals into innocent households and defraud wealthy buyers of their millions.

Holmes and I did not normally take our landlady so far into our confidence, and she listened to it all with the greatest interest. Then, our unwanted guest forgotten for the moment along with any thoughts of his fellow's return, we pored together over the extraordinary manuscript that they had brought with them.

"You see, none of this prefatory business happened at all," I complained, a little plaintively. "It's true that my cousin Emily wrote to me about her new baby, and, as you know, Holmes was kind enough to have my portrait of General Gordon framed, but all the rest is nonsense. Neither of us has the slightest interest in Chinese diplomacy, nor in this Hong Kong business. I've never been near China, and while Holmes has seen Tibet he's more interested in the power struggles of the East End than of the Far East. As for his trick of reading one's thoughts from one's expression ... well, he demonstrated it to me once, and very disconcerting I found it, but on that occasion I made him promise never to do it again, and he hasn't since. This yarn makes it sound as if he's at it constantly."

"I'd like to see him try it with me," Mrs Hudson sniffed. "I'm sure he doesn't know half of what must go through a housekeeper's mind each day."

"As for this," I said, "'I kept my temper and my silence, and held my tongue along with the newspaper'? What rot! I'd never write a sentence like that ... I say, though," I added pensively, "I believe that's a zeugma. Perhaps even two zeugmas. Or is it zeugmae?"

"I wouldn't know anything about that, I'm sure," said Mrs Hudson.

A patter of light footsteps came on the stairs, and the landlady quailed, doubtless anticipating the return of our second assailant. For my own part, ever hopeful, I cried out, "Holmes?" But the man who entered, after the most peremptory of knocks, was Inspector Stanley Hopkins.

"I came at once," the young police detective said breathlessly, "just as you asked ..." Then, seeing our state of undress, he flushed a deep crimson and said, "Oh, my word. I am so very sorry to intrude, Doctor, but the front door was unlocked, and your note seemed most urgent."

"It's quite all right, Hopkins," I told him. "Mrs Hudson's had a bad fright, that's all. We've had a pair of unexpected visitors … That will be one of them, in fact," I added, as the man on the bed in Holmes's room let out a low groan. "But wait a moment," I said, remembering something. I had intended to summon Hopkins, certainly, but then had been distracted by the false manuscript. Besides, there had scarcely been time for him to hear of the assault, from whatever source, and reach us. "To what note are you referring?"

He frowned, and pulled out of his pocket a scrap of paper, which he handed to me. It read, "Hopkins, please come at once. I must discuss with you a matter of unparalleled urgency. Watson." The writing was, once again, quite unmistakably my own.

I groaned. "Oh, Lord. It's exactly as you feared, Hopkins. We can't trust the evidence of our own eyes any more."

The Inspector stared at me. "You mean you didn't write this?" he repeated. "Good heavens. I would have sworn … but then, of course I would have. That's the whole point, after all."

"It's worse than that, though," I said, and showed him the manuscript, at which he stared in astonishment.

He flicked through the first few pages, then the last few. "So this entire document is forged?" he asked incredulously.

I said, "I haven't written anything up yet about this latest adventure. It is not my habit to, while a case is still in progress, as I never know what trivial detail I may have overlooked that Holmes will reveal to have been the key to the whole business. I have been taking notes, as I always do, but those are naturally very rough. They wouldn't read in anything like this polished way. Besides, I lost my notebook a few days ago. I only have what I've jotted down since then."

"Well, it looks as if somebody found it," Hopkins said. He looked more closely at the final pages, and whistled. "My word,

Doctor, this is incendiary stuff. And you've had visitors tonight, you say?"

I said, "We still have one. He's tied up in Holmes's room. It's Chops," I added, realising that in the confusion of everything else I had discovered, the significance of apprehending Bastion's actual murderer had completely escaped me. "I suppose you'll need to arrest him while you're here."

"I suppose I'd better," Hopkins agreed solemnly. "And they brought this with them, I suppose," he added, indicating the manuscript.

"And this," I agreed, showing him the note purporting to be from Holmes. He whistled again. In return, he showed me the reference to just such a note on the manuscript's penultimate page.

"I must say," the Inspector said, after I had given him a somewhat more comprehensive account of our activities that night, "it seems fairly clear what they intended, don't you think? They were to arrive here and do away with you quickly, Dr Watson, in Mr Holmes's absence. Where is Mr Holmes, by the way?"

"He went to the Diogenes Club," I said. "He had a summons from Lord Loomborough late last night. But that was many hours ago. He must be somewhere else by now."

"He went to see Lord Loomborough?" Hopkins repeated. "You are sure of that? This manuscript suggests that he was going to confront Mycroft Holmes."

"Well, we know how much that's worth," I said. "It was definitely Loomborough. A boy came with a message … Oh, for heaven's sake." I groaned again. "There was a message, in what I can only assume was a perfect facsimile of Loomborough's handwriting, asking for Holmes's immediate attendance, alone, at the Diogenes Club."

Hopkins shook his head in simple amazement at these successive revelations. "And where is that note now?"

"Holmes took it with him, I believe."

"Well, we must hope that he is safe," said Hopkins sombrely. "I suppose he is, though. It wouldn't suit their purposes to kill him."

"What were their purposes?" I wondered. "I still can't fathom it."

"Oh, I can tell you that," said Hopkins. "First, they would have killed you, as I've said. And then they would have hidden this manuscript," which he tapped for emphasis, "somewhere any half-competent search would find it. They would have placed the forged note from Mr Holmes somewhere prominent, to add credence to it, and if he'd left the one from Lord Loomborough, they'd have taken that away.

"And then I was to arrive, summoned by you to discuss an urgent matter. I would have found you dead, and this," he tapped the manuscript again, "telling me exactly why. They intended to make Sherlock Holmes the primary suspect for your murder, Dr Watson."

CHAPTER THREE

Hopkins summoned some men from Scotland Yard, led by the able Constable Vincent, and they came to take away the unprotesting Chops. Hopkins spoke to him first, of course, asking him most urgently where Holmes was, but he refused even to confirm the fact of our fight, the evidence of which lay all around him.

"You'll get nothing out of me, copper," was his only response. Since the man's speech was slurred, and he was either groggy from concussion or acting it well, Hopkins was unwilling to interrogate him further until he had received proper medical treatment.

While Vincent and his colleagues untied the man and placed him in handcuffs, Mrs Hudson and I dressed ourselves, and she managed, despite my protestations, to summon up a pot of tea, around which Hopkins and I reconvened once Chops had been dragged away. Hopkins instructed Vincent to send men to ask after Holmes at the Diogenes, and to scour the likely routes between Baker Street and the club for any sign of his whereabouts.

Still a little mortified by my earlier unchivalrous behaviour, and in view of her concern for the missing Holmes, I invited our landlady to take part in our little conference. I suggested also sending word to Mycroft Holmes asking him to join us, but

Hopkins's view was that we should first be perfectly clear about what we might and might not understand from the manuscript's efforts to incriminate him. "Ideally I'd also like Mr Holmes's opinion," he added. "Our Mr Holmes, I mean. But as there seems little prospect of that for now, let's see what we can find out on our own first."

We read through the manuscript together, systematically, considering between us which passages seemed to be largely reliable accounts of the facts, which were outright falsehoods and which mixed truth and lies. Some pages passed smoothly from actual to invented events and back again, while others, more poisonously, presented reality in a distorted form, often by glossing it with opinions from my supposed pen that were quite at odds with the ones that I actually held.

We soon concluded that those scenes where Hopkins himself had been present were represented more or less faithfully. "From my point of view," he said, "there's little to take exception to, which is sensible, of course, as it was me who this account was intended to take in first. They've taken a lot of care to reproduce our conversations faithfully, within the usual limits. With respect, Doctor, your stories are never perfectly true to the facts as I remember them, and nor would a reasonable reader expect them to be. You tidy up the things that people said to make them more readable, you skip over complications that turned out to be irrelevant, and so forth, as any decent chronicler would. Given those expectations, all of this – the parts with me in, that is – appear quite convincing."

I said, "I'm at a loss to see how they managed that. Even if they were working from my notebook as you suggest, most of what I jot down is intended as an aide-memoire to prompt my own recollection. It would be very difficult for someone who wasn't there to reconstruct an entire conversation from them."

Hopkins said grimly, "That is a worry to me as well, Doctor. And of course the notes will have left off at the point when you lost the book. But let's leave that aside for now. You say the opening passage is fictitious?"

"Up to the arrival of the messenger," I confirmed. "The message was as reported, but Holmes did not claim to have been expecting it. After that, the account of the conversation with Mycroft Holmes is accurate, up to Holmes's comments about dancing to his tune. Again, he never said such a thing."

"And then I recognise the description of your visit to the crime scene, and Probert's arrest," said Hopkins, "and our trip to Zimmerman's address."

"All that I might have written myself," I agreed, with a rueful respect for the forger's skill. "The scene at Sir Hector Askew's house is also largely accurate, although it describes him with less deference than I should have done. And I would not have compared young Windward to Shelley. He has a weak chin."

"That is perhaps more detail than we need get into," suggested the Inspector. "Which is the next passage to be substantially falsified?"

"Well, let me see." I flipped through the pages. "After that, Holmes and I returned to Baker Street, and had a conversation along the lines that are reported, but not in those exact words. That section must have been reconstructed speculatively from my notes. And I have not yet read Windward's story, I regret to say. I have been rather busy recently. But the next significant departure from fact comes when I mentioned the death at the Butcher's Apron to Holmes. He was most concerned, and feared that the victim was the man to whom he had been talking there. He guessed that the men he was seeking had got wind of their conversation and had handed out the beating themselves, to dissuade others from discussing their business. He was rather exercised about the matter, as I recall."

"Whereas here, he simply denies all knowledge of it."

"Well, quite. It's a very brief statement, but bears no resemblance to what he said." I continued to peruse the manuscript. "After that, there's little to object to until the end of our meeting with Graymare. In fact Holmes did not imitate Bastion's handwriting; he merely disagreed with Graymare's conclusions, and later expressed to myself and Mycroft his view that the man was a mountebank. Graymare was not humiliated in the manner described."

"I see." Hopkins made a careful note. "And after that?"

"Let me see …" I flicked through further. "Mycroft didn't try to dissuade Holmes from pursuing the forgery investigation, nor was I sceptical of it myself, as I am represented. I've shared Holmes's interest in the question throughout. The rest of that conversation, though, is more or less correct. The interview with Lucy Evans, of course, was as reported – including Holmes's unkind treatment of her, I regret to say. I admit that I was cross with him about that."

"As was I," Hopkins agreed equably. "And then?"

"Well," I said indignantly, "my supposed doings of that evening are invented from the whole cloth. I didn't meet with Jerome Windward, and I most certainly did not get drunk with him or betray Holmes's confidences. And this first encounter with Chops and Onions … that simply never occurred. The first time I clapped eyes on either man was three days later, when they accosted Holmes and myself in that alley."

"Interesting," Hopkins said. "I thought that passage seemed a little muddled. He seems to forget whether it's Chops or Onions holding you. He takes the opportunity to bring up the Butcher's Apron business again, though."

"These remarks about the pain from my war wound are wishful thinking, as well," I said. "It hasn't troubled me for some time now,

I'm glad to say." If it had, I would certainly not have done as well as I had during my most recent contretemps with those same men.

"Very well," said Hopkins, making more notes. "What did you do that evening, in fact?"

"I went out for a drink at my club," I said at once. "I met some army friends and we chatted for a while. When I came home, Holmes showed me the lock of hair that was found at Bastion's house. I didn't criticise his treatment of Lucy, though perhaps I should have."

"Well, never mind that now," sighed Hopkins. "Of course you wouldn't then have revisited the scene of the attack, since it never took place. Other than that, the succeeding couple of days seem solid enough to me. Is there anything that isn't?"

"A comment here and there," I said, "but mainly that Graymare did not request a further meeting with me. I haven't seen him since our first appointment, in fact."

"So where is the next major divergence from the truth?" Hopkins asked.

Again I leafed carefully through the manuscript. "Here," I said. "The attack on us both in the alley. We had no warning – that is, if Holmes was aware that we were being followed, he said nothing of it to me. We didn't lure them there, as described – it was simply a shortcut that Holmes knew. The first I knew of Chops or Onions being there – and, as I have said, the first time I encountered either of them – was when they cornered us. And then," I added, with considerable asperity, "this business of Holmes beating Chops to within an inch of his life is utter nonsense. You saw the man yourself, Hopkins. Did he look to you as if he'd been recently thrashed?"

The Inspector smiled. "Only by Mrs Hudson's formidable poker," he said. "No, there were a few older bruises, but nothing I'd consider evidence of a serious assault. What really happened?"

"Well, up to a point the conversation and the fight played out much as the manuscript says ... I suppose Chops and Onions themselves must have described them to the author," I said.

"And, I note," said Hopkins, "on this occasion they do not bring up the question of Daniel Maines's death."

"Nor did they," I said. "If Holmes is right and they killed him themselves, they would have little reason to. In reality, Chops fled shortly after Onions did, both with minor injuries, and left Holmes and me licking our own wounds."

"And we must assume," said Hopkins, "that one of them took your notebook with him. Which is why it becomes more interesting from this point onwards to look at what is accurate, rather than what isn't."

"Indeed," I said. "The account as a whole veers away into sheer fantasy, but there are still parts that stick closely to the facts. As I said, I didn't meet Graymare again, and the chance encounter with the Irregular is entirely made up. I know no lad called 'Sneaky'. My errands before our meeting with Lord Loomborough were simply a bit of shopping and a trip to the barber's, and none of the misgivings that are expressed about Holmes are ones I would share. I certainly wouldn't ask a street urchin for information about him behind his back! It's true enough that I was annoyed with him about the trick he played on Lucy, and for being abrupt with you that day, but neither of those are uncharacteristic of him. You know that as well as I do, Hopkins. He hasn't been more than normally violent or erratic lately, or given me any unusual cause for concern over his behaviour. Wouldn't you agree, Mrs Hudson?"

"Mr Holmes isn't always an easy man to have as a lodger," Mrs Hudson said carefully, and with what I suspected must be considerable restraint, "but he's done nothing over the past few days that's given me any more worries than usual. All this about his dark moods and his arrogance … well, that's just Mr Holmes. The rest is all stuff and nonsense," she concluded robustly. Her expression was angry and I recalled that she could at times be rather protective of her famous tenant.

"I didn't write it," I reminded her, rather weakly.

Hopkins smiled. "And after the invented meeting with Graymare?"

I considered. "Mycroft's remarks to us are more or less correct, oddly enough, but the meeting with Loomborough was not as this has it at all. He was far from kind and genial."

"What did he say, in fact?" asked Hopkins with interest, and I remembered that the Minister for Policing had been something of a thorn in his side of late.

"He warned us in no uncertain terms that we were barking up the wrong tree in looking into the counterfeiting affair, and that we were on no account to involve you in our investigation, or to draw upon the resources of the police in any other way. He was extremely stern," I added, wincing slightly at the recollection of our being told off like a pair of naughty schoolboys brought before the headmaster. To Holmes, of course, it had all been water off a duck's back, but my memories of my own schooldays are still vivid and rather painful.

Hopkins nodded. "I'm hardly surprised," he said. "Particularly since Mycroft Holmes warned you that that was what he would say. Nor did you reassure me of his support when the three of us met with Mycroft later. And that, of course, is a conversation that I *was* there for, and which seems to be accurate, as is the scene in poor Probert's cell. That I do find interesting."

Though the manuscript's view of Holmes's regrettable behaviour on that occasion was once more harsher than my own, I agreed with Hopkins that it reported it accurately. "The conversation with Dr Permenter is the last occasion when the manuscript seems to be drawing on the facts, however," I said. "Most of what was said at the Athenaeum was much as is represented here. After that ... we met with Professor Rames, certainly, and he *did* admit to being involved with the forging of the Shakespeare play, and for the reasons that are given, but not in the words that are put into his mouth. As for his co-conspirators, he flatly refused to say a word about them. Holmes did not bring up Mycroft's name, and nor did Rames. From then on, everything that happens up to the end is the most arrant nonsense.

"And, I might add," I concluded with no little annoyance, "this whole concoction is far more than I could possibly have written in a single night, however feverish or frenzied I was feeling."

"That, certainly, is a point of some significance," said a weary voice from the doorway, "and one that I can only hope my advocate would have raised in court."

"Holmes!" I cried in relief, as my friend walked in, grimy and bloody, and slumped down in his armchair. "Thank God you're home!"

"You may thank whomever you please, Watson," he replied, with some asperity, "but I found my own efforts more efficacious than anything in my limited experience of prayer."

"Your hands," I noticed. "They're bleeding."

"They were put to the disagreeable necessity of levering some very stubborn boards away from a window," he said. "But I am very pleased to see that you are well, Watson," he added, with feeling. "I had feared the worst."

He allowed me to apply some salve to his hands while I told him shortly of the attack, of Mrs Hudson's bravery, of Onions's escape and Chops's arrest. He listened gravely, and then said, "Mrs Hudson, I too must apologise if I have undervalued your most excellent services. The next time I am in need of a bodyguard, I shall most certainly know where to advertise." Then, perceiving the expression upon her face, he added, "No, I see that this is not a matter for pleasantries. You proved most capable at a frightening and disagreeable time, and I shall not make light of it. I thank you most sincerely for saving Dr Watson's life."

Holmes in turn gave his account of what had happened since I had last seen him. "I knew, of course, that there was some possibility of the message from Lord Loomborough proving false, but one cannot act as if every communication is suspicious. How else could I have confirmed his summons, other than by answering it in person? Any messenger I sent on my behalf could have been waylaid and the message intercepted."

"You could have telephoned," I protested. Holmes had only recently had the instrument installed in our rooms, and I heartily disliked it. Nevertheless, this seemed to me an occasion when its usefulness would have been unarguable.

"Not to the Diogenes Club, Watson. The members flatly refuse to have any such device upon the premises. Imagine the discomfort of knowing they might be called away from their peace and quiet at any moment to converse with another member of the human species! No, I had little choice but to go, and trust to my wits. I reached the club without mishap, but found Lord Loomborough absent. Apparently, however, I had only just missed him, and might yet find him awake at home. Mycroft was present, though, and I spoke to him for a little while about the progress of our investigation. He promised to look out certain items for me.

"I left the club and looked for a cab to take me to Belgravia, where Lord Loomborough resides. As is my habit when caution is called for, I sent the first two cabs away and mounted the third. As we pulled away, however, I heard the sounds of a struggle and a cry as my cabman was thrown upon the pavement. A moment later Chops was in the carriage with me, and it was being driven away at great speed by his comrade Onions.

"By now I was curious to see where they would take me, so I played along. They bound my hands, placed a sack over my head and took me to a street in Shoreditch (the rhythm of the paving there is unmistakable) where they bundled me out of the carriage and down into a coal-cellar. Then they left me and went about their business.

"It took me little enough time to free myself from my bonds, but escaping from the cellar was not so straightforward. The house above me was quite deserted, and my cries went unheeded. The door was locked and very stout, some heavy object had been placed over the coal-hatch, and my only means of egress was the boarded window I mentioned. They had taken care to leave me nothing with which I might lever it free, hence the painful expedient to which I was forced to resort.

"It was plain, though, that the cellar would not have held me permanently, nor had they troubled themselves to finish me off. Clearly their plans went deeper than that. If I was not their intended target, then their object in delaying my return to Baker Street could only be an attack on the house's remaining occupants.

"Given the *modus operandi* that they have evinced thus far, I had a shrewd idea of what they might intend. The possibility that I might return to find you dead, Watson, and myself condemned by your hand to hang, exercised me considerably, and lent additional urgency to my efforts to release myself. At length, I managed to prise away the boards sufficiently to squeeze through, and made my way back here as unobtrusively as possible.

"I had to evade several of your men *en route*, Hopkins," he added. "I had no way to tell whether they were seeking me in my capacity as an abductee or an escaped murderer. But I had to return here to learn what had happened, and to offer my help if I was not too late."

CHAPTER FOUR

Holmes wasted little time in reading the manuscript, skimming through it with such alacrity that I would never have believed, had I not known him, that he could be taking it all in. He consulted Hopkins's notes as he went, adding his own marginalia to Hopkins's notebook – not, at the Inspector's insistence, to the manuscript itself, which would have evidentiary value if the forger came to trial.

While he did so, Hopkins observed to me, "This little business goes well beyond forgery. It's conspiracy to murder, plain and simple. It's the connection we need to make the case that the forger was responsible for Bastion's and Probert's deaths as well."

Holmes murmured assent, and turned the page.

A little while later, he looked up and said, "The author takes some trouble to blame me for the killing of Mr Maines. I confess I must accept some part in provoking his death, insofar as his friends punished him for speaking to me. It is quite a fortuitous stick to beat me with, however, especially given that naturally nobody would testify to knowing who had really killed the man."

He continued to read. After a few minutes, he remarked, "I do not believe I called the forger a literary genius. Does anybody else recall my making such a remark?"

Hopkins and I agreed that he had not. "But that's a trivial point, surely," I suggested, "compared with some of the things the manuscript has you do."

"On the contrary," Holmes said, "it is notable because it occurs during a conversation at which Inspector Hopkins was present. The author of the document, who may or may not also be the copyist, seems to consider his own talents of sufficient importance to risk a remark that might have alerted Hopkins to his imposture. I dare say it would have passed without comment, or been dismissed as a whimsical invention of yours, Watson; the discrepancy is, as you say, a trivial one. But it suggests a character flaw in the forger that I should not have altogether expected."

An astonishingly short time later, he was finished. Turning the last page, he said, "It is apparent that this conspiracy, for such it surely is, has had us under surveillance for some time. Your notes would have been a windfall for them, Watson, but as you have observed they would hardly have been sufficient to reconstruct entire conversations with such a degree of precision. We have been eavesdropped upon repeatedly, I fear."

"Well, it certainly wasn't me," said Mrs Hudson, "nor the pageboy. He knows I'd skin him alive if I caught him doing such a thing."

"Fear not, Mrs Hudson," Holmes reassured her, "the conversations between Watson and myself when we were alone in these rooms are recreated only approximately."

"I've noticed that gentlemen aren't often really alone," Mrs Hudson observed. "I give you privacy in this house, Mr Holmes, as you've every right to expect. But when you're out and about I dare say you're generally surrounded by waiters and footmen and the like."

"Indeed," said Holmes. "I have little doubt that, if Watson

and I were to inspect every instance when our words have been reproduced with a suspicious degree of faithfulness, we should recall some assistant or servant hovering just about within earshot. In the case of our conversations with Mycroft in the Stranger's Room at the Diogenes, the attendant Jennings was often close at hand. We knew already that he was trying to better himself; I dare say the forgers found him not averse to a secondary source of income. Sir Hector Askew has footmen; at Boothby's there were attendants; at the Athenaeum, the waiter. Even cabmen may have sharp ears.

"It may be that our correspondence also has been intercepted, since I doubt that your notes made reference to your cousin's happy event, Watson. No? I thought as much. As for the conversations with Hopkins, here and at the Yard … Well, Hopkins?" he said, promptingly. "What is your view?"

Hopkins looked very grim. "I can account for some of it. The interview with Lucy Evans was written up in a report, for instance. I made notes for my own use of our conversation yesterday with Mr Mycroft Holmes, and after all the confusion following that terrible business with Probert, I couldn't tell you with any certainty where those notes are now."

Holmes said, "We may be confident that they are in the forger's hands. As Watson observed, this manuscript represents a considerable commitment of time, especially since it must not only have been written in the sense of being composed, as Watson would have done had this been his handiwork, but also copied in the most meticulous penmanship by whoever did the work of mimicking his handwriting. The notes of that particular conversation, then, reached the author's eyes at a late stage, and I imagine he must have been altogether quite alarmed that I had discovered the stylistic hallmarks whereby his work might be recognised.

"It was too late to alter the earlier pages, of course, nor could he omit the material in question, for fear of alerting you to its significance, Hopkins, but he does what he can to ameliorate the damage – suggesting, for instance, that Watson, too, spells *connexion* in the old-fashioned manner, though he has never done so that I have seen. You will notice that from that point onward the habits in question are rather carefully avoided, until he becomes overexcited, and I suppose hurried, on the final page. He even takes to using parentheses in place of dashes, though they had been notable by their absence to this point.

"But I believe I interrupted you, Hopkins."

Hopkins sighed bitterly. "I was just going to say that, with those exceptions, there was only one man present at most of those conversations, other than the three of us."

"Sergeant Douglass," I said, not wishing to appear the only man present dull enough not to have reached this obvious conclusion.

"He has betrayed the Yard's trust, and mine." Hopkins's face was stormy. "I'll see him face the full force of the law for this."

"He was, I assume, present at, and forewarned of, the arrest of Zimmerman?" Holmes asked.

"Oh, yes," said Hopkins, bitterly. "He's been part of all that from the start. He must have let these conspirators know that it was coming, and arranged for a false letter from Bastion to be found there."

"And he would, of course, have had every opportunity to purloin your notes of yesterday."

"So he would," Hopkins agreed. "But worst of all, there's poor Probert. If Douglass didn't kill him himself, he must have enlisted someone else who did. He's in this up to his neck. He's off duty at present. May I use your telephone, please?"

Hopkins called through to the Yard and instructed Constable Fratelli to cease the search for Holmes, and instead to send men round to Sergeant Douglass's home to bring him in, on Hopkins's authority. Knowing now that Holmes was safe, Mrs Hudson took the opportunity to retire, pleading a very understandable exhaustion. I insisted that she should sleep late, assuring her that Holmes and I would make our own arrangements for breakfast.

Replacing the receiver, Hopkins said, "I'm ashamed that I let that swine take me in. I should have better judgement by now."

Holmes said, "We should perhaps not be too harsh on the Sergeant, Inspector. We know that Probert was coerced into cooperation through feigned threats to his young relative, and Professor Rames spoke of similar inducements. Sergeant Douglass is a family man, is he not?"

"He is," said Hopkins. He did not trouble himself to ask how Holmes had deduced this point, and I, too, felt that we had greater concerns for now. "But if someone was threatening his children, he could have come to me."

"Doubtless he was warned that such a course of action would result in immediate harm to them," Holmes replied. "We are all familiar with how these tactics work. We may be sure that this conspiracy goes far beyond Sergeant Douglass, however."

Hopkins said, "Yes, I've been thinking about that too. As we've established, the manuscript takes great pains to ensure that I won't suspect its untruth. Their plan would have had you out of the picture, Dr Watson, and made me unable to trust you, Mr Holmes, leaving me no grounds to suppose that this account was fictitious. But what of the other people who appear in its pages? It seems several of them have been gravely misrepresented. Wouldn't they be able to testify to its falsehood – assuming, that is, that they're not part of the conspiracy?"

"My thoughts in a nutshell," said Holmes. "Professor Rames would not, of course, gainsay the absurd identification of my brother as the forger, for as we know he is in the conspirators' pocket. However –"

"But wait a moment," I said. "Of course I don't believe that Mycroft is the counterfeiter, Holmes, but is the idea really so absurd? The manuscript goes to great lengths to make it seem plausible."

Holmes sighed. "Really, Watson? Even if his indolence alone did not make it incredible, you have seen his hands. In his youth, I should have believed him capable of feigning another man's writing. I have some skill in that area myself, though I should not be confident of exercising it with sufficient proficiency to deceive the likes of Dr Graymare. However, Mycroft is no longer a young man – nor a slender one. Fingers as plump as his would be incapable of the manual dexterity required for such delicate work. Again, I would hope that any defence counsel worth his salt would make much of such an objection."

Hopkins frowned. "Unless it's a question of missing limbs or the like, it's very difficult to prove to a jury's satisfaction that a man isn't capable of something. Even if the defence shows him trying and failing, the prosecution can always argue that he's feigning."

"Very true," Holmes agreed, "and the manuscript is careful to leave open the option that Mycroft is not himself the forger, but the forger's paymaster. In truth, there is no compelling reason why those persons should be one and the same. A criminal organisation that consults with legal experts, military historians and literary scholars could quite reasonably employ separately a handwriting expert, a papermaker, a printer, a photographer and the like, as needed to fulfil the requirements of specific jobs.

"Be that as it may, we may place the manuscript's *dramatis personae* into several categories. There are those like yourself, Hopkins, whose actions correspond with those of their real counterparts and who we may therefore assume were intended to be taken in. There are those who we already know to be involved in the conspiracy, whose silence on the manuscript's divergences from reality might be relied upon. And there are those whose statements on the matter would have been either unavailable or untrustworthy – that is to say Watson, who was to have been removed from contention, and Mycroft and I, who would both have been implicated.

"And finally, there are three men whom we have not yet had cause to suspect, yet whose actions in this text differ markedly from those of their originals. Those are Dr Graymare, whose meeting with ourselves did not end as described, and who did not later meet clandestinely with Watson to call me a homicidal lunatic; Jerome Windward, who neither drank with Watson at the Criterion nor rescued him from attack; and Lord Loomborough, who far from being generous and accommodating attempted to warn us away from the case."

"Lord Loomborough." Hopkins looked shocked, yet also, I thought, rather delighted. "My word."

Holmes said, "It is not, perhaps, greatly less plausible that a government minister might be part of such a criminal organisation than a senior civil servant such as Christopher Bastion or Mycroft."

I said, "Holmes, we only met Windward for a minute or two, at Askew's house. In fact, you barely met him at all. Are you sure he's part of all this?"

Holmes said, "Since he could, if he wished, readily testify to the limits of our acquaintance, we must assume so. His chief role in the manuscript is as an early confidant for your counterpart's misgivings about my unpredictable and erratic behaviour. If he were to swear before a court that you had expressed no such fears, the case against me should be much weakened."

Hopkins said, "And it's perfectly clear how he would have been useful to the conspiracy, isn't it? He's an aspiring author. It must be Jerome Windward who has been composing these forged documents, and Carson Graymare, the renowned handwriting expert, who's been transcribing them. He may have told you that no-one could do so well enough to fool him, Dr Watson, but it wouldn't have been himself he was fooling. He certainly took in that other graphologist."

"Indeed," said Holmes. "I did him a grave injustice by describing him as a charlatan. The theories he propounds may be nonsense, but his technical expertise in handwriting is unmatched by anybody else whom I have met."

"Wait a moment," I said, suddenly excited. "I still have the story young Windward gave me somewhere. Might that shed any light on the matter?"

But Holmes had stood suddenly, his eyes widening in alarm. "I fear that it will have to wait, Watson. While we have been sitting here reading, a man's life has been in danger."

"Who do you mean?" I asked.

"Professor Rames," said Holmes. "His terror when we confronted him yesterday was obvious. The manuscript invents words for him, but it captures his state of mind very well. We may be sure that his role in the conspiracy has been consultative, providing the Shakespearean expertise the conspirators required, but having no involvement in the running of their organisation. Of those we suspect of complicity, Rames seems to be the least deeply involved, and thus the most likely to be persuaded to denounce this manuscript as a fiction. However, since the conspirators must know from their man Onions that their attempt on your life has been unsuccessful, and that we possess this manuscript, it is very likely that they have reached the same conclusion."

"I say!" said Hopkins, getting to his feet at once. "You're right, sir, of course."

"I confess that the point should have occurred to me before," said Holmes. He added ruefully, "I have had rather a trying night."

"We'd better get there as soon as possible," Hopkins said. "Constable Vincent has a carriage waiting. With your permission, I'll have the Yard send some men to join us," he added, reaching for the telephone once more.

While he dialled I said, "Loomborough must be the ringleader, I suppose. That fits with his reputation as a ruthless politician."

"We may very soon be in a position to prove his culpability," said Holmes. "That heavy tread upon the stair can be nobody other than brother Mycroft."

OPENING OF *THE ASSASSINS' DAGGER* BY JEROME E.
WINDWARD (UNPUBLISHED)

Captain Gilmore Montrose's display of memorabilia from his
service in the Indian Subcontinent was much admired throughout
_____shire, for both its intrinsic value and its historical and
anthropological curiosity. It had been shown off to many a visiting
professor, curator, and collector of Eastern curios, and it regularly
occasioned excited comment from the hopeful young ladies who
sojourned with their mothers or chaperones at his country house,
Montrose Court—for while Captain Montrose was no longer
young, he had never married—as well as many whose interest
lay perhaps more in these latter beholders than in the antiquities
themselves.

Pride of place, and the most envious glances of all, were given
to an antique Persian dagger, whose blade glinted like diamond
and whose hilt, set closely about with emeralds, sapphires and
opals, scintillated like a tropical ocean. Legend had it that it had
once been wielded by a cult of fearsome brigands, the legendary
hashishim or assassins, though Captain Montrose would assure
his more sensitive guests, with a gallant laugh, that despite this
historical connexion it had not been used to deal a killing blow
for a great many years.

But that was to change, one warm Spring Saturday when
the larks were at wing and the honeysuckle blossomed in the
hedgerows. Montrose Court was host to a weekend party, with
its usual complement of around a dozen guests, and on this
morning the Reverend Aleric Crichton—whose long habit it
was to rise early for his Morning Prayers—was the first to go
down to breakfast.

Mr Crichton's route from his bedchamber to the breakfast-
room took him past the turret-room which housed Captain

Montrose's collection, and which was habitually kept locked, but this morning stood wide open. This occasioned Mr Crichton little concern, as he assumed that Captain Montrose, too, had awoken early, and was paying his respects to his own Household Gods.

Knocking on the door, he stepped inside, calling a hearty greeting to his host, and then stopped dead—as unhappy a turn of phrase as of events—as the horror of the scene before him imposed itself upon his eyes.

For Captain Montrose lay face-down and unmoving upon the Persian carpet, next to an open glass case. Between his shoulder-blades, its silver gleaming with a crimson that was not that of rubies, projected the hilt of the Assassins' Dagger.

CHAPTER FIVE

It was by now perhaps five o'clock in the morning, and not at all a time when anyone who knew Mycroft Holmes would have expected to see him abroad. He was a creature of habit, addicted to his routines, and it took a grave crisis to rouse him from them. I supposed that a criminal conspiracy between police officers and a government minister, with the involvement of at least one foreign espionage agent, would probably suffice.

While Sherlock Holmes expended precious time, albeit in the most economical way possible, in outlining to his brother his conclusions so far, I looked for the story given me by young Jerome Windward, which I had not yet opened, let alone read. Our sitting-room had not been tidy even before it had been disarranged by the events of the night, and I had to search around for several minutes before alighting on the document wallet that he had passed me, days before, in Sir Hector Askew's hallway.

Mycroft, meanwhile, had brought a document-case of his own. "These took me some little effort to obtain, especially in the middle of the night, but the archivists and librarians whose help my associates sought were amenable, in view of the urgency of the situation," he said.

"We shall read them as we go," said Sherlock. "Windward's too, Watson – and bring the false manuscript also. We must waste no further time."

"I shall stay here and make myself at home," Mycroft declared, leaning back in his chair. "Would you place the telephone within my reach, please? Thank you, Inspector. I shall summon some men to guard my safety, and also to make me some more tea, so please don't worry on my account. But do call me here, if I may be of assistance in some less kinetic capacity."

A scant few minutes later, the Inspector, Holmes and I – Holmes still in his coal-stained, blood-speckled clothes – were in Hopkins's police-carriage, driven by the redoubtable Vincent and hurtling towards Kensington. My Enfield revolver, which I had thought at the last moment to retrieve from the strewn mess of my room, sat snugly in my inner pocket.

I cut the string that tied shut Windward's folder, and opened it up. Inside, as I had expected, was a thick sheaf of papers written out in longhand. Windward's own handwriting, for I assumed that this was indeed such, bore little resemblance to mine, nor to any of the others that we had seen imitated in the counterfeit samples.

I had been remembering with perhaps too much excitement some other cases of Holmes's in recent years, in which novels had provided clues to the resolution of mysteries. In one, a confidence trickster had drawn on a work of fantastical fiction for his more outlandish ideas, while in the course of another the draft of an unpublished novel had given a fictionalised account of a conspiracy involving its author. This time, though, if I had expected a secret confession or some other evidence of Windward's collusion in criminality, I was disappointed.

The title page announced *The Assassin's Dagger*, by Jerome E. Windward, and what followed appeared to be an overly sensational, though hardly original, novel of murder and sleuthing of the kind the reading public has seen in abundance in recent years.

Between the clatter of the horses' hooves, the jolting of the carriage, and the rattle of the wheels across the paving-stones and cobbles, I read the opening pages. "Well," I said, "I count an *occasioned*, a *connexion*, some superfluous capitals, a parenthetical remark with dashes, and something that looks moderately like a zeugma. Is this enough to mark Windward as our elusive author, Holmes?"

"Unless we are to entertain the possibility that this, too, was for some unfathomable reason forged," Sherlock Holmes agreed. "But I hardly think that probable." From Mycroft's document-case, he drew a number of papers. "Your opinions, gentlemen?" he asked as he passed them around.

Each was handwritten, in three very different scripts. As I skimmed them, the same familiar formulations presented themselves, now almost unbidden, to my attention:

"To expenses occasioned during April of 1893 ..."

" ... reciprocating the Tender Regard that you have shown me during our connexion ..."

" ... he has, 'in one fell swoop', abandoned his principles, his country, his party, and any hope of convincing his members not to do the same to their foundering ship."

"More of our fellow's handiwork, I suppose," I said. "But what are these, exactly?"

Holmes replied, "They are the evidence leading to the three separate scandals which propelled Lord Loomborough into his current position. Each of these communications brought down a colleague of his, whose shoes he deigned to fill shortly thereafter. Here are some letters from a woman of unsavoury reputation; here, receipts issued for some illicit income; and here, the submitted manuscript of an article castigating their party leader for his inadequacies."

"And all, I suppose, written by Jerome Windward, and transcribed by Carson Graymare," Hopkins said. "How old would you say Windward was, Dr Watson?"

I considered. "Not older than his mid-twenties, surely. How old are these documents?"

"The earliest dates back seven years," said Holmes. "Either Mr Windward is maturer than he appears, or he was a precocious youth."

"Loomborough himself is an author, though," I remembered. "A memoirist, like myself. Why would he need Windward's services?"

"You assume that he wrote his memoirs himself," Holmes noted drily, over the noise of the carriage. "It is not unknown for rich men to employ amanuenses to scribe their autobiographies for them. The arrangement is less overt than your chronicling of my own adventures, Watson, but it is perhaps little different in other respects. It may even be how the two men met."

He drew from the document-case a clothbound book. "We might find out, if we read this latest volume of Loomborough's reminiscences. Mycroft thinks of everything. However, I hardly think it necessary. We have all the information that is germane, and what is more we may expect to arrive at Rames's family house at any moment."

With a final lurch, the carriage drew up outside the townhouse that Holmes and I had visited some twelve hours earlier, on the occasion of our recent interview with Professor

Rames. We alighted hurriedly, and Holmes (with scant regard for the fact that it was Hopkins, not he, who was the official presence here) strode up the steps and rapped thunderously at the door with his cane. As I followed, I noted with concern that a window on the ground floor had been broken.

"I see it, Watson," Holmes told me, before I could bring it to his attention. "I fear that we may be too late."

It took a minute for the family butler to answer the door. His eyes narrowed when he saw Holmes. "Why, it's you!" he said angrily. "I hoped we'd seen the last of you yesterday. Be off with you!"

"We are with the police," said Hopkins, stepping forward smoothly and ignoring the man's rudeness. "Inspector Stanley Hopkins of Scotland Yard. May we see Professor Jonathan Rames, please?"

"Ah, Inspector, I'm so sorry," the butler said, reverting at once to a deferential professional character. "I'm afraid the Professor won't be awake yet. We servants have only just risen."

"It's imperative that we see him on a matter of the utmost urgency," said Hopkins, just as Holmes asked, "What, pray, has happened to that window?" Both were interrupted, however, by a bloodcurdling shriek from inside the house. Holmes pushed past the butler at once and ran into the hallway. Hopkins and I were close behind him, I pulling out my revolver, the butler protesting feebly behind us.

We quickly traced the scream, which continued unabated, to the drawing-room, which lay on the ground floor at the front of the house. Its source was a housemaid, clinging convulsively to a feather duster, standing stock-still and staring down at the rotund body of Professor Rames, the cause of her loudly vocal horror. The eminent Shakespearean scholar lay on the carpet at the centre of a scarlet stain, his bald head caved in by a killing blow. A blood-smeared lamp lay on the floor beside him, and a vase lay smashed nearby, its flowers scattered, its water mingling with the late scholar's blood. Other signs of disarray littered the room.

"There, now, miss," Hopkins told the girl at once, and took her by the shoulders. "It's quite all right, I'm a policeman. You can leave everything to us. See that she's looked after," he added to the butler, as the poor woman's frantic screams subsided to sobs, "but stay here yourself, if you please. We'll need to ask you some questions."

I knelt to examine the late scholar, but it was perfectly apparent that there was nothing to be done for him. "We're too late," I said. "He's been dead an hour at least." He wore a nightshirt and dressing-gown, and clutched in his hand an old-fashioned nightcap.

Hopkins had crossed to the shattered window, glass crunching beneath his feet. "Has anything been taken from this room?" he asked the butler. After a hasty survey of the debris, the man confirmed that some candlesticks and a rose-bowl, both silver, appeared to be missing.

"Well, it looks as if the Professor came down and surprised a burglar," Hopkins said.

"Come now, Hopkins, you surely –" Holmes began impatiently, but the Inspector interrupted him, mildly enough.

"I said that that's what it looks like, sir. I'm well aware of how surprising it would be if the appearance matched the facts. Where is the Professor's room?" the Inspector asked the butler.

"We have him in the main guest bedroom, sir," the man replied shakily. "It's on the second floor, on the street side."

"Easy enough to throw some gravel at his window and wake him, then," Stanley Hopkins continued. "He'd see the fellow waiting there, and come down to let him in. It must have been someone who knew where he was sleeping, and whom he recognised. Presumably Onions, since this happened after Chops was detained at Baker Street.

"He brought Onions in here to speak to him, and a fight ensued, during which the thug stoved in the Professor's head with the lamp. Then he grabbed the most expensive and portable items he could see and left, pausing only to smash the window from outside before making his escape. The whole thing was intended to look like a burglary, and as I say, so it does."

At first Holmes had appeared irritated at having the role of explicator of the crime scene usurped from him, but as Hopkins continued with his recital he had begun nodding, and now smiled in almost paternal pride. "Just so, Hopkins, just so," he said. "The guest bedroom is above this room. Had this scene played out in the way we are invited to imagine, the Professor must have been aware of the intruder before he came down. Either the window breaking would have awoken him, or, if he had been already awake, he would have heard the noise. Yet a man who heard a burglar in the night would surely rouse others before going to investigate, or at least bring with him some more formidable weapon than a nightcap. No, that explanation will not do at all, whereas the one you have outlined fits the facts quite comfortably."

"Forgive me if I can't take much satisfaction from that, Mr Holmes," Hopkins said. "This is another member of the public who we've failed to protect. My word," he said, suddenly, "you don't suppose that Windward and Graymare are in equal danger? After all, they too could testify against Loomborough."

"I suspect that for now their value to the conspiracy is too great to dispense with them," Holmes replied. "I doubt that there is another forger of Graymare's calibre in the country, for instance. To kill him would end the whole operation at once. I hope that they are not yet that desperate."

"Even so," said Hopkins. "I'd better have them brought in, to be on the safe side."

He put a telephone call through to Mycroft, who was best placed to co-ordinate our efforts. Quickly Hopkins instructed that men should be sent to Dr Graymare's home and others to Sir Hector Askew's house, where we assumed his cousin would still be staying. Police constables would need to come and take statements from Rames's servants. They should also arrange for the Professor's body to be taken to the police morgue, like those of Zimmerman, Bastion and Probert before it.

Constable Vincent and the carriage would accompany us to Lord Loomborough's, where we would be going without delay.

CHAPTER SIX

Lord Loomborough lived in Mayfair, a short ride away from Rames's relations' Kensington pied-à-terre. As befitted a man of his distinction and stature, the Minister's house was lavish and grand, with a view across a verdant square to one of London's most beautiful eighteenth-century churches.

I expected Holmes to mount the stairs to the front door and knock as insistently as he had at the Rames house, but this time he held back. He said, "I feel that a less direct approach might benefit us in this instance. The servants' entrance, I think, Hopkins?"

"Very well," said the Inspector, "if you think so. Vincent, you keep watch here. If His Lordship comes out, collar him."

"With pleasure, sir," replied Constable Vincent stolidly.

We circled round to the side of the house and down the servants' stairs, where Hopkins tapped discreetly at the door. The kitchen-maid who opened it looked between us in confusion, unsure of how she should respond to three gentlemen arriving in this unconventional manner, and in Holmes's case still very grubby and dishevelled.

Again Hopkins introduced himself, explaining that we were there on police business. "Please allow us into the house, miss," he said. "No need to trouble your employer for the moment, if you don't mind."

The servants were busy about the many tasks that occupy the attention of a household of such size, and in the kitchen we found the cook and another maid making breakfast in a great bustle. "Oh, Lord," the cook declared when she saw us. "More gentlemen abroad, at this time in the morning! Are you for breakfast too, then, sirs?"

"Lord Loomborough has guests, then?" Holmes asked.

"One, sir, a young gentleman. He arrived just a little while ago, and Mr Sacks the butler had to wake His Lordship up. They've called for breakfast."

"Then we shall certainly join them," said Holmes, adding kindly, "though please do not trouble about us; we have already eaten." I wished that that were the case, but for the moment we had more immediate concerns. "Where shall we find His Lordship?"

Confused still by our arrival, but willing enough to be of service given Hopkins's credentials, the kitchen staff directed us to Lord Loomborough's morning-room. We proceeded there, my hand resting warily on the gun in my jacket pocket.

As we approached, the sound of angry whispering reached us through the morning-room door, which stood ajar, and Holmes raised an urgent hand for us to pause. We stood in silence and listened.

"This is unconscionable," Lord Loomborough was hissing, and again I winced as I recalled his diatribe of the previous morning, castigating Holmes and myself for our frivolous misuse of the time and effort of his police force. "You should never have ordered such an action without consulting me. Rames is a pillar of the academic establishment, and his death will be an insupportable loss, bringing all kinds of attention. At such a critical time it will also create suspicion, suspicion that we most certainly do not need!"

Calmly, a voice I recognised as Jerome Windward's retorted, "Figgis made it look like a burglary. If it occasions anybody any deeper suspicions, they're scarcely likely to conclude from the killing of a man who supported the sonnet's authenticity that it was faked. Where would be the sense in that? We can simply blame it on Sherlock Holmes's uncontrollable fury, as we did Maines's death."

Figgis, I presumed, was either Onions's real name or that of some other hired thug. I was surprised, however, to learn that young Windward had taken the initiative of ordering Rames's murder. It must surely be beyond his purview as the operation's wordsmith, and it was small wonder that his principal was angry with him.

"Holmes will know!" Loomborough cried, forgetting himself, and then continued quietly again: "He or his interfering younger brother. What steps have you taken to recover that manuscript, eh? That should have been your objective, rather than stilling the tongue of a discreet man like Rames. He has said nothing untoward so far – why should he now?"

"Well, now we can be perfectly sure he won't," said Windward nonchalantly. "The situation with the Watson manuscript is complicated, thanks to Figgis and Smith's botchery, but not irretrievable. I'm told the Baker Street house is swarming with Mycroft Holmes's men. We must assume that both brothers have read the manuscript, but they would deny its import in any case. A bigger difficulty is Inspector Hopkins. Our best chance now is to get rid of him along with Watson, and ensure that the manuscript reaches another Scotland Yard detective, ideally a less astute one. That would include most of the rest, from what I gather."

The three of us exchanged glances, and at Holmes's nod I pulled my gun from my pocket.

"Meanwhile," Windward continued, "we must remove anyone else who might discredit the Shakespeare texts until they're sold. Remember, that money is an insurance policy. We can't be sentimental or half-hearted about this. Rames had to go, and so has Graymare."

"*Graymare?*" Loomborough repeated, aghast. "You've gone quite mad. Graymare is irreplaceable. His skills are essential to the success of the whole operation."

Holmes shot Hopkins a contrite look. I hoped that Mycroft's men would reach the fussy little graphologist in time.

"The operation, as you call it, has run its course," Jerome Windward replied, still in the same even tone. "The Watson manuscript may yet fulfil its purpose, but if it doesn't, the Holmes brothers won't be caught in the same way twice. In the meantime, we must hold our nerve, our ground and our tongues until that sonnet is sold."

"Oh! I should never have listened to your absurd schemes," Loomborough complained. "I should have realised you were out of control when you had our men eliminate Bastion."

"Control, Loomborough?" said Windward quietly. "I was never under your control. I've found it useful to harness your career to my ends, that's all – a career I gave you, let us not forget. I can take it away just as easily, once I have the money from Boothby's. If the Watson manuscript fails, then all the other fakes can come to light as far as I'm concerned. It's nothing to me."

"Ah, but if it succeeds yet," Loomborough cried, all thought of discretion evidently abandoned now, "what then, eh? You won't want any of this business to come out then, will you? Not while Mycroft Holmes is alive, and might be restored to a position to have you tracked down and apprehended. It is hardly likely that a man with friends like his would hang, whatever happens to his brother. I can bring you down yet, my boy."

"You're right," said Windward, every bit as calm as before. "And that's why you, too, are a liability, Your Lordship."

Hopkins and Holmes reacted at the same instant, each diving for the morning-room door, where they collided. In the moment it took them to disentangle themselves from one another and throw the door open, the sound of a gunshot rang out from inside the room.

Unfortunately I, the only one of our party with a weapon of my own, had been slower to recognise the danger, and for the moment I was stuck behind them, unable to see the scene they had uncovered, let alone to bring my revolver to bear. Realising this, Hopkins ducked down in front of me, to allow me to sight over his shoulders, while Holmes stepped forward.

I saw that the morning-room extended from the house into a conservatory, the floorboards giving way to paving studded with various exotic plants in pots. A glass door stood open to a garden, a sizeable one by London's standards.

Jerome Windward stood with a smoking pistol raised towards Holmes. Between them, next to an overturned chair, Lord Loomborough's lifeless body lay sprawled upon the floor, his resemblance to Abraham Lincoln grotesquely exaggerated in death.

"Put the gun down, Windward," said Holmes sensibly. "You can see that Watson is armed."

The aim of Windward's pistol swung between Holmes and myself, but seeing that I was largely inaccessible behind Hopkins's body he trained it downwards at the Inspector. "No, *you* put the gun down, Watson, or I shall shoot Inspector Hopkins. It would occasion me great satisfaction if one or both of you died. Holmes I can take or leave, but I'm sure we can work him convincingly into this little scene. Evidently he killed Lord Loomborough to protect his brother, then eliminated the two of you as witnesses. As long as the manuscript you're holding reaches the eyes of one of the Inspector's suitably pedestrian colleagues, the inference should be clear enough."

I held the pistol aimed unwaveringly at Windward. "If I disarm myself," I pointed out, "there's nothing to prevent you from killing all of us. Forgive me if I prefer to keep that impossible."

"That's commendably rational of you, Doctor," said Windward. "In that case, you compel me to eliminate the impossible – and Mr Holmes."

He turned his gun arm quickly towards my friend, his finger already tightening on the trigger, but as he moved, I fired. I hit him in the shoulder, throwing off his shot, which shattered a plant-pot holding a tall aspidistra. At the same time Holmes leapt, as did Hopkins, while Constable Vincent, alerted by the earlier gunshot, immediately appeared behind me. Windward struggled savagely, but between them the two men wrestled him to the floor, where Holmes's strength was sufficient to pinion him.

I quickly examined the wound I had made. It was a clean shot, and presented no immediate danger.

"Jerome Windward," said Hopkins, regaining his breath, "I am arresting you for the murder of Lord Loomborough, for conspiracy to murder Jonathan Rames, Christopher Bastion and Gilbert Probert, and for the attempted murder of John Watson. That isn't the half of it," he added cheerfully, as he hauled his captive roughly to his feet and handcuffed him, "but it should do for now, I think."

"If we are enumerating murders only," suggested Holmes, "there are still others to be added to the list."

"Well, there are Griffon and Macpherson, and no doubt others," said Hopkins, as he pushed Windward into Vincent's brawny arms. "Maines too, perhaps. But we'll establish that in time, I'm sure."

"I am alluding," Holmes said, "to those who died in the arson attacks you were investigating previously, notably Konrad Wendt, whose demise first alerted you to the espionage dimension belonging to this current affair. You will, I am sure, recall the other names?"

"Of course I do," said Hopkins, confused. "But I don't see the connection. We all understood that Zimmerman …"

"Insofar as there ever was a Zimmerman," said Holmes, "he is standing before us at this moment."

Despite his bleeding shoulder, a sly smile spread across Jerome Windward's face.

LETTER TO SIR HECTOR ASKEW

Kennetfell
7 April 1898

Dear Cousin Hector—

I suppose you will be surprised to hear from me, as it has been so many years since we last corresponded, and you have, I suppose, imagined me quite the invalid these days. In truth I have not been well, and have rarely had the energy to write.

But I am writing now to introduce to you a distant connexion of yours—my grandson, my late daughter Bertha's boy Jerome Windward. It is likely that you have not heard of him before now—he has lived with his father in Devon since Bertha's death, and my illness has prevented our having much communication—but he has recently stayed with me, and quickly shown himself to be the most cheerful and enlivening company. He is a writer like yourself, and in my opinion a most promising and talented one, whose literary gifts and works will soon, I have no doubt, be widely appreciated.

He wishes to spend some time in London in the Summer, and I suggested that you might be willing to act as his host. So confident am I that you will accommodate my wishes and him that I am sending him this letter to bring with him as his introduction to you.

I am confident that you will find that he occasions you very little inconvenience, and a great deal of Good Cheer, during his stay.

Your affectionate cousin
Reginald Askew

CHAPTER SEVEN

"My suspicions on the point were first aroused," said Sherlock Holmes, "when you, Hopkins, described the corpse you believed to be Zimmerman's as having been in reasonable health.

"A man who never left his room would quickly become unfit," he admonished the Inspector. "Even Mycroft walks a hundred or so paces each day, and nobody would call his body a healthy one. The landlady at the property spoke of visitors arriving and departing in disguise, but on further enquiry, and the application of liberal amounts of money, she confirms that she was well aware that 'Zimmerman' was no single individual, but a succession of men, each of whom occupied that room for a week or so at a time. All would have been agents of Windward's, with the one you arrested being the last and unluckiest."

Holmes, Stanley Hopkins and I were ensconced in the sitting-room at 221B Baker Street. Holmes and I were smoking companionably, though the Inspector did not partake. At my eventual pained request, Holmes had abandoned the experimental rose-scented brew that he had favoured of late, and reverted to his habitual shag tobacco.

Two days had elapsed since the arrests of Jerome Windward

and John Smith, alias "Chops", and the news had swiftly followed that Dennis Figgis, alias "Onions", had been apprehended entering Dr Carson Graymare's property in Hampstead with nefarious intent. Sergeant James Douglass had also been in custody since that night, as was Dr Graymare himself, and further members of the extended counterfeiting ring, its associates and enforcers were still being brought in.

Holmes had summoned Hopkins to hear his final conclusions on the case, before handing over the more tedious processes of the law to the police, as was his wont. Though Mycroft Holmes had been invited to join us, he had declined. The urgent crisis over, his indolent habits had reasserted themselves entirely, and he had expressed the fervent intention of stirring no further from home than the Diogenes Club for the remainder of the year.

In deference to her valiant intervention at the time of the burglary, we had also asked Mrs Hudson to be present, and she felt sufficient interest in the outcome to accept, though she kept hopping up to ensure that we were supplied sufficiently with cakes and tea.

Setting aside his cherrywood pipe for now, Holmes continued, "Jerome Windward is no older than he seems, though his name is not, of course, Jerome Windward. He is Anthony Sperrington, an unhappy child from a wealthy military family who disappeared from his school in Hampshire at the age of sixteen in the autumn of eighteen eighty-nine, and has not been heard of since. It seems that he ran away to London, where he came into the orbit of the late Professor Moriarty, and the latter, detecting the lad's gift for parody and imitation, devised with his usual baleful ingenuity a twisted end to which it might be put.

"This explains the boy's precocious criminal career. It was Moriarty who arranged for him to enter into partnership with Carson Graymare, who since his university days had been supplementing his legitimate earnings with the forger's art, and it was Moriarty who, shortly before his final, fatal sojourn to Switzerland, put both his protégés in touch with Lord Loomborough, who had reached what would have been the summit of an undistinguished career as a backbench peer.

"Loomborough had decided that the scope of his ambitions lay beyond such an ambit, and had enlisted Moriarty's help in realising them. Loomborough and Sperrington, along with Graymare and others whose assistance was equally technical, formed an alliance the outcome of which you know. To provide a legitimate excuse for their business together, Sperrington also wrote Loomborough's memoirs, published under His Lordship's own name.

"Though Moriarty was its instigator and took his percentage of Loomborough's fee, their enterprise survived his demise and the dismantling of his criminal organisation. Between them the collaborators expanded its scope, putting their various talents to use for clients both old and new, and bringing others into the scheme, through bribery or coercion, whenever additional expert knowledge was needed. Whatever the others believed, however, young Sperrington was always the chief partner in their relationship – the author, if you will forgive the pun, of their conspiracy. Moriarty had taught him well, and he considered Loomborough, Graymare and the others nothing but willing and useful pawns, to be sacrificed should the time become appropriate."

"The poor boy," murmured Mrs Hudson, to my surprise, but Hopkins nodded his assent.

Holmes continued, "They carried out the various schemes of which we are aware, along with numerous others. Their clients included Robert Foxon, of course; Alastair Mineheart, Sir Lester Lesborne's grandson; the man, still unidentified, who burgled Lord Kerwinstone under the name of Percival Campion; and

Jonathan Rames, who wished to cite in his research a historical record that did not yet exist – but not, interestingly, Leonard Griffon, the Barraclagh claimant.

"In that instance, having now had the opportunity to examine both, I am convinced that it was the marriage certificate found later that was forged. Our friend Fitzalan Gerraghty was quite correct in his belief that the first to be uncovered was genuine, and Griffon should, by rights, now be sitting in the Lords as the fifth Earl of Barraclagh. It was the present custodians of the estate, not wishing a new Earl to return to claim it, who had the second and supposedly earlier certificate created to invalidate the first. Unfortunately, poor Griffon began investigating the fraud on his own account – which was why he expressed an interest in speaking to you, Hopkins – and Sperrington had him removed, while doubtless allowing Loomborough to believe that the decision was his.

"Last year, it seems that Sperrington was approached by a foreign intelligence agency, who wished him to turn his skills towards a most particular job. They wished three men either eliminated or removed from their current eminence, who had been thorns in the side of their spying network for many years.

"These men were Konrad Wendt, a former agent of theirs who had defected to a rival power, Christopher Bastion, whose organisational abilities had enabled a number of efficient operations against their agents in the Empire, and the nearest person they could identify to a British spymaster-general, Mycroft Holmes. Removing Mycroft from the picture, in particular, would strike a blow against the very heart of the British government, leaving its spying operations fatally weakened.

"Sperrington's interest in writing crime fiction was perfectly sincere; it was, in fact, what had led him to seek the society of Moriarty's associates in the first place. No ulterior motive led him to write that *Assassin's Dagger* yarn, Watson, nor to place it in your hands; he was genuinely, though quite perversely given his intentions, interested in your opinion. This fascination was at once engaged by the novel problem facing him, and he constructed a plot that would have put Arthur Morrison or Max Pemberton to shame.

"First he built the legend of Zimmerman, hiring his room and populating it with these anonymous agents, detailed between them to carry out a routine intended to suggest covert spywork. Then he hired Chops and Onions – or, as we should properly call them, Smith and Figgis – to implement the arson attacks that would disguise the assassination of Wendt. He suborned Douglass, through threats to his family, to act as his agent in the police, and through him he kept track of your investigation into the arson, steering it perhaps with hints in his desired direction."

"Oh, Douglass helped the work a great deal." Stanley Hopkins shook his head bitterly. "What a fool I've been," he said.

"Not at all, Hopkins, not at all," said Holmes, with no very convincing show of feeling. "There is not a single one of your colleagues whom I should not expect to have been fooled," he added generously, which given his oft-expressed opinion of the other Scotland Yarders, I imagine came as little comfort to the young man.

He pressed on. "Anthony Sperrington's planning was meticulous – or Jerome Windward's, as we may now say, for by this time he had inveigled himself into Sir Hector Askew's house in that persona, by dint of yet another counterfeit letter, so as to gain an introduction to Christopher Bastion. Bastion in turn he introduced to Miss Adorée Felice – not, to be sure, a spy, but an ordinary gold-digger whom Windward found through very ordinary channels. Bastion's affairs were habitual and expensive, but on past occasions he had been able to draw upon his family's wealth as a recourse against any potential bankruptcy. With the accusations made against him, however, I imagine that his brother was more reluctant to oblige this time.

"There was, in fact, no requirement for Sergeant Douglass to plant the evidence of Bastion's forged letter at Zimmerman's house, since Zimmerman was wholly a character created by Windward. The dupe who was to be the final Zimmerman was instructed to ensure that it survived the destruction of the other papers, and so he did. He must have been warned also not to talk to the police when arrested, and perhaps promised as well that Douglass would secure his freedom. Had he not attempted to escape nevertheless, or had his attempt been thwarted in a less fatal manner, I have no doubt that he would swiftly have met Probert's fate. As things fell out, his death was accidental, though like the others in this case it must ultimately be laid at Windward's door.

"With Bastion's downfall in train, Windward was free to concentrate on Mycroft Holmes – and his plan for him was the most fiendish of all. He took advantage of Mycroft's family connection to me, and of my friendship with our age's most famous writer of crime stories – albeit of histories rather than of fiction. From his own talents and activities and those of his associates, he spun a tapestry of facts and lies that was to culminate in the permanent cutting-off of Watson's thread, with my own left to hang. He would expose his own crimes, laying every one of them at Mycroft's door, and then suggest that I had killed my friend to protect my brother.

"To do that, he first needed a crime for me to investigate – and that, not any romantic jealousy or unpaid debt, nor any need to silence him, was why Christopher Bastion had to die rather than being merely disgraced.

"My actual actions he incorporated into his plot as I made

them, as he was quick to do with the unauthorised thuggery of his men at the Butcher's Apron. It would be Watson's words that condemned me, and no man other than myself or Mycroft – the chief suspects-to-be, who could hardly be disinterested in the matter – would be competent to prove them wrong."

For a moment Inspector Hopkins looked dismayed, and then, remembering how his own detective instincts had failed him in the case of Douglass, shook his head ruefully again. "I'd have been horrified," he said, "and I'd have wanted more than anything for it to be untrue. But the manuscript painted a very convincing picture, Mr Holmes. I hope that, given time, I'd have noticed the language clues, but I wouldn't hold out much hope of convincing anybody else at the Yard on that basis."

This time Holmes seemed to realise that he had been ungracious, and said, "I am certain that you would have made every effort, Hopkins. Had you been willing to listen to advice from a suspected murderer, I should have done my best to guide you. But with Lord Loomborough's oppressive influence constraining your superiors, I, too, doubt that you would have made much headway."

He continued, "The late Lord Loomborough had his own reasons for wishing to see Mycroft removed. With his intellect dominating the halls of Whitehall, the risk that Loomborough's criminal activities would be discovered would have been ever present. His Lordship was very happy, therefore, to go along with Windward's plans, especially with the forging of the Shakespeare works, which promised to be very lucrative indeed.

"As we know, he was quite unaware that Windward, having become bored with the whole business, intended to take the money and move elsewhere, presumably under the protection of the foreign government that hired him, having first exploded his own counterfeiting operation.

"Had Loomborough indeed been the instigator of the affair, we may imagine how differently Windward's 'Watson manuscript' might have read. As it is, it accurately represents Loomborough's reputation, his interference with police business, and his route to power, despite none of these being strictly relevant. Indeed, it does so in rather greater detail than I suspect you should have been capable of or interested in giving, Watson. It suppresses his role in the conspiracy only so far as concealing the fact that he warned us away from our investigation, whereas a text that Loomborough himself had overseen would have taken greater pains to absolve him of any blame.

"In fact, I suspect that Windward hoped to use Loomborough as a scapegoat, in the event that it was discovered that the manuscript was forged. Why else would it have been a note from him, not Mycroft, that summoned me to the Diogenes on that fateful night?

"To be sure, Loomborough could have testified that Windward, or Sperrington, had been his accomplice throughout – but by then the man could have been living elsewhere under quite a different name, perhaps using his newfound leisure to pen crime novels, since that seems always to have been his primary interest.

"Wheels within wheels, gentlemen – and Mrs Hudson – scheme upon scheme. Windward was certainly a protégé after Moriarty's own heart, though he proved a less formidable opponent in the end."

After a moment's thought I said, "It baffles me, though, that the manuscript mentions Windward at all. We barely met him at Askew's house. He played no role in our investigation, and his version of me could easily have confided in some other person. If he'd kept himself out of the matter altogether – and if you, Mrs Hudson, had not come so valiantly to my aid at the crucial moment

– then you might be in gaol now, Holmes, awaiting a capital trial, and nobody the wiser about your having ever met him."

Holmes smiled. "It baffles you, Watson, because you are that most contradictory of creatures – a self-effacing author. Jerome Windward is not. As I have said, there was no reason for him to pass you his own novel, other than sheer self-aggrandisement. He almost certainly hoped, by locating it at the scene of what was to be a most notorious murder, and ensuring that it was mentioned in a central item of evidence, to gain the interest of publishers and the public in his legitimate work."

His smile became a smirk. "You might even have contributed to the publicity: 'a gripping yarn, mixing peril and tension … astonishing talent and promise … Great Things in his future – John H. Watson, M.D. (deceased).'"

"That's hardly in the best of taste, Mr Holmes," Mrs Hudson admonished him.

"It certainly would not have been," Holmes agreed, unabashed. "What is quite clear is that Windward's high opinion of his own talents, and of himself, is expressed each time he appears in the manuscript. He puts inveterate praise into your mouth, Watson, for everything from his appearance to the charms of his company, and most extravagantly of all for his novelistic endeavours. He even has me – shortly to be condemned as a murderer, let us not forget, and hardly known for my literary interests even under usual circumstances – praise him for a genius. He goes so far as to write for himself a wholly fictitious scene in which he is the hero, bravely rescuing poor crippled Watson from the cowardly thugs!

"No, he could never have written a story from which he was absent. As a mere contributor to forged documents, nor as a pale imitator of the late Professor Moriarty's criminal mastery, Jerome Windward would never receive his due. What he yearns for is honest literary recognition. His attempt to emulate the genius of Shakespeare shows the extent of his self-conceit.

"Yet it is not that that I find the most unforgivable," he added, with a smile. "What staggers me most is his unjustifiable belief that he was worthy of adding his own work to the Watsonian canon. In the end," concluded Sherlock Holmes, as he set about refilling his pipe, "it was his author's vanity that led to Jerome Windward's downfall."

EPILOGUE

Dear Mr Bodley,

I am grateful to you for the loan of the enclosed documents, which have served as a reminder of a most interesting episode.

The entire matter is one in which the public would, I imagine, be most interested, were these documents to be published, but this course of action is one that, to my regret, I cannot recommend. This is not indeed because of the scandal attaching to senior parties in government. Lord Loomborough has been safely dead now for decades, and all those guilty persons who survived the case received, and in many cases served, their sentences long ago.

Nor is it because of any disparity with the facts: on the contrary, I can attest that the second and shorter narrative is authentic and substantially true, within the usual parameters of Dr Watson's artistic licence.

No, my reservation relates to Anthony Sperrington, alias

Jerome Windward, who still serves at His Majesty's pleasure, having escaped hanging thanks only to his relative youth, his early corruption by Professor Moriarty, and the services of a smooth-tongued defence lawyer.

Both his names have long been forgotten by the world outside his gaol, but the publication of this narrative would bring him renewed fame and notoriety. It might even create a market among the more prurient reading public for his novels, which I am told he has continued to produce apace, though he has never succeeded in interesting a publisher sufficiently to bring them to a wider audience.

I should not wish to see him prosper, especially not through his attempts to exploit the fame of the late Dr Watson. He remains as irresponsible as Watson was conscientious, as self-interested as Watson was respectful of others, and as arrogant as Watson was humble. It is unconscionable that such a man should profit from the Doctor's good name, and so I must advise you most earnestly not to give this shabby imitator the publicity he craves. Instead, I urge you to desist from publication.

I ask this in the name of the memory of your late client, my good friend, and "the best and wisest man whom I have ever known."

Yours,

S. Holmes

ABOUT THE AUTHOR

PHILIP PURSER-HALLARD is the author of two previous Sherlock Holmes novels, *The Vanishing Man* and *The Spider's Web*, and of a trilogy of urban fantasy thrillers beginning with *The Pendragon Protocol*. He also writes novellas and short stories, edits anthologies, and is an editor of and contributor to The Black Archive, a series of critical books about Doctor Who. He tweets @purserhallard.

SHERLOCK HOLMES
CRY OF THE INNOCENTS
Cavan Scott

It is 1891, and a catholic priest arrives at 221b Baker Street, only to utter the words "*il corpe*" before suddenly dropping dead.

Though the man's death is attributed to cholera, when news of another dead priest reaches Holmes, he becomes convinced that the men have been poisoned. He and Watson learn that the victims were on a mission from the Vatican to investigate a miracle; it is said that the body of eighteenth-century philanthropist and slave trader Edwyn Warwick has not decomposed. But should the Pope canonise a man who made his fortune through slavery? And when Warwick's body is stolen, it becomes clear that the priests' mission has attracted the attention of a deadly conspiracy...

PRAISE FOR CAVAN SCOTT

"Many memorable moments... excellent." *Starburst*

"Utterly charming, comprehensively Sherlockian, and possessed of a wry narrator." *Criminal Element*

"Memorable and enjoyable... One of the best stories I've ever read." *Wondrous Reads*

TITAN BOOKS.COM

SHERLOCK HOLMES
THE LEGACY OF DEEDS
Nick Kyme

It is 1894, and Sherlock Holmes is called to a Covent Garden art gallery where dozens of patrons lie dead before a painting of The Undying Man.

Holmes and Watson are soon on the trail of a mysterious figure in black, whose astounding speed and agility make capture impossible. The same suspect is then implicated in another murder, when the servant of a visiting Russian grand duke is found terribly mutilated in a notorious slum. But what links the two crimes, and do they have anything to do with the suicide of an unpopular schoolteacher at a remote boarding school? So begins a case that will reveal the dark shadows that past misdeeds can cast, and test the companions to their limits...

PRAISE FOR NICK KYME

"A highly enjoyable book with plenty of action." *Fiftyshadesofgeek*

"An engaging and exciting story." *Talk Wargaming*

"An entertaining read." *SFF World*

TITAN BOOKS.COM

SHERLOCK HOLMES
THE RED TOWER
Mark A. Latham

It is 1894, and after a macabre séance at a country estate, a young woman has been found dead in a locked room.

When Dr Watson is invited to a weekend party where a séance is planned, he is prepared to be sceptical. James Crain, heir to the estate of Crain Manor, has fallen in with a mysterious group of spiritualists and is determined to prove the existence of the paranormal. Confronted with a suspicious medium and sightings of the family ghost, Watson remains unconvinced – until James's sister, Lady Esther, is found dead in a room locked from the inside. Holmes is called to investigate the strange events at Crain Manor, but finds that every guest harbours a secret. Holmes and Watson must uncover the truth, and test the existence of the supernatural…

PRAISE FOR MARK A. LATHAM

"Great fun… with a setting we love spending time in." *Barnes & Noble*

"Lose yourself in nineteenth-century London – you won't regret it." **George Mann**

"Victorian London comes alive in ways even Conan Doyle could never imagine." **James Lovegrove**

TITAN BOOKS.COM

SHERLOCK HOLMES
THE DEVIL'S DUST
James Langrove

It is 1884, and when a fellow landlady finds her lodger poisoned, Mrs Hudson turns to Sherlock Holmes.

The police suspect the landlady of murder, but Mrs Hudson insists that her friend is innocent. The companions discover that the lodger, a civil servant recently returned from India, was living in almost complete seclusion, and that his last act was to scrawl a mysterious message on a scrap of paper. The riddles pile up as aged big game hunter Allan Quatermain is spotted at the scene of the crime when Holmes and Watson investigate. The famous man of mind and the legendary man of action will make an unlikely team in a case of corruption, revenge, and what can only be described as magic…

PRAISE FOR JAMES LOVEGROVE

"Lovegrove tells a thrilling tale and vividly renders the atmosphere of Victorian London." *Guardian*

"Another impressive read based on the iconic detective." *Starburst*

"Delicious stuff, marrying the standard notions of Holmesiana with the kind of imagination we can expect from Lovegrove." *Crime Time*

TITAN BOOKS.COM

SHERLOCK HOLMES
THE VANISHING MAN
Philip Purser-Hallard

It is 1896, and Sherlock Holmes is investigating a self-proclaimed
psychic who disappeared from a locked room, in front of
several witnesses.

While attempting to prove the existence of telekinesis to a scientific
society, an alleged psychic, Kellway, vanished before their eyes during
the experiment. With a large reward at stake, Holmes is convinced
Kellway is a charlatan – or he would be, if he had returned to claim
his prize. As Holmes and Watson investigate, the case only grows
stranger, and they must contend with an interfering "occult detective"
and an increasingly deranged cult. But when one of the society
members is found dead, events take a far more sinister turn…

PRAISE FOR PHILIP PURSER-HALLARD

"A master craftsman. His stories are both cleverly
constructed and wrought in the sharpest prose,
and he's always a joy to read." **George Mann**

"A startlingly original premise with some
bloody good storytelling. I'm in for the long run,
and you should be too." **Simon Morden**

TITAN BOOKS.COM

SHERLOCK HOLMES
THE BACK TO FRONT MURDER
Tim Major

It is May 1898, Sherlock Holmes investigates a murder
stolen from a writer's research.

Abigail Moone presents an unusual problem at Baker Street. She is
a writer of mystery stories under a male pseudonym, and gets her
ideas following real people and imagining how she might kill them
and get away with it. It's made her very successful, until her latest
"victim" dies, apparently of the poison method she meticulously
planned in her notebook. Abigail insists she is not responsible, and
that someone is trying to frame her for his death. With the evidence
stacking up against her, she begs Holmes to prove her innocence…

PRAISE FOR TIM MAJOR

TITAN BOOKS.COM

SHERLOCK HOLMES
THE MANIFESTATIONS OF SHERLOCK HOLMES
James Langrove

Maverick detective Sherlock Holmes and his faithful chronicler
Dr John Watson return in twelve thrilling short stories

The iconic duo find themselves swiftly drawn into a series of
puzzling and sinister events: an otherworldly stone whose touch
inflicts fatal bleeding; a hellish potion unlocks a person's devilish
psyche; Holmes's most hated rival detective tells his story; a
fiendishly clever, almost undetectable method of revenge; Watson
finally has his chance to shine; and many more – including a
brand-new Cthulhu Casebooks story.

PRAISE FOR JAMES LOVEGROVE

"Pitch-perfect. Lovegrove tells a thrilling tale and vividly
renders the atmosphere of Victorian London." *Guardian*

"The reader [is] in no doubt that they are in the hands
of a confident and skilful craftsman." *Starburst*

"Lovegrove has become to the twenty-first century what
J.G. Ballard was to the twentieth." *The Bookseller*

TITAN BOOKS.COM

SHERLOCK HOLMES
THE SPIDER'S WEB
Philip Purser-Hallard

It is 1897, and Sherlock Holmes is investigating a murder
that took place during a society ball.

Holmes and Watson rush to the scene, but are shocked by the flippant
attitude of the ball's host: the wealthy Ernest Moncrieff, a favourite
of high society who was found in a handbag as a baby. Suspicion
naturally falls upon the party guests, but the Moncrieff family and
their friends – including the indomitable Lady Bracknell – are more
concerned with the inconvenience of the investigation than the
fact that one of them may have committed murder. But behind the
superficial façade, Holmes and Watson uncover family secrets going
back decades, and a mysterious blackmailer pulling the strings…

PRAISE FOR PHILIP PURSER-HALLARD

"This ranks among the top novel-length
Sherlock Holmes pastiches" *Publishers Weekly* **(starred review)**

"A very good locked-room puzzle" *Morning Star*

TITAN BOOKS.COM

For more fantastic fiction, author events,
exclusive excerpts, competitions, limited editions and more

VISIT OUR WEBSITE
titanbooks.com

LIKE US ON FACEBOOK
facebook.com/titanbooks

FOLLOW US ON TWITTER AND INSTAGRAM
@TitanBooks

EMAIL US
readerfeedback@titanemail.com